FLAT SURF

BAER CHARLTON

MORDANT MEDIA

Rogena Mitchell-Jones, Literary Editor
RMJ Manuscript Service, www.rogenamitchell.com

Published by Mordant Media, Portland, Oregon

IISBN: 978-1-949316-16-2 [ebook]
ISBN: 978-1-949316-17-9 [paperback]

10 9 8 7 6 5 4 3 2 1

01 RED SAND

The one half-opened eye was blind with sleep. The two eyes of the coyote, a foot away, watched the man twitch in his nightmare.

The heat was always the same—intense and rising. The door never opened—until it was too late. The window continued to crack—a hundred pieces became a thousand that became a million. The dashboard would always balloon from the engine toward the two detectives. The unused radio would become a missile. Darkness became yellow-white heat as the small bomb expanded from the firewall's engine side, turning the moonless night into the sun itself. The freeway overpass loomed as the undercover car now turned fireball followed its given track to destruction...

The twitch always saved him. His shoulder was violent. But his naked butt cheeks told him he was already sitting up. The sweat needled his skin as his hands hung between his knees. He waited as his breathing returned to his slowed rhythm—his heart would follow a minute later.

The fangs of the coyote were still bright white. The pink and black of its tongue curled at the back of the lower fangs. The canine stood just inside the door. Frank was never sure if the coyote was sizing him up for breakfast or just checking in. The bowl of food was sometimes eaten and sometimes went weeks with only a biscuit or two consumed. The water bowl was under a constant drip, refilling the bowl in a couple of hours. The dog turned and stepped outside the open door. It was their arrangement. The door was open. Frank would roll over some nights in the winter, and the pup would be curled in a ball behind his knees like he had the first winter—*five hundred eighty-seven days before*. Frank didn't keep track, but something in his mind had turned on with the accident. He didn't care, but he now knew how long ago.

Two thousand five hundred and fifty-two mornings since the night his life changed. *Two thousand five hundred and twenty-seven* mornings since they told him he would live—they just never told him how. *Two thousand five hundred and forty-five* mornings since they had buried his best friend from second grade on. *Two thousand four hundred and two mornings* since they told him he would walk again—they just didn't tell him what it would take to do it without a walker or cane.

Two thousand mornings since he had sat on the edge of his bed and rubbed the nightmare from his face—again.

He slid from the side of the bed. His toes bent as the heels rose to touch his butt cheeks. He rested until he felt the muscles in his legs relax and soften with the stretch. With his hands on the edge of the mattress, he gently pushed as he unfolded and sat back on the bed. He gently eased his body forward to lie along the faces of his quadriceps. His nipples hung suspended an inch above his knees. Slowly releasing a breath, they touched and then lay squished. As the crosshatching of scars on his back gently stretched, he allowed himself a dozen slow breaths.

He opened his eyes. The pattern of the ancient Persian rug, bracketed by his feet, was always the same. He noted the pale-pink nail polish on his right big toe needed to be touched up. Maybe it was time to get a complete pedicure. But for now, a cool shower on the porch would have to be enough.

Frank rose and padded his way out the open door. Turning left, he pulled the lever for the shower.

As his friends called his house, the *shack* was the last building at the end of homes built long before building codes came to the bohemian enclave of Crystal Cove. Before he insulated the walls, the shack had been nothing more than a cover from the cruel winter winds raking the point and shelter from the hot sun of Southern California.

Frank glanced at his closest neighbor. The yellow house—six hundred twenty-seven feet away. Three hundred and twelve of which was now State Park. The rest would come when he was finally gone.

Frank stepped into the stream of the cool shower. The warmth came from a looping of black hoses lying on the roof. In less than three minutes, the water would be pure cold county water.

Taking a shower in the afternoon was an act of desperation. There was no way to mix cold water to temper the scalding heat from the sunbaked hoses.

Frank rinsed his hair in the now-cold water and turned off the shower. The cold finish was always refreshing. Frank thought of it as the same as the stinging brace of aftershave lotion he no longer needed.

He sat on the wooden office desk chair to dry off. He waved at the woman standing on the deck of the neighboring house. She didn't wave back. Frank figured she would complain about the naked man, and the long-suffering park employee would have to explain the facts of life. The lone building sat in the middle of one of the last clothing-optional parts of the California coast. There was nothing the state or the park could do about the man who showered on his deck overlooking the spectacular coastline he also surfed.

His stomach growled.

He pulled on the next T-shirt on the three-foot pile. The florid image of a buxom bikinied surfer on a fourteen-foot old-school board bracketed between the words *Surf or Die*. It was one of his favorite shirts and the oldest. His physical therapist had given it to him *one thousand six hundred and seventy-two* days before. He fluffed it out over his weathered board shorts.

After slipping his feet into the rainbow-painted huaraches, he lifted his right foot and checked the remaining tread. Most of three tires had basically survived the explosion. He had asked the watch commander to secure the tires for him. Why waste good tire tread? One of the precinct's finest had made him a fresh pair of huaraches from the tire tread. Since they knew how he felt about his longtime friend and partner, and to show him that they were okay with the man's sexual nature, they had dyed the leather in a rainbow. The pink toenails were Frank's idea and contribution. At six-foot-four and still built like a running back, nobody ever questioned his clothes or toes.

The old beater of a Bentley convertible still rode solidly over the gravel road. The old track led almost directly to the shack's side of the café, but Frank wanted it to grow over to discourage any tourists from taking a back route to the headlands. The new road wandered across the fourteen hundred acres he had inherited on his twenty-first birthday. He signed a promise with the state to never develop the land and to leave it as a nature refuge in exchange for access to his house, his café—also called 'The Shack,' free power, water, and no taxes. On his death, the entire refuge would escheat to their control and remain a reserve. Everyone else just thought he was a squatter or a surf bum.

He pulled the Bentley behind the Shack. The screen door squealed—daily routines.

The light through the south-facing window was warm on his right foot. Without checking his watch, he knew it was close to eight. The kids would be clustered off the point. The weather last night would have brought in swells from Alaska. The short boards would be carving up the four-to-six-foot rollers.

HE SCANNED through the Dow Jones as he reached for his mug. A thin finger and thumb gently stopped him at his wrist. He looked up at the tall, emaciated waiter.

"I figure you're going to need this instead."

Frank looked down at the steaming cup of espresso, and then down the small restaurant to the only windows looking out at the large parking lot.

The golden-brown Taurus with the hubcap-free black tire was obvious. There was only one detective left in Orange County who insisted on driving the old Taurus.

Frank growled. "Just go lock the door."

Danny mocked shock. "That is no way to treat your only son. Besides, it's too late."

The tall man sashayed his six and a half feet of what looked like only a skeleton through the restaurant. "Good morning, Mickey. Did you want chai while you beat the old man?"

The young Italian slicked back his hair with one hand. "Morning, Danny. Um, to go… for both of us, please."

Danny turned at the pass-thru between the coffee station and the counter. He backhand-snapped his towel in the air. "Grumpy has already had breakfast, so you don't have to treat him to steak and eggs at the leather bar."

The detective rolled his eyes. "I've seen him eat before. Trust me—I don't want to see it again."

"Just sayin', sweetie. Save your money for new shoes."

The young detective adjusted his tailored suit as he sat in the chair that Frank had pushed out with his foot. His middle finger and thumb pinched the button through the hole.

"You're out of your district."

The one fleek eyebrow rose. "Danny was right. You are grumpy this morning."

Frank glowered at the young detective for the pace of three slow breaths. "Welcome to Happy Tuesday."

"It's Thursday. The Alzheimer's is making you forget days."

Frank leaned back in his chair with a deep sigh. "I should

have run you over when I had the chance."

The young man grumped back. "The tricycle would have dented your cruiser, and you would have had to explain it to Dad. Besides, Mom wouldn't have liked it."

"Your mother's lasagna was the only thing saving your sorry ass."

"That and Dad having a habit of losing at your Wednesday night poker games."

Danny placed a tall paper cup with a lid and a pink-sequined thermal tumbler mug in front of the two men. "Have him home in time for his nap, or he's going to be cranky."

The young detective pointed at the bright-pink mug. His face was a sour question mark.

"It's your chai tea. Don't be a dick."

"Pink?"

The tall waiter threw his hip out and rested the back of his hand on it. "Your tea doesn't come in condensed espresso shots like his double quad-shots." He waved his right hand at the tall paper cup. "Besides, I lent you a perfectly fine aluminum—"

"It got a bullet through it."

"And you didn't replace it. So I lent you Frankie's personal undercover brown—"

"A bus ran over it…" The young detective was now growling. Frank was leaning back with only a hint of an amused smile.

Danny was nicely wound up. "I think we're starting to see a trend here. I loan you nice things, and you treat them like shit. I'd beat you with a stick, but I can't trust you to take off that Goosy belt and reciprocate. You just can't be trusted with nice things. So you get the one even I wouldn't be caught dead with."

"It's Gucci."

"Just what I said—Goosy. And you don't." He turned to Frank. "Don't bring him back. He's dead to me." He passed his palm down the air, spun on his heel, and stormed off.

"Who said I was leaving with him, anyway?"

Frank watched the waiter disappear into the back. A moment later, he came out with a tray loaded with a food order and backed his way out the front door to the deck. He frowned and turned his attention to the young man sipping on the pink tumbler. "What are you doing down here anyway?"

"We have a body."

"Tough shit. I don't work for you guys anymore. Do I have to show you the fourteen-inch scar up my spine to convince you?"

"Is that the one crossing the twenty-two-inch scar where you got skegged on Redondo Beach?"

Frank growled. "I deserved that one. I was on his beach and jumped the wave ahead of him. I was trespassing."

"What about the three-inch knife wound?"

"Left or right side?" He smiled as he sipped the last of his espresso in the porcelain cup.

"Left."

"Your mother apologized for it years ago."

"God… you *are* getting old. She dorked you on the right side. The left was the dope dealer."

"He apologized with his dying breath. What's your point?"

"Well, Mr. Zipper, this one is on your beach."

Frank glanced over his shoulder out the window. His frown was superior instead of drama.

"No, Newport. Out on the point. An elderly couple and their little dog found it this morning."

Frank squinted one eye. "That's not your jurisdiction, either."

"No, but we think the victim might live up in my district."

"Why me?" Frank pushed the handle on the small cup.

"Because you have enough special insight that we can justify a consulting fee."

"How big a fee?"

"Your five hundred a day started an hour ago."

"I don't need it." His face was stone. He knew the negotiations and what was a reality in the big cities of Orange County.

"Okay, eight Frankos, but you're paying for lunch." Mickey stood and buttoned his center button.

Frank remained seated and then turned to face out the window at the ocean. "It's gonna be a great day on the water."

"Jeezus. Okay, I'll spring for my own lunch."

Frank turned back. Sipping on the empty cup, he eyed the younger man. He put down the cup and stood. Sliding his feet into the huaraches, he looked up. "A full large, and I choose the choke-and-puke."

The right lip of the younger man curled. "Slut. I told the sheriff you wouldn't come for under twelve hundred."

Frank smiled a toothy smile. "Done." He put his hand out toward the door. "Fifteen big it is. But I'm not changing my clothes, and we're taking your car. I don't want to get mine dirty in the city."

The kid smiled and picked up the pink tumbler.

"And make sure you get Pinkie back to Danny. It's the one your dad gave Kahuna when he made detective."

Mickey held the newish tumbler up. "You're so full of shit."

Frank growled. "Just make sure Danny gets it back. It's his favorite, but I think he's sweet on you."

As they climbed into the sushi-smelling undercover car, Mickey snickered. "Danny isn't sweet on me. I don't wear enough leather."

"Your belt's as close as he'll ever get to his fantasy of going to a leather bar."

Mickey pumped the pedal twice and turned the key. "Why?"

"He's afraid they'll hurt him."

Mickey frowned as he backed the car. "Have you ever watched him compete in tae kwon do?"

Frank nodded. "I was also there when he got his third-degree black belt in karate."

02 SKINS

Mickey eased the Taurus right onto A Street. The short street looked recently scrubbed, and the walls of the buildings had fresh paint. Frank guessed the taggers hit on Friday and Saturday night, and the landlords prayed at the altar of their money with rollers and paint on Sunday.

Mickey watched in the rearview mirror after they passed two young women wearing only flip-flops and thong bikinis. From the corner of his eye, Frank could tell both were sporting newer West Coast saline jobs. Probably one of the surgeons in Fashion Island. He didn't care if the surgeon had also done a bottom job as well. After the wreck, he'd stopped looking—or caring.

"You're going to run over the cat—" He could see the low-speed bump had startled Mickey... but only for a moment. His eyes returned to the driving. They could see the black-and-white blood clot at the south end of the parking lot. The uniform stood where he could turn the tourists and media around or away.

Mickey eased to a stop beside the officer. "How bad is it, Riley?"

The man leaned down and looked over his mirrored aviators

at Frank, then looked back at Mickey. "Did he come with the instructions and bottles of strained food for every two hours?"

Frank sighed softly. He'd heard it all before. "Hey, Riley? Tell your mother to call me after she puts your father in his diaper for the night. Unlike you, I don't need any little blue pills."

The man stood. "Fuck you, Pounds, and the ugly goat you rode up on."

Only the other side of Frank's mouth twitched. His left finger rolled in the air just over his knee. Mickey slid his foot off the brake and let the heavy car roll.

FRANK STOOD and scanned the expanse of the beach. The Balboa Pier was over his right shoulder. The blue canopy was already over the body under the yellow tarpaulin. He didn't have to look. He knew there were at least a dozen cameras on the pier with lenses longer than his arm.

"When did you change beats?" Frank asked.

Mickey closed the trunk and walked over. He leaned against a Shamu as he pulled hospital booties over his shoes. Frank thought about saying something but figured the shoes were handmade and cost more than he was making for the day. He let it go and slipped out of his huaraches.

Mickey pulled the back of his right bootie above the ankle. "I didn't. They requested me to handle you." He stood and started walking. "I accepted because of the combat pay."

Frank blinked a slow shrug and bent over. After picking up his huaraches, he followed.

More to himself, he commented on the surf. "Flat. Dead flat."

The medical examiner in the blue jumpsuit stood. He buried his fists at his kidneys as he bent backward. Frank harrumphed silently. The move hadn't helped the man twenty years ago and wasn't going to help him today.

"Give it up, Oz. Nobody is ever going to buy the bad back routine. You're going to have to put in your forty like every other dumb slob."

The white mane shook softly as the man turned around. The large walrus mustache was equally white and just as impressive in its size.

"Says the man who doesn't work." His hand stretched out. "Good to see you, Frank. I just wish it were over a beer or good scotch instead."

"What have you got?"

"Neither." His eyes twinkled for only a second. "Oh, the body. You tell me." The Australian stepped back to reveal the body.

The body was encased in a winter-thick wetsuit from the booties to the gloves and up to where the head should have been. The only anomaly was it being summer, and the liver thermometer was still stuck in the corpse's back.

Frank studied the size of the large diver. He figured the person was a comfortable six feet from the bottom of the booties to the truncated neck. Loosely, he thought the living diver would stand close to six-ten and weigh close to three hundred pounds or more. He took a breath and looked at the white-haired examiner. Closing his eyes, he turned and looked down the beach. As he opened his eyes, they scanned past the uniformed officers standing around.

"Who found him?" Frank asked a uniformed officer.

"It was called in at five-fourteen this morning. I was the first to respond." The uniform's accent was a soft New York as he stepped up. "Stevens. Dirk Stevens."

Frank looked him over. The two stripes told Frank it probably wasn't the man's first body or crime scene. But, with cities being what cities are…

"Did you puke on my crime scene?"

The uniform smirked under his reddish mustache. "I worked my way through college as the night pickup for one of the busiest mortuaries in Queens. Bodies are bodies—complete or just parts." He nodded at the headless body. "My partner and I looked around but didn't find the head. She dived the dumpster and the five cans on the beach while I sheltered the body, but no head. Just dive tanks and a broken shortboard that probably wasn't his."

"Why do you say that?"

"It was only a fifty-six. There's no way he could stand on it. It would sink with even me. It's a kid's board."

Frank pulled at his lower lip as he thought about the information. "Bag it and tag it anyway. How many tanks?"

The officer poked his jaw to one side. "That's the strange one. He was running a triple, and the sticker says they're for mixed gas." He pointed at the ocean. "Where the hell's he going to use a triple tank of mix?"

Frank looked at Mickey. The young detective put up both hands. "I don't dive."

Frank looked at the officer. "Mask, fins, anything else?"

"Not yet. We held off until they got you here."

"And that's another thing. Whose wisdom was it to drag me out of bed for an ax job on a diver?"

The officer pointed at the medical examiner.

"Oz?"

The examiner skewed his mustache and shrugged. "Let's just say I have a hunch."

Frank held up his right finger and turned to the officer. "Stevens, I want you to set teams to pull every bit of shit out of every dumpster or trash can within three blocks. I want the mask and anything this diver might have used. Even if it's a pink macramé ditty bag with lipstick and a wig—if this guy could have used it, touched it, or pissed on it—I want it bagged and tagged. Got it?"

"On it."

Frank watched as the young man explained and then deployed his teams. Turning, he dropped his hand and finger.

"Why?"

The medical examiner chewed on his lower lip for a second. "I think you might know the vic."

"I don't know many divers."

"I think he might have been more of a surfer than a diver."

Frank frowned. "How so?"

"The wet suit." He pointed at the seams. "It's an O'Neal. Custom, but still an O'Neal."

The angry sturgeon in Frank's stomach rolled over in a flop. The chances of a body turning out to be someone you know are slim to none… but with only a few hundred surfers, who are mostly scrawny kids, the odds start to skew. Frank didn't like where this was going. There were only a few surfers who were giants. Frank could name and count them on one hand, leaving the thumb for himself.

Frank lifted his dark glasses onto the top of his head. "Have you rolled him yet?"

"Was just about to when you finally wandered in. Care to do the honors?"

Frank looked at the slight smile under the pure-white broom of a mustache. The man was the oldest looking ME when he graduated from med school and went to work for the county. The story went that he was hustling across the center park of UCI in a bad storm. The first bolt of lightning had hit him just before entering the tunnel under the main ring road. The second bolt had struck him as the young Japanese student helped him stumble out the other end. Both he and his wife had turned white when they were juniors. Two days after they graduated, they flew home to her parents in Japan and were married by the family priest.

Frank growled. "They don't pay me enough."

The examiner shrugged and turned to the body. Crossing one foot over the other, he reached under and pulled upward. The body rolled like it was trained.

The green patch and red number one were all Frank needed to see. "It's Mary."

Mickey looked at the obviously male body and pointed to the letters. "It says he's a brother…"

Frank looked at the kid and his thousand-dollar suit. The three letters *BRO* curved over the top had nothing to do with being a brother. He looked down at the booties over the custom shoes.

Looking up, he slid the aviators back over his eyes. His voice was only for the three of them. "No, it says he served with the Big Red One. His name is Mary Shores. He served four tours of duty in Vietnam. He owns a bar in Orange. He's a surfer, not a diver." He looked down the long beach. "The patrol was right about one thing. The shortboard wasn't his. He always rode a fourteen-foot long gun with hard rails and a double set of triple skegs. The front ones were metal and sharpened. Something is all wrong here, and it isn't about locos and barneys."

"How can you be sure it's him?"

Frank slowly pulled the mirrored glasses to the end of his nose. Mickey wasn't even sure he was breathing, but he could feel the ten-count.

Frank held the eye-lock as he spoke to the examiner. "Hey, Oz, can you split the right sleeve to expose the bicep?"

The man grumped. "Because they don't pay you enough."

Frank held his hand out. The ME slapped the scissors into his palm. Three seconds later, the same patch and sentiment were shown in a larger, more-detailed tattoo. Mickey read the block-lettered words and looked at the two pieces of bread in a toaster. "What the…?"

Frank rested his hand on the younger man's shoulder and leaned in. "Toast of the Army."

He fished his wallet out and handed his card to the ME. "Have the uniform call me if they find his board, car, or anything else. If it helps, he used to drive a gray one-ton van.

We'll be up at the Rusty Pelican. Junior is buying lunch. Mine is coming in a rocks glass."

"Fair dinkum, Frank. Sorry about your friend."

Frank's head bobbed only slightly. His face could have been chiseled in stone. "Thanks. Take care of him."

As they cleared the canopy, Frank turned back. "Hey, Oz?"

The man stood from being bent over the body. "Yeah, Frank?"

"Did you work out the time of death?"

"About two-thirty this morning. The wet suit kept the heat in… but before three."

The older detective's upper body wavered with the news. His mind was trying to place the time and location and come up with why the winter wet suit and gas-mix triple tanks. He blinked and fanned his hand.

"Thanks, Oz. Keep us in the loop."

They stopped at the edge of the sand while Mickey took off his booties. Both men were looking at the bigger picture of the beach and pier. Mickey huffed as he pulled the second bootie off. "What are you thinking?"

Frank let out his breath through his nose. "I think your wallet is going to scream almost as loud as your commander by the time I'm half as drunk as I want to be."

The waitress set down the second round of oysters Rockefeller, a Virgin Mary, and a double Glenfiddich straight up in a bucket. "Anything else for you two?"

Frank looked at the young, tanned brunette over his mirrored glasses. "Have them fire one last round of the oysters. And give the chef my compliments."

She nodded and left. The restaurant didn't open for another half hour.

Mickey put the shell back on the plate. "Why go surfing in

the middle of the night? Or should I be asking more like, would he?"

Frank looked down at the couple walking on the dock below them. From the man's age, he guessed they were headed for the larger power launch at the end. The woman was barely old enough to be his daughter... or secretary. Frank looked back at Mickey. A couple of mixed age, on a boat at noon, on a weekday, was none of his business, and he didn't want his mind going back to his years in vice.

He picked one of the oysters and brought it to his mouth. His hand stopped. "Only an idiot would go surfing in black skins on a moonless night in the dark. He wasn't surfing."

"Then what was he doing?"

Frank shrugged and looked south into the back marina. A large blue-water power-sailer was just coming out of the deep. The two masts of the ketch rig were sleek but fat. He figured the waterline at well over fifty meters. Nobody was obvious on the deck. It was rigged for the clipper-class solo racing. There would be only one person aboard in a race around the world, all the rigging controlled from within the cabin. He remembered reading about the captain who was over twenty hours ahead of every other boat when he ruptured his appendix. With only local anesthesia, he removed his own appendix and stitched himself back up. He finished fourteen hours ahead of second place. Only after winning did he release the video he had shot of him doing surgery at sea.

"Frank?" Mickey spoke. "Frank?"

He shook and looked up. "What?"

Mickey thought about asking where the man had gone but thought better of it. "I asked... if he wasn't surfing, what was he doing?"

Frank quickly slurped the last two oysters as the waitress took the plates and replaced them with the next two. "He was diving. But I don't know why."

Frank's phone buzzed in his board shorts. He pulled it up but didn't recognize the number. Thumbing it, he answered.

"It's your nickel... What did they find?... North or south of the pier?... Where on the pier?... Did they find the van?... Still no head?... Anything else?... Makes sense—it would have been dark... I don't know. I'd have to see it... Okay. Keep at it and keep me in the loop... Thanks, Stevens." He hung up, then captured the number and attached a contact. He made a couple of marks in the notes.

"They found the mask in a can on the pier—at the end—still no hood, head, or van. There was a water torch in a can at the north end of the upper parking lot and a clear waterproof case, but he didn't know what it was for, but they bagged and tagged it all."

Mickey pushed back from the empty plate and sipped his Virgin Mary. "So he's suited for cold water, rigged for depth, and a torch to light his way... Where the hell was he going?"

Frank shrugged and slushed the last of his drink. He eyed the retreating boat. Part of him wished he were going with it. He looked over at Mickey. "What...?"

"I said, because you have a relationship with the victim, you'll probably get bounced."

Frank thought about the regulation that had ruled his life for so long. His eyebrow pushed up as he sucked the last sliver of ice from his glass. "Except, this time, I'm a consultant because I may have intimate knowledge about the victim." He crunched the ice for emphasis.

03 OUT OF LANE

The traffic on the 55 was light, even for the middle of a weekday. Frank's focus kept sliding over to the middle and concrete bollards dividing the freeway. He remembered when the first fences went in. Every month someone took out hundreds of feet of fence. The company had lost a hundred bucks with every mile they had installed, but they also had locked-in the repair at union scale for the following twenty years. By the end of the second year, the company subcontracted the job of doing the initial install and was cleaning up on the repairs. One of the county smarties had figured they would probably replace all the fencing by the end of the second year. The smarty quit his job as a county supervisor and started his own company with a single machine built and used in Germany. It could make in place a mile of concrete bollard a day. By the end of a month, he had bought four more machines.

The first company saw a need to separate the traffic. They figured out a way to exploit the market. The second company saw a way to make a better separation—driving the first company out of business. The first company then saw how the bollard created an attraction to see what was on the other side. So they designed a machine to drill the bollards and install a short fence pre-woven with green slates to block the view. Eventually, they gave up on the visual and just left the bollards.

He realized where Mickey was going when the man put on the turn signal to get onto the 405 South. "Don't. Keep going. I want to go up to his bar."

Mickey looked over. "He had family?"

Frank joggled his head. "I don't think so, but I doubt if anyone thought to go find out."

"So where are we going?"

"The bar is just up from the circle."

Mickey looked over at Frank. "So where were you?"

He pulled at his left earlobe as he watched the incoming merging traffic. "What do you mean?"

"You were off in la-la land."

"I was watching the center divider."

Mickey looked at the concrete wall and short green fence. "What about it?"

Frank settled deeper into the seat. "I don't remember."

They rode in silence.

The front of the building had once been an Amtrak dining car. The wheels were fake, but the car was split down the middle and butterflied to run the length of the building's face. The windows were paintings of silhouetted people engaged in a wild party behind the drawn shades. Across the top, a sign of welded scrap steel and iron left to rust in a post-industrial look. The rust-and-grunge sign was jarring in its juxtaposition over the glass and shiny polished stainless-steel railcar halves.

"Eat, Drink, and be Mary? What kind of place is this?"

Frank chewed at his lip as he slid out of the car. "The kind of place you can take Danny for dinner, and nobody would care."

Frank pulled on the door. It swung open as the sign said. He held it for Mickey, who hesitated and then took off his dark glasses and stepped into the gloom.

The woman behind the bar had shorter hair and more muscles than most men or even gym rats. The large circle-of-words tattoo was prison appearance by design. The *Hurray for Me* read upside down on the bottom and would typically show just below a standard T-shirt. But with the sleeveless shirt stretched over the sports bra, pierced nipples, silicone, and covered hard muscles, the *And Fuck You* was exposed. The black-and-blue rose dripping blood from the stem was a whole different story.

The smile was jarringly out of place with the gravelly voice. "How's it hanging, Frankie?"

"Living the dream, Pussy. Just living the dream."

She put down the glass she was polishing and nudged her chin toward Mickey, hanging back and looking around. She lowered her voice to a stage-whisper. "Who's the door bitch?"

Frank rolled his eyes and ended with a wink. Pussy was Mary's first employee. He had hired her when the bar was a shack down on Fifth Street, and she was a skank in the back ally with a needle in her arm. "Pussy, this is my partner for the day, Mickey Romero. Mickey, this is Pussy Galore, and don't make any bad James Bond jokes."

Mickey hesitated and then just nodded.

Pussy snorted air. "Timid and afraid. I like that in a corner dolt. Let me see if I can find you a pink ball harness."

Frank took a breath. "For God's sake, shake her hand. She doesn't bite, and for all the time your dad spent in this shithole, she could almost qualify as your sister."

Mickey glared at Frank as he stepped forward and raised his hand.

The woman's hand was large and comfortingly warm. Her attitude shifted to a softer tone. "You can call me Pussy or Puss. I know a lot about you. Your dad was proud of you and talked a lot. He was peoples to all of us freaks—treated us all like family or normal. We threw him a big sloppy, sobbing mess of a retirement party. We understood when he moved down south… but there isn't a day goes by we don't miss him. Mary, especially—they were like brothers."

Mickey cleared his throat. He hadn't expected the turn of the conversation.

Frank pulled out one of the stools and sat. "That's why we came up. It's about Mary."

She grimaced as she pulled her hand back. "He wasn't here this morning. He usually comes early and throws the beer they leave in the locked cage out back. The surf must be running hard and tall somewhere."

Frank gently shook his head with a slow sigh. "Nah, it's flat all over. They found his body early this morning out near the point on Newport."

The "Oh, shit" was small and quiet. Puss leaned back and grabbed at the back bar. "What happened?"

"Sorry, but I figured it would be better coming from me than just a phone call or a uniform."

Her eyes were on the bar, but Frank knew she didn't see anything.

"Puss? We're trying to figure out what he was doing down there. We couldn't find his van or his long gun…"

Her face scrunched on the right side as she blinked and looked up. "The van is here. He blew the motor or something the other night. He had it towed up from Dana Point. He had to hit the till for a few hundred for the driver. It's in the garage… I can give you the key…"

"What was he driving?"

"He borrowed Pauly's '59 Nomad. They got it re-piped, and Mary was dialing it in."

"What color paint?"

"Mostly, it's bastard black, with a surfer on each side in a curl."

Frank thought a moment. "Any rack on the roof?"

"Nah, you could slide a dozen long guns in it and still have room for a few stiffs." She blinked and twitched. "Sorry… I didn't mean—"

Frank put up his hand. "It's okay." He pulled out his phone.

Mickey adjusted on the stool. "It's parked up on A Street, north side of the drag. I noticed it when we went past down to Balboa. I used to turn there when I was taking Dad to the Tail of the Whale."

Frank's head jerked. "Hey, Stevens? It's Frank Pounds. You're not looking for the gray van. He was driving the 1959 Nomad parked up on A Street. If you can't find any keys on Mary—" He waited. "Okay, go ahead and slim-Jim the locks. We can bring the keys back for the two guys if they need it."

He rolled around until his back was against the bar. "Nah, we're up at his bar. His van is here, but we were just getting into that." His eyes sparkled from the wet and the tiny twinkling Christmas lights woven in a fishing net hanging from the ceiling. "Yeah, we'll get with you after roll call in the morning. Have a good night."

He closed his phone and rolled back around. "Fuck it." He looked at Mickey and then at Pussy. "I don't wear a uniform. Give me a couple of fingers of Fiddish." They looked at Mickey.

He held his hand up. "I'm driving... Club soda."

"Ice?"

He looked at the bar and thought. He looked up. "Nah. I'm a man. I'll take it straight up."

She looked at Frank, who rolled his eyes and shrugged.

She poured two sodas and the scotch. She softly touched her glass to Frank's.

He nodded and growled. "To one hell of a guy."

They moved to the office once the other bartender arrived. The office wasn't what Frank had expected from Mary. There were a few photos—a beat-up poster of a surfer on a giant wave, the skeg trail drawing a white line straight down the black face of the wave. He had seen the photo elsewhere. The wave off Portugal hit the record of well over six stories high. Scrawled on the top in Sharpie philosophy: Do Epic Shit.

There were photos with Mary in a tuxedo standing with musicians. Frank recognized Yo-Yo Ma, only because of the cello. He had to lean close to figure out the signature of another: Leonard Bernstein. He had addressed it to his good friend, Mary.

The photo closest to the desk was a black-and-white photo of four young soldiers leaning against a blown-up tank. Frank guessed it was Vietnam, and the tall guy with the long 50-caliber Barrett rifle was Mary. It almost looked like a toy in his hands.

There were only a few pieces of paper not related to running the bar. Even there, the paperwork was sparse. Frank fluffed the thin stack of receipts. "It appears he ran the business a little loose."

Pussy shrugged with a slow blink. "I think there was mostly cash flowing around. The credit card machine could be working one minute and break the next. Most nights, it never worked."

Frank nodded. He understood what sort of business a less-than-Main Street bar could be. The Shack was a cash-only business. The sign by the door of the Shack was large: *Order what you can afford. Eat what you order. We don't have any plastic for you to take home, and we don't take plastic.*

Frank only had three people resort to washing dishes, floors, windows, and the deck with all the chairs and tables. The last one, Danny, still worked for him.

"So who takes over the business now?"

She leaned against the desk. "I never heard him talk about any family, and his only relationships were surfing and here at the bar. I don't even remember any buddies from the army coming by, and I've been with him since '93." Her face froze, and then, as her eyes got large, she sat down heavily.

Frank knew the look. "Yeah. Time hits ya hard sometimes."

She looked up, dazed. "You aren't kidding. I've been wiping a twat so long I've forgotten what it feels like to hold a cock."

Mickey started to say something but leaned back against the doorjamb. As he looked down the short hall, he folded his arms.

Frank frowned. The penny for the young Italian had finally

dropped. He was sure there would be a question about his father down the road. He turned back to Pussy. "They found a set of triple tanks rigged for gas—had Mary mentioned any deep, long diving lately?"

"I know he dived occasionally, but mostly he just surfed." She pointed at the photo of the blown-up tank and men. "He mentioned a few times doing diving in 'Nam. But I don't know much about it. I just always thought it had to do with him being a sniper."

"Any other pictures lying around that you know of?"

"Just the one out by the register. He was particularly proud of it." She pointed at the photo of the giant wave in Portugal. "It was taken just after he pulled this stunt."

"What's it of?" He couldn't remember seeing a photo by the cash register.

"It's just a snapshot of him and a buddy in Tangier getting arrested as they walked out of the sea. They swam across the Strait of Gibraltar with paddleboards and fins. They were getting arrested for unlawful entry."

Frank raised an eyebrow. "It wasn't prearranged?"

Pussy shrugged. "I guess not. But the reporter had intervened and told the police it was a publicity stunt by the guy who'd just surfed the tallest wave in Portugal. Luckily, the surfing was televised and popular with the police chief, so they put them on the ferry the next day and sent them back."

"Who was the buddy?"

"One of his BRO buddies."

Frank stood. "So what happens to the bar now?"

She cocked her head. "I guess I just keep carrying on." She waved her hand at the desk. "How hard is it to pay the bills and throw beer?"

He looked at Mickey and back at Pussy. "I'll stop by in a few days. We'll see if we can figure this out."

The ride back down to Crystal Cove was silent. Frank let it go. He knew Mickey had a lot to think about.

04 DEEP DIVE

The tips of the small waves were just starting to turn pinkish-white with the new light. The roughed-up end of Frank's board rose a few inches and fell. His slow breathing matched the steady rhythm. Most of his mind was busy with what he always thought of as playing with blocks—ideas stuck together, formed solid blocks that his mind randomly pushed around, stacked, spread out, or moved to one side.

The black block in the middle of everything was a set of triple air tanks. Not the ones they found, but the ones Uncle Sam had issued him *eight thousand four hundred and fifty-seven days* before.

The gray block with yellow waves moving along the surfaces was the gas-mix table for depth, weight, temperature, and time. The block wouldn't move, and he couldn't manipulate the scales to match Mary—even if he knew where Mary had been diving.

In the dawn light, the surf was by any surfer's opinion *flat*. Frank hadn't come to surf, but to think. Since his sophomore year in high school—*eleven thousand six hundred eighty-three-days ago*—he had found his most productive thinking in the mindless up-and-down of the surfboard, sitting on the water in the morning light.

"Dude."

The blocks wouldn't behave. He tried to push a box with a head in it. It only sunk into the water below.

"Hey. Old man."

Frank looked around. The bald surfer with the pure-white goatee was slowly breast-stroking his board toward Frank.

Frank gently closed his eyes and returned his face toward the sun. He let the weak beginning of the day's heat soak through his skin.

"Damn, Frankie. I was above the north point, and I could still hear you thinking down here. What the fuck, dude? Have some respect for other people's quiet." The man pulled up alongside and sat up. His voice lowered and lost all severity. "I suppose, with your connections, you heard about Mary Shores…"

Frank dipped his head. He wasn't ready to talk to other surfers about the man—especially another Vietnam vet and long-gun rider. The family was too small and close. He could feel the man slump in on himself.

"A nasty piece of shit…"

Frank turned one eye on the man. "I don't want to talk about it."

The man with only one hand and half of the other bobbed his head. "If I hear anything about a wake or service, I'll leave word with Danny at the Shack."

Frank sighed and thought about the gesture. "Thanks. I'd appreciate it. And, if I hear anything, I'll post a notice at the Skeg."

The man realized Frank would probably be the first to know anything. Even being retired from the sheriff's department, his connection would run deeper than the VA or any brotherhood of surfers. His thanks was soft and almost lost as he laid down on his board and started paddling toward the cove.

Frank looked north toward an unseen spot about ten miles away. He looked back at the retreating older surfer. The man's browned back only showed a few pink nicks and bumps, but Frank knew the man was just as scarred as he was—sometimes, the person was a lot deeper than the sum of their skin.

"Hey, Trevor?"

The man sat up and looked back over his shoulder.

"Do you dive?'

The man chuckled and looked at his long surfboard riding high and buoyant on the water. "Kinda hard to do on a long gun."

"No. I mean scuba dive."

"Why would I do that? All the fish I need is down at the Safeway. And if I want sushi, I can always go to a bar."

Frank's smile drew tight on the one side. The truth of old bachelors. "So you wouldn't know where to get equipment for deep dives…?"

"Nah." The man lay back down, paddled halfheartedly, and then looked back over his shoulder. "There is a red flag thingie on 17th near Newport. Isn't the red flag thingie where bubble-heads go?"

Frank rocked his body and head. His voice was soft and absentminded. "Yes… yes they do." He looked up and laid down on his board and started paddling toward the south of the cove. "I'd forgotten about the place. Thanks, Trevor. I'll be in touch." He watched the man wave his truncated hand. The sniper's bullet had taken the three fingers between the thumb and pinkie, plus a scoop of the metacarpals. The man's right hand was a permanent surfer's sign for *hang loose*.

THE ARTIST COLONY of the nineteen twenties and thirties lined the south wall of Crystal Cove. Surfers took over the row of garages in the sixties and seventies. Many stored their heavy long-gun surfboards there in the days of honor and inability to haul them around. Then there were the squatters using other garages as camping shelters. As most would say, they were a little better than sleeping on the sand, as they were a long row of leaking roofs. Only one pair had seen repair to the roof. Max and Frank had patched the roof so Max could live where he fixed and reshaped boards. The man had always smelled of fiberglass and resin.

The two garages were the only privately owned garages—both had been part of Frank's inheritance. The middle rack along the south wall was the only rack Frank still used. The other fifteen held boards of friends long gone. The board with a lei of Hawaiian flowers on it rested right above his. His partner had rarely used it, but it reminded Frank of their solid and special partnership.

Frank looked at the empty rack at the bottom of the back wall. Somehow, it seemed like it had always been waiting for Mary Shores' fourteen-foot balsawood long gun. It would wait until Frank could get it released from evidence—after they solved his murder.

As he closed the garage door and secured the lock, one of the houses' semi-permanent residents walked past. She was one of the few who worked—most were just tourists. The white canvas espadrilles didn't match the sheer nylons and two-piece pinstriped suit, but he knew the correct shoes would be in the larger bag matching the purse. Even when relaxing on the beach, Frank had never seen the woman without some form of silk scarf wrapped at her throat.

This morning's scarf, fluffed at her neck, matched the suit's gray, but with accents of powdery lavender. The red piping edge was her signature—everything was soft and pretty until she slit your throat and drained your bank account.

Still holding the large lock, he turned. "Good morning, Bitsy."

She looked over, distracted. "A fine morning, Frank. But if I were you, I would not even bother with the surfboard. It looked flatter than the 405 Freeway." She half-glanced back down the alleyway toward the beach. "I don't think those waves would even wash the top of your big board."

"Good advice, counselor. Maybe just a little waxing and then more coffee."

"Wise choice, young man. Wise choice. Have a good day."

"You too, Bitsy."

She raised her free hand as she turned up the hill. "Court day. Screwing assholes in court is always a good day, Frank. Best sex there is."

Frank sighed. He had run a background on her years before. He knew her hair color came from a well-controlled set of bottles. She could afford to live anywhere she wanted, in any size house she wanted, and drive anything she wanted—or be chauffeured. The woman had started practicing law when women were still expected to be demure and quiet. He wasn't sure if he could afford or would ever need her services. But he did know in his soul that if he ever needed a shark in his corner of a courtroom, the seventy-three-year-old woman, walking up the mile-long hill to her 1974 BMW 2002, would be his choice. Last he checked, she had spent well over a month's worth of nights in jail for contempt of court.

"IT AMAZES me you even know how to turn on a computer." Danny wiped the table and chairs carefully with an eye at sanitation. His contempt for young couples bringing children to the Shack, clothed only in diapers, and plopping them down on his chairs, rode only below the few hairs on his arms.

Frank didn't have to look to know the knuckles on his fist holding the rag were blanched with rage. Only once had a child demonstrated a leaking dirty diaper. But the once was burned in the fastidious germophobic mind of the tall man. Frank never said a word about the few times the one-man force of iron-will had stood at the door and told a sloppily dressed parent with a child dripping from their arm how the health department had just closed the Shack because of hoof-and-mouth, anthrax, or some other made-up disease designed to scare a parent. Frank owned the business and building, but it was Danny's home, life, and empire. Under his bony guiding hand, it had never had a negative week.

Frank's growl was only a low rumble as he continued to poke at the keys with his two index fingers. It seemed the back-space, at times, got the most use. The black dish in the plastic key undoubtedly accounted for something.

With the last chuff from the man leaning forward as if he could intimidate the information from the inanimate machine, Danny threw the rag on the table, sat, and spun the laptop around.

Looking at his boss's snarled face, he backed off from his usual taunting about Luddites in the twenty-first century. "What exactly are you trying to find?"

Feeling the hidden affront, Frank growled. The passive face didn't change. "There was a set of triple tanks found near Mary's body. They had a mixed-gas sticker on them..."

The long, slender fingers were already dancing across the keyboard. "And you want to know where he bought them... or at least got them filled..."

The man turned the laptop back around and stood. "It looks like you have a busy day ahead of you—starting with the three shops in San Clemente and seven chandlers or dive shops in San Pedro."

Frank frowned. "What makes you think he would have gone all the way down to San Clemente or up to Pedro?"

Danny straightened his body to his full height. "Same reason Mickey will be wearing storm-gray socks this morning." He turned and walked back to harass the cook for the three orders for his customers. Frank saw the nose of the tan Taurus ease into the parking spot.

He returned his attention to the list of shops. There were three flags in San Clemente and four in Dana Point. As the medium-gray slacks appeared in his peripheral vision, he noted the sliver of the darker socks. They weren't dark enough to be black—just dark enough not to draw attention. Mary might not have wanted his purchase or movements known.

Mickey asked, "Where to first?"

Frank slid his finger on the pad, forcing the interactive map to scroll. There were only two flags. "Let's drop down to Pendleton."

Mickey rolled his eyes. "Why not waste more time and go all the way down to Del Mar or La Jolla?"

Frank rose and brought his nose within a few inches of the younger man. "I don't get paid enough to let you get so close to El Chicano or the track."

Mickey snorted softly. "You're just afraid I might talk you into Jose Domingo's, and they would make you eat in the parking lots with those shorts."

They walked past a stoic Danny. Frank flipped his head. "Tell him, Danny. He's just jealous I have better-looking legs than him."

Danny barely moved his lips. "Mickey has legs? I thought they were just jelly sticks."

Mickey walked past with his left hand and middle finger rubbing up and down behind his ear.

05 TANKS A LOT

The armful of seemingly random tattoos had long turned green with sun and age. The solid white of the brush-cut hair screamed gunnery sergeant. The soft voice and easy flow of information showed a man relaxed in his world and one who loved what he was doing.

The fingernail was cracked but trimmed close. "This set of numbers will tell you what the mix is, but based on what you're saying, I'd say he was diving the shoulder. But why he was doing it at night is beyond me. If I went hunting over the edge, I'd want all the light I could get. There are lots of dangerous animals out there these days."

Frank's mirrored aviators eclipsed the bottom of his eye. "Sharks?"

"For one. Barracuda and the two-legged kind come to mind also."

Frank frowned with curiosity.

The man snorted with a soft growl. "What, you thought all the pirates were above the surface?"

Mickey came out of the office. He watched the old diver and Frank. His right hand absently picked up a metal tool of some sort. He studied the small mass of metal—turning it over and around. He brought the price tag closer to his eyes and frowned. Mouthing the word *ouch*, he carefully placed it back in the bin. He dramatically withdrew his hands as if he were apologizing for touching the tool. And looked over.

The gunny snorted. "Expensive piece of titanium alloy, isn't it? But if you're a rigger, that there tool can save your life."

Frank rolled his eyes and squinted out the window. A large swathe of white sail slowly moved through the channel. He blinked and ground his head around. "Find anything?"

Mickey shook his head. "He didn't buy them here."

Frank looked at the former marine. The man shook his head. "There will be an expiration date for the tanks, but no way really to trace where someone bought them. They're not as bad as hand weapons with gun shows and all, but it's close. We probably have a dozen singles here that have been through at least a dozen hands. The closer they get to their end date, the cheaper they are. Eventually, someone will buy a tank for the metal or cut the bottom off and make a gong. Other than that, they're just a container for air or gas. Nobody really gives a shit whose they are."

Frank stuck his hand out. "Thanks, gunny. You've been a great help."

"No problem. Anytime you want to go get some bugs or abalone, come on down. I've still got a pass onto the nuke land, so we don't have to hump the equipment."

"I appreciate the offer. It's been a few years since I rustled up some bugs to grill."

As Mickey nosed the Taurus onto the northbound onramp, he glanced at Frank. The man was watching him with his knee pulled up on the seat. "What?"

"What did you really find?"

Mickey leaned toward the window as he watched the side mirror with his blinker on. The truck passed, and Mickey eased into the next lane. His head turned only partially before he started watching the faster lane. "Nothing. And I mean strangely—nothing. It's as if they're selling rutabagas. There is no tracking from the hole in the ground, the picker's hand, or even the box they end up in."

"There should be some semblance of tracking…"

Mickey settled the large car into the fast lane, then glanced over. "There is… normally. But the system seems set up so they get to be as loose as they want. They can sell a bunch of controlled new equipment, but there is no tracking for the used equipment."

"Who would want used equipment?"

Mickey peeked up at the mirror. "Same person who wants a cold untraceable weapon."

Frank bobbed his head as he leaned against the door. His finger tabbed the window control, and his words flushed away in the rush of air.

"A nun going to a garden convention…"

His sarcasm got lost on the diesel fumes as they passed a slow-moving truck. He eyed the white plate as he scanned for a matching California plate—there was none.

"When did they start letting Mexican trucks run this high without a California plate?"

Mickey bit on his lower lip. "About the same time they let them across the border without having to pass a reasonable smog test."

THE CHANDLER'S shop was small but neat and busy. Frank and Mickey waited their turn as they watched two men and a woman manhandle the computer terminals with efficiency and speed. One customer's jumpsuit had more grease and rust than blue cloth showing. The white in his brown buzz-cut was in patches. Frank had seen the type of head injuries causing the patches. He was amazed by the man rattling off a long list of supplies as the woman typed.

"Can I help you men?"

Frank and Mickey turned. The man looked more like a yacht lizard than anyone who could help them. The white shorts were pressed, and there wasn't a wrinkle or stain on the light blue polo shirt. Frank looked down at the slip-on deck shoes over bare feet. The smile floating in the sea of freckles under the dark glasses and red curls hadn't changed.

"You two don't look like you're here to place an order." The man pulled his glasses and hung them from a single stem in his shirt. "My guess is either cops or a bored stock trader wanting to cut the cost of his nose candy by outfitting an old rummy sport fisher to run a few kilos up from Baja."

"Why not a teacher who wants to just treat his dad to a new doo-dad for his black hole in the water?"

The man snorted and waved at their shoes. "The custom McDoofus slippers and hemp slacks aren't the uniform of the day for any teachers I've met." Moving his hand up and down Frank's body like an elevator. "This is the Goodwill dregs teachers can afford. So what do you cops want?"

Frank held up a photo from better times. "Any of these guys come in here?"

"Sure. Dick Nixon was a regular customer. He lived just up the hill from here. The short fuck is doing time in Soledad or San Q… I can never keep track… He moves around a lot." He looked back up at Frank with a pure poker face.

Frank's slimmed mouth pulled to the right in a half-smile. "Orange County Sheriff's Department. The guy you referred to as a short fuck was killed night before last."

"Shit." The man hollowed. "Crap. Mary was one of the nice guys. What happened?"

Frank glanced at Mickey to make sure he wasn't overstepping. The young man's face was still hard from the McDoofus slap. Frank rolled his eyes back to the chandler.

"That's what we're trying to find out. There was a set of triple tanks…"

The man looked at the silent Mickey and talked to Frank. "One hour mixed for a hundred to a hundred-twenty feet." He looked at Frank. "What do you need to know?"

"Do you know where and why he was diving?"

"Sure. He was diving the shoulder, and I always assumed he was going after bugs and shells."

Mickey stirred. "Shoulder?"

The man grabbed at the air as he slid past them. From a large flat file, he drew out a large map. His hand passed over the area of light blue and the darker. "This is what people are familiar with when looking at the continental shelf." His hand flattened in the air as he talked. "According to general maps and people's beliefs, the shelf goes out a mile or so and then drops straight down for two thousand feet."

Frank pointed to a slender series of numbers running up on the outside the demarcation. "What are these numbers?"

"It's the shoulder. It's too narrow to draw on most maps." He leaned over and opened another drawer. Fingering through the stack of maps, he finally withdrew one and laid it out on top of the original. It covered a much smaller area. "This is a dive map. If you're a power swimmer, you could swim from top to bottom in two hours." He waved his spread hand over the whole map. "Or you can take a single tank and have a great time chasing bugs and fish all over here for half an hour or so. But..." His finger drew along a narrow path between two lines. The lines separated three numbers of depth.

Frank leaned forward. "So the shoulder is about thirty or forty feet deeper than the shelf..."

"Exactly."

Mickey leaned in. "What's there?"

The man leaned back to give Mickey more room. "For most people—nothing."

Frank frowned half of his face as his mind raced. He had lived most of his life on the other side of 'for most people.'

"But for other people...?"

The man shrugged. "Mostly nothing... but then... there are the larger fish, and larger predators."

"What sort of predators?"

"What sort are you looking for?"

"The kind to leave Mary Shores' body on Newport Beach."

The man leaned against the map chest. As the color returned to his face, he turned, took four steps to a bait bucket, and lined the inside with his lunch. The woman looked over, and Frank held up his hand. She dipped her head and went back to her computer.

"Jeezus." The man wiped the back of his hand across his mouth. "I wanted to believe you were joking... Sorry. I realized you wouldn't have driven down if this was a joke." He considered the bucket again but held up his hand instead. "Let's take this outside." He grabbed the bucket as an afterthought.

They sat on the weathered bench. Mickey leaned against the rail with his back to the boats in the marina. The afternoon had reached quiet. The yacht moms had finished their shopping and were bracing themselves with a late gin and tonic or Bloody Mary before maneuvering their three-ton SUVs to pick up the kids from school. Any real sailors were out for the last breeze and sun of the day, and the wannabe businessmen were back at their offices worrying about paying their bills and only dreaming about the day they might take on the black hole in the water called a yacht.

The walkway was empty other than the two seagulls fighting over something dropped earlier. Trash dirtied the water, but food disappeared via the rats of the sky.

"He bought the tanks and fins about three weeks ago. Said he was going to take a look at the bugs along sailor's shelf. Everyone knows the shelf gets the warm flow from the nuke plant, so the bugs are larger, but the abalone are what people are really after. When California outlawed the shells from overfishing, the locals in the know knew the shelf was still full. It was just a matter of getting them and not getting caught."

This wasn't new to Frank. He had done his share of poaching in the dark of night. "Explains the flood torch and night, but the point off San Onofre is a far cry from Newport."

"Was he killed there… or just dumped there?"

Frank rose on his one hip as he fished for his phone. He squinted at the screen as he searched for the number. Poking it, he put the flat slab of technology to his ear and leaned back to the building.

"Oz. Frank. Did you figure out where he was killed?"

His face was impassively hard as he listened. Their years working together had created an understanding between the examiner and the detective. The one knew what information the other wanted and didn't want to waste time questioning a fool.

He animated by crossing his right sandaled foot on his bare left knee. "Yeah. He bought the rig down here in Dana Point. They were under the impression he would be poaching abalone where the nuke plant dumps its warm wastewater out onto the shelf. He never talked about Newport."

Mickey turned his head to watch a large Zodiac glide by. The woman driving the boat looked like she was driving her convertible sports car with the top down through her neighborhood streets. The afternoon sun lit up her dyed neon-red hair with pink spiked tips. The wraparound black glasses gave her more of a rakish look than a bandit. More than a yacht club pirate. She was more of a hunting marina shark. The two large outboard engines destroyed any misconception of the inflatable as a convenience dingy of the meek—this was a sport in her own league. A force of nature astride her badge of right. As she got to the turn, she goosed the engines to drift the large boat into an expert flip turn. The lone woman, combined with the engines' weight, left the light front to slap around the center point. It was an impressive move with no more time or effort than a person raising their arm to flex their muscle.

As she approached the 'No Wake' marker, she opened the throttle to let the engines snarl. The boat lifted onto the top of the small waves and turned for the ocean and the lowering sun. Mickey could almost imagine her drawing a saber and laughing to her pirates, commanding them forward to raise all sails, for it was time to kill and plunder another ship.

The chandler chuckled and quietly stepped over to the rail. "She's just as wonderfully powerful with her two feet on the dock."

Mickey frowned a question at the man.

"Her name is Mary. But for the way she swirls life around her, she might as well be named Molly Boone."

"Molly…?"

"The female pirate. She was just as bloody as Blackbeard. But a lot more fun. She ruled the Dry Tortugas." He waved his hand in dismissal. "But that was another lifetime ago."

They turned as they heard Frank stand.

"We have an appointment."

Mickey looked hopeful. "Dinner?"

Frank shook his head. "Another body."

Mickey's face fell and darkened. "Does this one still have a head, at least?"

Frank's head twitched to one side as he put his hand out to the chandler. "Thanks for your help. I'll be back. I'll need the same setup as Mary. Maps would be a good place to start."

"I'll start gathering everything. Are you going to need a suit too?"

"Everything but my baggies."

The man laughed. "Baggies don't fit under skins. I'll pull shelf maps from here to Seal Beach. You might want to take Stevie to lunch and tap into her expertise in diving the shelf. She was the one at the counter."

"I'd rather keep this as quiet as possible."

"She's the most qualified diver of the shelf to where it runs out in Ventura. She's also been keeping my secrets for thirty-eight years."

Frank shook his hand one last time. "Works for me."

06 WRECK

He stopped the searing heat for the first time. The orange blossom became a multicolored orange ball in front of him. He could sense the rising hands of Kahuna, his partner. But he couldn't turn his head to take a last look. He could only sense the feelings of fear, shock, and understanding of loss. Beyond the ball of ignited explosive and gas was the final deadly buttress of concrete. The 5 Freeway continued northwest, the 57 Freeway swung over top continuing northeasterly, but their unmarked car and his partner's life would end in a hundred and fifty-three feet.

Frank's eye shot open as he realized that he didn't know how many days it had been for the first time since the crash. The hot breath was an inch from his nose. The tongue washed over his face in three quick laps of relief.

Frank reached out and kneaded his fingers in the fur. "I'm okay, buddy. In fact... I think I'm getting better." He tried to find why his heart wasn't racing, why he wasn't sweating, and why he felt relaxed and rested. He scooted back on the bed and patted the mattress in the curve of his body. The wild coyote oozed into the invitation. With a last lick at Frank's chin, she curled into a ball with her nose buried under her paw. Soon they were both asleep as the dark sky pinked and then grayed.

"Jeezus… when did you get a dog?" Mickey's voice was irritated as he stepped up the last step and peered into the small, dim shack.

Reflectively, Frank's hand went to the rib cage of the thin animal. It rested down the two inches it had raised in warning. Frank knew the character of the young man. He wouldn't enter, he wouldn't threaten, but he also wouldn't run.

"Is that a coyote?"

Frank grabbed the dog to him and rolled over with the dog on top. The dog squirmed as he was now placed on the human's safe side, away from the new human. Frank snuggled his nose down in the nape, growling in an old game of theirs. The dog licked his nose and then half rose, resting her jowls on the man's chest. If her human was okay, then she was okay.

Frank growled as he kneaded at the one ear. "She's my coyote. Go get your own." He sat up. The coyote licked one more time at his mouth and jumped down. Padding to the large box, she escaped through the winter doggie-door leading under the shack.

Mickey withdrew his head from watching the dog use another way out. "We have an ID on the body."

Frank gently pushed him out of his way as he walked out onto the porch—naked. "Not before breakfast, we don't. I worked late last night."

Mickey's head snapped toward the neighboring house, a couple of football fields away. Frank turned on the shower, stepped into the water, and started peeing as he shampooed his hair.

Mickey started, "What about—?"

"Shut up. I have sixty-seven seconds to get this done."

Mickey drew his wristwatch up to his view. The second hand just swept the seven.

The growl was garbled by the hands pushing water around the face. "Fuck you, asshole."

The sweeping red hand passed the four as Frank shut off the lever and waved a large sprinkling of water at the light gray linen suit. The morning light shined off the many surgical scars, surfing dents and dings, and baby-fist holes of missing meat. He flopped into the wooden chair to air-dry.

Mickey looked around for another chair, but his scrutiny was also drawn back to the man's front side. He wasn't sure which had been more abusive to the man—his duty to his country, his addiction to the waves, or his retirement by concrete abutment. His father had told the young Mickey about his friend and fellow SEAL, but seeing the physical evidence confirming the stories' truth was always jarring.

"Counting the stitch marks again?" One morning after a good drunk, a waking hungover Frank had found the fingers of a five-year-old Mickey counting the stitches on his body. Over the years, the reminder was sure to rouse a flush on the young man. It didn't disappoint.

"Don't you have a towel or something? We're burning daylight."

Frank turned his head to the young man and snorted. "Somehow, it doesn't sound the same as when it came out of your father."

"Fuck you, old man." The finger rubbed along the side of his nose.

Frank pushed himself erect. "Now you sound more like the punk we all knew and loved to irritate."

A minute later, he stood in the doorway in boardshorts and a Grateful Dead shirt. He leaned his shoulder against the door-jamb as he pulled on a pair of deck shoes.

"No sandals?"

He lowered his mirrored aviators onto his nose. "Going formal today." He thought about the blue booties over the man's shoes. "Where did you park your car?"

"There's a ditch crossing the road down here from the Shack."

Frank smiled. "Glad you were smart enough not to try to drive through it. I buried caltrops in the dirt."

Mickey lowered his head and looked over his dark glasses. "I found them. We're taking your car."

"You do know my daily includes expenses."

"So...?"

Frank stepped off the end of the small deck. "The Bentley will cost you a double-buck each mile. She kind of likes her premium gas."

"The Bentley also has a ridiculous blown and milled 427."

As they slid into the topic of conversation and Frank lit the engine, he goosed the gas enough to make good use of the exhaust system and leaned toward his friend. "Your point being...?"

Danny heard the big engine and placed the coffee, tea, and breakfast on the southern table. He was still pouting and didn't want to talk to Mickey. The silence at the table was solid. Mickey respected the conditions. The sparkly pink coffee travel mug disappeared and returned, clean and full. After Danny had retreated to the kitchen, Mickey checked. There were four or more bags of tea in the steaming water. He replaced the lid. The small smile was only a flash.

Frank continued to eat as he read the report. He closed the folder and grabbed the last of his toast. He pushed the bread around the plate, mopping up the last of the orange evidence of his poached eggs. His focus was out the south-facing window to the edge of the ocean and sky. The fine edge was a hard blue-gray of the ocean and the soft blue-white of the sky. One distant puff of condensation floated halfway to the distant islands.

"They may be connected, but I doubt Mary knew this asshole. Latino scum from Santa Ana wasn't his style."

Mickey looked up from reading a text on his phone. "Style of what?"

Frank brought his attention around. "Of anything. Sex. Social. Hanging. You name it, and they weren't within a mile of each other."

"What did he have against Mexicans?"

"Nothing. He loved surfing up and down the Baja back in the day. He was more fluent in Spanish than you or me."

Mickey frowned. "I don't speak Mexican."

Frank raised his hands out as he stood. "I rest my case." He turned toward the kitchen. "Danny."

The soft voice floated out from the back. "They're in your beater, boss."

As they walked out to the Bentley, Frank noticed the trunk was ajar. He raised the lid and checked to arrange the three tactical bags. Only one had been in the trunk since the wreck and his forced retirement. The other two were locked away in what passed for the Shack's office. The large floor safe was under a small rug gifted to Frank after the first sandbox war. His fourteen words of Farsi had saved a family. The mayor of the village had tracked him down and showed up at the airport as Frank was boarding the airplane with his company. Holding the small roll, he had ridden in the C-130 to Germany, embarrassed by the largess.

Somewhere over Turkey, a sergeant had wandered back down the noisy cavity of the transport. He sat down next to Frank and held his hand out, asking permission to look. He had only pulled back one corner. After thinking quietly for a moment, he looked at Frank. He explained how a family like the mayor had only two things of value: his family and the family rug passed down from father to son for generations. He said he wasn't sure, but he would guess at the rug's age to be somewhere between four and six hundred years old. The pattern was definitely after the second Crusade. Frank had watched the face of the man whom he had thought was just another Latino. His eyes fell to the name tag: Al Sadat.

After he had recovered from the nine surgeries and restored

the Shack, he used the rug to cover his secrets. Only Danny knew about the safe and knew the codes.

As Frank nosed the heavy car onto the highway headed north, he thought about how much Danny had become his family. Every bit as much as the wild coyote.

Mickey dozed as Frank cruised the quiet car up the coast highway. Frank wasn't complaining. His mind was pushing blocks of information around. The block with the head still sinking, the block with the triple tanks not moving, and a fresh-grown cube with overtones of gray continued to bother him. The new sand-colored cube was small but still moved too easy. Like the first short surfboard he had picked up. *Ten thousand forty-three days.*

He jerked the steering wheel. The heavy car lurched and then wallowed. He wrestled the weight to the center of the transition underpass ramp from the northbound 55 to the northbound 5. He remembered it was Sunday. The investigation may not take a day off, but Pussy would if the bar was closed.

Still mulling over the sand-colored cube and how easy it pushed around, he tipped the blinker and flowed with a small white car onto the northbound 57. He had stopped trying to figure out who made what car. He had become his mother. Cars were just cars and their color. Trucks were simply what they had stacked in their back bed. If it had lawn mowers, rakes, and leaf blowers, it was a gardener truck. Large racks with lumber made it a carpenter truck. And, if it was empty, it was an empty-head or testosterone truck.

He took the Chapman offramp and headed west.

THE DOOR SWUNG IN. The gloom of the curtained apartment softened the woman's appearance. "It took you long enough to find me." Pussy's open hand grabbed at the air while she turned. "The girls were just making breakfast. Bloody Mary or coffee?"

Frank stepped in with Mickey following with fear. "Coffee

for me, but I think Mickey only needs a few slaps and a spanking for drinking his piss-water tea."

A short pixie with pink hair and a nose ring leaned out of the kitchen. "Oolong, Lapsang Soo Chong, or Earl Grey?"

Mickey brightened. "Oolong, please."

Her head retreated to giggles. "Dishwater, and we'll let Connie piss in it."

Frank peeked in at the two young girls. The identical twins both wore long T-shirts emblazed with "No, I'm the other one." He had met them a couple of times before. He wasn't sure if they were really old enough to work at Mary's, or even which was which, or who was who—so he never asked. He wasn't even sure if they were female or something else. He nodded at their mirrored finger waves and mouthed *Good morning*.

He dropped the thin file on the table and pushed it at Pussy. She opened it. He watched her eyes. She scanned it loosely and then went back to the beginning and read it with interest.

Mickey looked at the blue-haired pixie as she presented a glass mug of steaming water. The teabag was just starting to create curls of color. He fingered the label tag. The pixie snorted haughtily, hip checking his shoulder. Frank was surprised when the young man just smiled. The tiny hip did not affect the slender man.

Pussy softly closed the file, staring at the cover. Her voice was soft so as not to leave the table. "I'm sure there's a reason you showed me this guy's file. But he sounds like a real creep."

"They found his body yesterday."

She glanced at the twins in the kitchen, who were far from paying attention. "Same way as Mary?"

Frank nodded.

"And you want to know if he'd ever come into Mary's or if I'd ever met him?"

Frank nodded.

Her hair jiggled. Frank could feel the tension in her head and neck. Revulsion could do that.

Mickey shifted on his seat. His mouth was pursed with bitterness. "There's a connection somewhere."

Pussy leaned into his face as she stood to get more coffee. "Mary did *not* associate with asshole slime." She pointed back at the folder, her sports bra and T-shirt stretched over the defined muscles. "That is the slimiest of the fecal eaters the world can produce." She huffed into the kitchen. The twins stood quietly out of her way. "Frank." Her voice more of a bark. "More coffee?"

His only reply was rolling his head and raising his mug.

She filled his mug, set down the carafe, and sat down. Frank could tell the storm had blown over with a last drawn-out sigh.

"Have you thought more about the bar?"

She held up a finger as she leaned back.

The twins stopped behind her. "We're going for a run."

"Okay... Where?"

"We were thinking down to the river. They laid new cover along the east side, so we were thinking down to the back yard, around the nearside of the park, and back up from the Katella trail."

"Okay, but take your phones."

They kissed the top of her head and walked as one into the back of the apartment.

Pussy's head snapped at another thought. "Tink?"

The two heads appeared back out of the room.

"If you bring home a cat again, I will skin you both and make throw pillows."

The two voices were in clear harmony. "Got it, Mommy." The heads disappeared.

"And be home in time to clean up for the one thirty matinee. I don't want to miss the coming attractions this time." She listened to the silence. "You got me?"

"Got ya."

Mickey frowned. "Back yard?" He knew the river would be

part of the Southern California water districts' concrete-lined riverbeds, which were little more than flood control.

The woman's face paused, replaying the conversation. It lightened as she got to where the girls had said where they were running. "They work for Disneyland. The Back Yard is the area along Ball Road where the warehouses and repair sheds are."

Frank smirked. "What do they do at the park? Zipline?"

Pussy smiled with half her mouth pulled back. "Tink zips, but the other Tink is a cast member on the concierge level of the hotel."

Mickey coughed. "They're both named Tink?"

The woman's face washed blasé. "Other than the coloring in their hair. Can you tell them apart?"

"No."

"Neither can Disney, but the health benefits are the most important. The pay is good, and nobody knows how to control them, so they enjoy their lives."

Frank cleared his throat with a sip of coffee. "Are they identical twins?"

Pussy nodded. "Born four states and twenty-seven days apart. But they are cousins. Their mothers were identical twins. They've been dressing alike, doing their hair, and forcing the appearance since they were about ten. One is about an inch taller, but don't ask me which."

Trying to understand a world he had never been close to, Mickey waved his spidered hand in a circle over the table. "The family dynamic between you three...?"

Frank growled softly. "Is fluid and only their business."

Mickey's head snapped to a grumpily passive Frank. The man's eyes were cold hard stone above the rim of his mug.

"We're in their home, and it's none of your business." Frank quietly placed the mug on the table. "The bar...?"

She leaned forward and pulled out her cell phone in a leather pocketbook shell. Opening the cover, she withdrew a business card and spun it across the table to Frank. As he read it, she explained. "He was Mary's lawyer. He had made some provisions for other parts of his estate, but the bar was never mentioned. He's going to draw up a conveyance of hostile takeover in case anyone tries to make a stink."

"So, you'll just continue—business as usual."

"Business that's unusual as usual." Her smile quirked to the left.

Frank nodded with a small knowing smile. Times change but remain the same.

07 SHOULDER WORK

The work boat was almost as old as Frank's shack, but with decades of paint, chip, mink coat, and more paint. The back deck ran straight into the water. The restraining transom was only a rope from one side to the other. The style was self-bailing.

Frank sat with his back to the cabin. The line of white-frothed water trailed for almost a quarter mile behind the boat. The run from Dana Point to the point off Newport Beach wasn't far on the map, but he knew the work boat would be doing good if they could maintain a steady seventeen knots. The current washed south down the entire seven thousand miles of the West Coast. The occasional bay, harbor, spit, or point served to slow then speed the flow. The surf beds lined with board-riding addicts were named for the accelerating point or the deadly termination point. The areas following the beach's name, such as Malibu or Newport, were made famous by Hollywood or took the name of the beach city. They were breeding grounds for serious surfers. The surf runs mild to medium. Spread over a wide area, they support newbies, wave troughs, surfers waiting for their driver's license, or a car to haul their boards and friends to more challenging locations.

Frank could still smell the slowly rotting interior of his friend's 1963 Volkswagen Transporter bus. The mold of their stitched and restitched—and only rarely laid out in the sun to dry—used wet suits compounded the other wads and piles of discarded shirts, towels, and baggies. The original VW factory-gray carpet had turned to compost and replaced with used shag carpet. Eventually, it was carpeted over with crude-woven blankets gathered on surfing safaris to Baja California.

The four friends pooled their money for gas and the occasional used tire with some rubber to the tread. The three with mechanical understanding had all but memorized the spiral-bound book *How to Keep Your VW Alive*. The fourth had gotten a part-time job at the Little Engine Shack for the employee discount and the occasional five-finger discount on the often needed 7mm or 10mm screw, bolt, or nut.

The pressure of the cabin against his back, the sound of the engines throttled back, and the surge of the following surf washing up and over the deck shook Frank from his memories of growing up on the water of Southern California. He turned his head toward the flying bridge. The weathered face of the woman leaned out.

"I think this might be a good place to get you acquainted with diving the shoulder."

Stevie turned and started down the ladder. "Paul can keep the boat on station, but also come to us when we come up." Her deck shoes touched down on the wet deck. "We'll be packing double tanks so we can cover some serious area of the shoulder here. The water has been clear for a few days. We can probably track the centerline and see anything or at least any anomaly from the wall to the drop." She opened the cabin door. "Let's go over the map to get you oriented to why we're here."

The soft pencil mark had been marked before. "Paul will stand station here. As you can see, we come here often. The bugs on this wall are fat but also meaty from the cold wash caused by this canyon. We call this part of the shoulder 'Maytag' for the washing-machine action going on from here to here." Her finger and thumb showed the spread. Frank noted the three small canyons creating the currents.

"This is how wide?"

She moved her two fingers to straddle the X of soft graphite. "The shoulder here is only about twenty feet wide. There is some rockfall as the shelf wears down." As her fingers moved north, they followed the lines. "As we get up here, we'll be weaving back and forth to cover the almost one hundred feet of shoulder, but the rockfalls are less and fewer. We should be able to see anything strange or out of place along the flats. The shoulder tends to be relatively flat as it probably was the old continental shelf. Anything that isn't flat should stand out even if it's the same color as the surrounding silt."

She picked up what looked like a kid's toy. "There will be one of these clickers hanging on your rig. It's amazing how far the sound carries underwater. When we're separated over the wider sections, we can get the other's attention with the clicker."

The speaker on the wall squawked. "We're on station. The sonar places the wall right under us."

Stevie reached over and depressed the lever. "Thanks, Pauly. We're all set, and we'll be right out."

As they got their wet suits ready, she held out a large tube of Vaseline. "If you lube your lower legs, they will stay warmer. Your booties slide on easier, too. Just cinch your straps tight on your fins because they can also slide off easily." She smirked. Frank figured she had firsthand experience.

Frank had forgotten how diving in deep water felt a lot like flying. When there is no bottom, and you're deep enough, the sensation is more of floating in space. You dive deeper, but the scenery doesn't change. You hang in the water, and you don't know if you are rising or sinking. Your buddy is your only point of reference unless a fish or trash floats by—both of which usually stick closer to the surface.

Stevie had set their weight belts to create a slightly negative buoyancy. Later, they would aid their ascent back to the surface with small balloons. Buoyancy was a dance of small adjustments.

As they worked their way down the continental shelf wall, Frank scanned the crevices and cracks. The few lobsters he saw were larger than what he would want on his plate. But he knew many divers would come over the edge to impress guests who judged more by size than quality. Even though the bugs were from colder water, their size made them tough and tasteless.

The shoulder spread out ahead of them. As Stevie had described, the floor was strewn with rocks and boulders. As they lowered, some of the small shadows moved. Frank wasn't sure if the almost transparent shrimp were ghost shrimp or just lacked color because of the dark. He glanced at the digital depth meter on his left wrist, finding they were floating just over the floor at eighty-seven feet deep. The floor would be closer to ninety-three or four.

As the shoulder widened, they rose to get a better view. The tumbles of rocks were mostly at the base of the wall, with a few heavier rocks having the energy to roll out across the middle. Only a few of them were larger than the size of a head or a body. Most of the larger ones showed signs of having fallen many years before with enough time to start growing a new deep-water neighborhood.

The divers progressed steadily.

The clicking disrupted the constant flow of the sound of his breathing. It was as crisp as a cricket in his shack as the morning warmed the dark weathered wood. He turned in the water and didn't see Stevie.

She rapidly clicked a series of three and then a slow beat of one every second. Frank slowly spun in the water—searching. As he focused on finding her, he realized he was floating in the water too high to see the shoulder, too deep to see the surface, and far enough away from the wall to know where the shelf was.

His first reaction was to panic.

Click.

Click.

Click.

He listened and concentrated on the beat. He could feel the calming as his own heartbeat slowed to match the clicking.

He drew his left wrist up to his mask. The second dial, next to the depth, showed direction. He swept his right arm to align his body in the northwesterly direction the shoulder went. The depth was only fifty-four feet. He bent forward and headed as close to straight down as he could.

Slowly the shelf came into focus. The tiny light clicked. The clicker produced enough piezoelectricity to power the small red LED. The light he could barely see in the boat cabin now stood out like a searchlight in the dim nether light of the shoulder. His eyes drifted closed in relief as he clicked his clicker. He thought of the fireflies of Camp Lejeune on a moonless night. *Ten thousand, nine hundred seventeen days.*

As he drifted to the diver sitting—floating—on the hood of an old car, Frank realized he had missed much human trash littering the shelf. He looked around at what looked like a semi-crushed refrigerator and something that may have once been someone's pride and joy with polished shiny paint and possibly chrome—whatever it was.

He turned back to Stevie. Behind her mask, and by the mass of bubbles, he could tell she was laughing at him. He dramatically shrugged with his arms.

She held up a small whiteboard with writing on it. *You got mesmerized.*

He nodded. It wasn't the first time. When scanning an unchanging roll of desert while watching for insurgents, he had missed the three women in burkas leading a donkey packed with rifles and rocket launchers. He had expected men crawling out of the wasteland, not three women walking along the road. In police training, there was a famous video. The scene was a typical city sidewalk café. You were supposed to ring the buzzer when you saw the criminals make contact or exchange information. The sound was as garbled as a real stakeout from a block away. Everyone focused on the man in the striped suit. The waiter brought him water and took his order. The man read his paper. After a few minutes, a woman sat down at the next table. The waiter brought the man's coffee and Danish roll and then turned to take the woman's order. She asked for water but was waiting for a friend. The waiter left. The man in the striped suit folded his paper and sipped at his coffee. The woman looked over and asked if he was finished with the stock report.

As the man handed her the thin section of the paper, the room full of highly trained observers started pounding their buzzers.

Not one of them flinched at the people on the sidewalk behind the diners. A man in handcuffs, dressed in a gray prison jumpsuit, walking in a shackled shuffle, met a person in a gorilla suit. By their actions, the gorilla asked the prisoner for directions. The prisoner had held up his chained hands and pointed back down the way he had come. It was a natural movement and scene on a busy street—only the characters were unusual. The entire room had focused on the person they assumed was the criminal but had missed the real criminal and his exchange of information.

Mesmerized by expectations.

Stevie tapped her wrist. Their time was up.

They gently swam up to forty feet and hung in the water. Frank wrote on his tablet. *Good lesson.*

She raised her hand in the okay sign and then thumbed up. She held a small balloon in her left hand. She squeezed the end to her mask and released air into the balloon. Frank rested his hand on her forearm as they began to rise. The closer to the surface they got, the larger the balloon became. The streams of exhaled air bubbles from the two divers were constant. Their fins wagged loosely under them. There was no hurry as their bodies became adjusted to the lack of depth. They hung at fifteen feet of depth. The water was bright, and the surface was so close. But the result of hurrying could be deadly. Frank drifted with a smile over all the times he had hung for the three minutes, waiting. He would take the sunny water over the black of night—any time.

The sunshine felt good as they peeled the wet suits. Pauly had marked where they left off their search. They would pick up again later with no wasted backtracking.

"It's common with searching. There are many reasons for always diving with a buddy or in groups. Becoming mesmerized to the point of drifting is only a minor one. At least you didn't reach into something or under something, only to find an eel chomping on your last finger." She laughingly held up her hand with two fingers comically turned down. "Five beers, bartender."

"It's still amazing how I could miss something as big as a car or refrigerator. Why would they stay on the shelf? And how the hell did they get there?"

"How they got there and why is a mystery. If the car were a legitimate wreck, I would think the salvage would have been more than the cost to haul it out and dump it. Same with the fridge. So, I like to think there was a body in one of them at one time." She smiled at the former detective. "As for why they are still there… it would take an extremely hard storm to produce enough storm surge deep enough to wipe the shoulder clean. So long before they go washing into the depths, all the boulders the size of bodies or heads will have to get flushed out and over the edge." She pulled at the toe of her bootie and with a grunt. Her bare foot glowed in the sunshine.

As Frank sat thinking in the warm sunshine, he subconsciously stretched his arms and back. The swimming had felt good. The movement had loosened him up.

Stevie stood over him with a bottle of water held out. "Here. You'll need this." He took the bottle, and she sat on the other bench. Her head and shoulders rocked gently with the boat's movement through the waves. "How's your back feel?"

He squinted one eye as he used the other. "Good. The dive loosened it all up nicely."

She nodded in acknowledgment and knowing. "Yeah, check in with me the day after tomorrow. If you're still loose and pain-free, we can try triples."

"How much did we do today?"

"From what Paul has marked, we covered just over a mile."

Frank collapsed his bottle as he sucked the last of the water. "Not bad, but I had hoped for more."

She snorted. "I'd say we flew through the shoulder—considering you haven't dived in what... ten or fifteen years? And then there's your back..."

Frank stared at the deck and the pattern of the water. "Nine thousand eighty-nine days."

She laughed. "Not nine thousand or nine thousand and ninety-days..."

He shook his head. "Nine thousand eighty-nine days. Strait of Hormuz. Cloud cover and only a sliver of a moon. It came up about an hour after we were feet dry and two men short."

She studied his face. She stopped any thoughts of teasing the man.

08 PEDRO

Not all books have the same cover. Not all books with similar covers have the same pages, stories, or characters.

Frank sat poring over the newly expanded file on the second headless body.

When Mickey walked into the Shack with a slim leather attaché case, Danny slowed. His mouth turned from smartass dig to a small mew of appreciation, and his trailing hand danced near the leather.

Mickey shifted the shoulder reports. A salvage friend of Frank's had trolled eighty miles of the shoulder with a metal scanner. He had also gotten his hands on the mapping scan the coast guard had done the year before. When Frank stopped smelling like horse liniment, he and Stevie could make better use of their time. They would still chase down the occasional car or refrigerator, but the dredging report would also allow them to skip over many acres wiped clean by the tides. An empty shelf was a waste of time, gas, and allowable muscle.

"Is there a way to overlay these two sets of scans?"

Frank flinched. The break in the silence was like a shot resulting in the image he was looking at. The French division of Interpol had recovered thirty-eight bullets from the two bodies.

The heads had turned to mush. Only through intensive work had they been able to identify the male.

He replayed Mickey's question in his head.

"Do you know any computer whizbangs at UCI?"

Mickey leaned back in the chair. His right eyebrow knelt in a frown. "Why? What have you heard?"

Frank sipped on his coffee as he returned his focus to the report. He randomly stabbed in the dark just to tease. "You're almost old enough to be her father."

Danny stopped behind the dapper man. His face was one of shock and interest. In his condition, he would hold the full pot of coffee stationary to hear any juicy dirt.

Danny blushed defensively. "For your dirty mind, she's twenty. Well, next month. It's mutual, and she approached me first."

Danny silently rolled his eyes and shook his head like a black church lady being told about an errant grandchild. His free hand was waving the finger of accusation.

Frank grumped with a smirk. Teasing the young Romero went back many years. "That's what you get when you troll those Sadie Hawkins dances. Bait."

"It doesn't matter. She's not a computer science geek."

Frank looked up as he held up his mug, forcing Danny to give away his presence. "Maybe she knows someone at her halfway house who knows how to turn on something bigger than a cell phone or a vibrator."

Mickey looked through his eyebrows at the older man. "You're starting to sound like an angry old man." He looked up at Danny. "Or Danny has been lacing the coffee with caustic soda. Either way, it doesn't suit your usual dower-sunshine act. Find anything new on Pedro?"

Frank flipped through the few pages and photos. "Nothing of substance." His face shrugged at Mickey. "I think it's time for me to go surfing down south." He looked up at Danny, who had been trying to snoop about what they were working on. "It's complicated. When I can make sense of it all, I'll fill you in. Now be a good little waitress and make me a bag and a couple of thermoses—I'm going to Mexico."

The man spun on his heels, the center being the coffee carafe. The coffee, hardly feeling the rotation, was stationary in the glass globe. Frank smiled at the tai chi trick as Danny stalked to the coffee station, restored the pot into its place, shot Frank a pouty look, then pushed into the kitchen.

Frank smirked as he straightened the new paperwork into the folder. "Is this the only copy?"

Mickey's head rose with closed eyes. One eye opened. "As a complete package? I think so."

Frank stood. "You want a copy as long as I'm making them?"

"Just don't lose this one."

"I'll leave it in the safe." Frank looked at Mickey's pensive face. "What?"

"The sheriff called me this morning. Evidently, he gets to the office at a quarter after five these days."

Frank knew this wasn't just random chitchat. "What did he want?"

Mickey took a deep sigh. "The usual. Wrap up a murder by Friday. Have the report on his desk by Sunday night."

Frank looked out at the flat surf in the cove. "The man was always an asshole, but now he's a greedy asshole."

"He said he had to answer to nervous constituents in the wealthiest part of the peninsula."

Frank tapped the files on the table. "If he calls again, tell him I've been logging twenty-hour days and calling in favors from L.A. to Mexico. Just don't tell him to go fuck himself—that's my job."

Mickey picked up Pinkie and weighed the fullness. Shrugging, he stood and scooped up the two shoulder reports. "If I need them, are these on a thumb drive anywhere?"

"In the office. The navy is old school. Billingsly burned me a disk."

Mickey's eyes and shoulders slumped back. "Oh, great. Now I have to find a gray-haired computer forensic person with last-century technology."

Frank stopped mid-turn. He pointed at the two-inch stack of paper in the younger man's hand. "No. That's what's in your hand." He turned. "Don't be an asshole. That's my job."

THE RIDE DOWN to Playa de Rosarito or, as most surfers called it, *Rosy*—had taken longer than most trips would have taken. The five-minute cruise at the border became a thirty-minute old-home week with American border guards and some older Mexicans. Some recognized the board, few recognized the Bentley, but all had recognized the surfer cop. Frank and his partner had been regulars across the border. Mostly on their days off, occasionally on business, and even the rare day of hooky while conducting a background investigation—*wink, wink.*

The apron windows were run-up to the eaves for the season. Only the severe stormy season would cause the owner to lower them to shed the rain or close them against the cold month.

Frank slowly spun the coffee cup in the saucer with his thumb and middle finger. Although the briefcase was next to his chair, his mind was blank and soaking up the sunshine's warmth. The sounds of traffic, people, seagulls, and memories blended into a pleasant melody of lightly colored gray noise.

"Still, he comes to Rosy and orders only coffee." The man pushed his elbow onto the windowsill next to Frank's table. "Senior, your car has some dents and needs to be washed. If you insist on this path, it will make my street look like the barrio."

Frank stretched his feet out and crossed them on the opposite chair. "Maybe it just means you need to wash your street more often, *gandul.*"

The man shrugged his eyes as he looked at the small waves of a dead surf. "Ah, you say 'slacker,' and I say 'mayor.'"

Frank snorted at his old friend. "The day you get elected mayor is the day I know the whole of Baja has turned to corruption as a way of life."

The man grabbed his Panama off his curly chestnut head and held it over his heart. "Through my heart, you shove the stake of slander and probably twist it as I lie mortally dying in the filthy street."

"Your words, Ralph. It's a filthy street. You really need to clean it up."

The man put his hat back on as he stepped over and looked at the longboard lying where a passenger would sit reclined in the Bentley. "For this conversation, I need a beer."

Shuffling into the bar, he held his hand up at the waitress. She nodded to her boss and uncle.

Ralph looked at Frank's feet on the chair. "*Cochino.* You talk of a dirty street and treat my furniture like it was your pigsty." He jerked the chair, and Frank lowered his feet. The man thought and swapped it for a chair from the next table.

Frank adjusted his bulk on the chair with his elbows spiked on the table.

"You look like shit. When was the last time you caught a decent wave?"

"Thanks. You look like the ravishing Marilyn Monroe yourself. When was the last time you even touched a board, much less got on one?"

"This afternoon."

"Bullshit."

The man smiled up at his young niece as she set the Corona in front of him. She waved her finger back and forth at the two men.

"Are we eating, or is this just a social visit?"

Frank looked up at the girl. "We'd better eat. Anything lobster is good for me."

The large Mexican nodded. "Same, *mija*." She nodded and left.

Frank pulled his aviator glasses down slightly with his middle finger. The man smiled. Things rarely changed.

He pointed out at the Bentley. "I just touched your board."

"Fuck you." The aviators were pushed back with the same middle finger.

"It doesn't look like it still be fourteen feet?"

"Nah. I've chiseled some off the nose a few times. More like eleven-five or six now. They must be working the hell out of you. You're up, what… twenty kilos or more?"

The man removed his hat and scratched hard at his head as he scrunched his eyes and face. He sighed and wiped his forehead with his hand. "I got married again about ten years ago when they made me the chief of detectives. Her first husband died of a bad diet. She swore she would make sure I was well-fed."

"What kind of diet did he die of?"

The man squinted as he looked back in the bar. "He ate too much lead."

Frank nodded. An all-too-common malady in Mexico. "Was he a cop too?"

The man nodded with his mouth on the bottle. "I got his job."

"Risky business."

"It depends on what you investigate. There are many crimes where solving can cause greater grief in both camps. Then too, there are crimes in the solving, make the city safer, knowing which is the secret to a longer life, my friend."

"Does this make you corrupt?"

Ralph held out his hand, and it was steady. "There is a fine line between being discreet and being corrupt. My bank account says I'm of the former, not the latter. For this, my wife is happy. I sleep at night without a *pistola* under my pillow, but my retirement will be the bar I earned as a young man." The man shifted forward into his arms. "But you did not drive down here to surf, eat bugs, or talk about my life."

Frank craned his neck as he looked along the flat surf. "I can at least go sit on my board out there…"

"You can do this shit at home. You burned a hundred gallons of expensive gasoline in the beast out there to get some answers. What are the questions?"

The two hot plates arrived, held by toweled hands. The man only paused a moment to make his point and then leaned back.

The man watched his niece return to the bar, then his head ground around. "Now."

Frank furled his lower lip and cocked his head before picking up his fork. "Eat first. It was a long drive."

As they ate, Frank pushed a photo across. Ralph studied it. He squinted as he chewed. "He fits the profile… but I don't recognize him. Maybe his name?"

"Juanito Pedro Garcia y Espinoza. If he was one of the cartel boys, he came via his family in Pico Rivera, California. He was okay in Catholic school. But then, the money ran short, and he went to public school. When he went into the system, he was a peeper for the local gang. When he graduated, he came out working for more money."

Frank dropped the copied file on the table. Ralph skimmed over the first few pages as he chewed. Eventually, he put the fork down and picked up the file.

Frank leaned in. "John Taylor. Also known as Three-Toes. I believe you were responsible for the other two?"

Ralph gently put the papers down. Frank watched his eyes bounce from table to air and then in the other direction and back to three places on the table. The man was searching for answers he didn't have.

Ralph took a sip to clear his throat. He pulled his phone out of his pocket and held up his one finger as his thumb searched for the number. Pressing, he placed the phone to his ear as he looked at Frank.

"He left here about two years ago. Some thought he *morta*." His flat hand in the air flipped over. "Others said he was down Chihuahua way. Rumor had it there was a girl over in San Felipe with an uncle who ran a boat. The rest—" The ringing stopped. Frank could hear an official female's voice. Ralph turned, sheltering the phone.

"*Comandante por favor*... Rafael Garcia."

Frank gave up interest when it became clear the conversation would be faster than he could understand. He finished the last few bites and leaned back with his coffee mug. The small throat-clearing at his shoulder was soft. His heart skipped a beat, but he smiled when he looked around. The pot was full, and the young girl's smile was reassuring. She was used to her uncle and how he conducted his police business.

"*Como se llama?*"

She laughed lightly. "Your accent is terrible. You need to come surfing more often. They call me Mari with an *I*. It's short for Mariposa. The monarchs fly every year through our backyard. My mother used to put a chair in the yard so she would be washed by the millions of butterflies as they flew to Northern California."

"Your English is better than most kids growing up in Orange County."

"My father is from Fremont, California, and my mother teaches English at the high school. If I ever got less than excellent grades, they threatened to send me away to my aunt and her twenty-nine children in a foreign land."

Frank sensed some of Ralph's humor coming. "Where is that?"

"Botswana. My aunt is a nun and teaches in an orphanage there."

Ralph hung up and turned back around. He was curious why his niece was there and then realizing his beer was almost empty. He thought about the phone call. "Maybe I had better switch to coffee too."

She pulled a mug off the other table and filled it. The two men's silence was stupefying. As she walked away, Frank locked eyes with the other detective—mayor, friend, and former surfing buddy. He shoved his chin at the cell phone in the man's hand.

The phone gently clicked down on the table. The man raised the mug to his lips and softly slurped. Placing the cup back on the table, he eased forward until they were a few hands away. His whisper was more air than noise. "What are you involved with? What you bring to my city? My house? My…?" He stopped and looked back into the dim of the bar—looking for his niece.

"Maybe these will help." Frank spun the two photographs onto the table. Both bodies stopped short.

The man picked them up and examined them. Rubbing his thumb on the edge of one photo he looked with a question. "Pedro?"

Frank nodded. "According to fingerprints… Pedro."

The man looked back down at the other photo of a body on a beach. "And this diver?"

"If he ever came down this far, you would remember him as a giant surfer. His name was Mary Shores."

Ralph squinted at both photos. "And he was in the drug trade?"

Frank cocked his head. "Why would you think that?"

"*El Hacha.*"

"The ax?"

"Si. Pedro was known to my friend as a front man for the Sinaloa Cartel in your Orange County. Two days ago, he turned up dead and chilling on your coroner's table. Well, according to rumors my friend heard, most of him was there. His thinking is of some falling-out with the cartel, and he loses his head. The man for this job is a man named Maximillian Cortège—also known as *The Ax*. Or *El Hacha.*"

"And he's an enforcer for the cartel?"

"He is judge, jury, and executioner, from what I hear. I try to keep Rosarita far from the doings of these people. I prefer dealing with small-time surfers buying a bag of pot. Or maybe an older man dropping dead from an evening with a young lady."

"So if someone loses their head...?"

"*El Hacha.*"

Frank frowned and shook his head at the young woman approaching. She turned and went back to the bar. "Do they ever find the heads?"

"My friend did not mention this." The man ran his hands over his head and looked out at the surf. "All he mentioned was unusual activities. So, something has happened." He looked back at Frank.

"Can you get me photos of this guy? And maybe anything else your friend can provide?"

"I'll see what I can do. Do you still have the falling down beanery on the cliff? The one with the *flako* tall guy?" Frank nodded. "I will have it dropped off there."

Frank thought as he stacked the thin folders and stuffed them in the briefcase. His lips were furled in frustration. "Ralph, you've been great. I enjoyed meeting Mari, and as usual, the food was worth the drive." He pushed the chair back and stood with his hand out.

Ralph mirrored him, and they shook. "What will you do now?"

"Somehow, Pedro, Mary, and this ax guy are connected. I know for a fact Mary didn't take much more than aspirin, so the drugs and cartel don't make sense. But it's my job to figure it out."

"Just don't lose your head over it."

Frank pointed his finger at the man. "Don't even joke."

"I'll call you when the surf is up. You can bring the big gun and come eat bugs with me."

Frank snorted breathily. "Ralph, you are so behind the

times." Frank smiled as the young woman slid up beside them. "Mari, tell your *tio* why he doesn't have to call me about the surf here."

She smiled and shook her head. "There's an app for that."

Frank nodded his head at her and smirked at his old friend. "But give me your card so we can stay in touch."

"You can always call here. It is the same California phone number it always was."

Frank covered his one ear. "I don't want to know if you have ever gotten a phone bill in all these years."

The three laughed. They all knew most of the bar's business was from Americans. And it was better not to have a phone line easily tapped by the government.

09 THE SMELL OF FLOWERS

"Why didn't we eat at the Shack?"

Mickey glared at Frank as they leaned back against the pillar and partial wall. The McDonald's was busy and reeked of fat. The sound of a dozen or more teens bubbling with hormones, sugar rush, and over-the-top loads of caffeine ricocheted off the hard surfaces. It didn't help to ease Mickey's attitude. Nor did Frank's calmness. And especially the heavyset woman dressed in a rough work shirt and pants standing too close to his fresh-cleaned silk suit. Everyone was casually waiting while watching the multiple slow-moving train wrecks behind the counter.

Frank's gaze rolled to the side edge of his unmoving head—watching the door open as he drew a small photo out of his shirt pocket. He smiled at the three young teenagers with bouncy ponytails, tight tank tops, and matching compression leggings above their choices of high-top cross-trainers and scrunchy socks. His smile pulled harder as they walked up to the counter—ignoring the three people waiting quietly for their turn.

As Mickey's mouth opened and his finger rose, Frank covered his hand with his and pushed it down. As Mickey scowled at him, Frank mouthed *Watch*. He nodded his head toward the oblivious girls.

The brunette at the end turned her hands backward as she pushed down on the counter's edge and rose on her toes. She looked first at the scurrying workers and then at the taller blonde to get her lead.

The blonde cracked her neck in a small reflective snap. With her hands flat on the counter, she pushed back as she bent over, exposing the tight muscles of her butt and thighs. Frank guessed at cheer squad or gymnastics or possibly both.

The third girl, with curly mousy-brown hair on the edge of frizz, was quiet. Frank guessed if the blonde was the Alpha, she was the Omega. Her calm and silence marked her as the complete follower—gymnastics, not the cheer squad.

Frank could feel Mickey's frustration coming to a boil. He suspected Mickey had suffered people cutting the line in front of him many times as a child. He was not going to suffer these three young girls.

Frank leaned over and nudged Mickey. His voice was low, but he knew his voice would carry to those who were always listening because they were insecure. "It's called *pretty privilege*. The cuter or prettier they think they are, the more they believe they're next in line—it's their birthright of privilege."

The mouse turned in horror. "Were you in line?"

The blonde turned with less of a look of horror and more of a slight blush. The brunette stood frozen and didn't want to look.

The husky woman in a green khaki work shirt and pants barked a laugh. "No, honey cakes, we were just standing here, making bets on when you three would notice one of you has a split seam on your butt with no panties to hide your cookie." The woman hacked her throat and pretended to spit on the floor as if she were chewing tobacco.

The three froze in horror. For a moment, they wanted to reach to check their seams or have the others look. The situation proved too much, and they hurried sideways back out the door. They disappeared to the left but not out into the parking lot. Frank smiled at the thought of them stopping and feeling each other's butt seams.

Turning to the now-smiling woman, who was bouncing up and down on the balls of her feet, he chuckled. "You're an evil woman. Does your mother know I love you long time?"

The woman's head cranked around with a throaty, gravelly chuckle. "You just love my flowers, Frank." She stopped and scrunched one eye. "It is Frank, isn't it?"

He nodded as he remembered. "Do you still have the flower stand?"

"Six days a week. The seventh I make deliveries."

Frank moved his finger back and forth. "This is my partner, for now, Mickey Romero. Mickey, this is… I'm sorry, but I never could remember your name…"

Turning, she pushed her hand and arm out. "It's Azola, Azola Granger."

Frank watched the young man's confused look as the dynamo of womanhood forcefully shook Mickey's hand.

"Kahuna and I used to stop by her flower stand every Wednesday just before we got off shift." Frank turned to her. "I thought it was funny. His allergies would give him hell whenever we had a case in people's gardens. But he always stopped."

Her mouth rolled in indecision. Finally, her head notched to one side as her hips notched the other. "The petunias didn't bother him so much, but they were his boyfriend's favorite."

Frank's eyes narrowed. "Boyfriend?"

"Paul. You were his partner, weren't you? And you didn't know about Paul?"

"There was… something about… he was always down at Hoag Hospital…"

Her face pulled unscrewed. "He was in a coma. He was in the coma for over two years before Kahuna died. Then suddenly, two months after Kahuna, Paul had a massive heart attack, which cascaded into a stroke and an embolism in his lungs. Now I deliver flowers to both graves."

Frank ignored the middle-aged woman now standing at the counter. "Who pays for the flowers?"

"Nobody."

His tongue rode his lower lip hard. "Can I help with it?"

"Why? Are you a filthy rich saint or something?" Her voice was as crusty as her appearance.

Frank gently wagged his head. "Certainly, no saint."

"Do you remember him?"

Frank pointed at his pink toenails sticking out of his rainbow sandals. "Everyday."

Her eyes still on his toes, her arm rose, and the hand found his arm and squeezed gently. Her voice had an increased huskiness. "Them toes are payment enough." She looked up. Her eyes were awash. She patted him on the arm, then left.

Frank watched the door close. The smell of flowers faded as if it followed Azola out the door. *Two thousand five hundred and sixty-three days.*

"I know I shouldn't expect normal with you, but what just happened was weird, even for you."

Frank looked at the kid. His growl was throaty but clear. "I'm not hungry now." Three strides, and he shoved at the panic bar and pushed his way outside.

They sat in the Bentley in silence. Mickey looked at the small photo as he kept tapping it on his thumbnail. His voice was soft and wispy. "You know… some days, I'm really dense, and it takes a long time for me to see what's in front of me…"

Frank smirked sadly as he leaned forward and started the engine. The large Chevy engine rumbled under the Bentley hood. "You're just now figuring this out?"

Mickey shot him a cold, sharp look. "This has nothing to do with my being a detective—"

Frank held up his right index finger as he backed out of the parking space. "The youngest ever to make detective." He put the car in drive and slipped on his sunglasses. "With or without a father on the force. And don't ever apologize about it. You earned it on your own merits."

As the beast nosed out onto Harbor Boulevard, Frank motioned like he was slipping on his dark glasses as he watched the side mirror. The gray sedan he had noticed sitting in the next parking lot pulled out a block behind them.

He smirked at Mickey, who was still in confusion. Only a single pencil-thin strand of hair ruffled in the convertible's wind. "I take it this isn't about the day I pulled into the driveway and stopped instead of running you over when I had a chance?" He saw the small hiccup in the young man's chest. The smile or laugh rarely followed. "You and the red tricycle would have been little more than a bug splat on the Pontiac."

"Mom would have never let you in the house again."

Frank looked over his sunglasses as he bent forward and fumbled with the radio. The gray car was the third car back without enough traffic to hide it.

"I would have found another girlfriend in a month. In those days, I was surfing hard and a slut." He leaned back and reeled his right arm out along the backs of the seats. "So, what's the question?"

Mickey held up the school photo of the young boy. The narrow black tie and poorly fitting suit coat didn't need the letters at the bottom. *Central Catholic School 9th Grade, Fullerton, California.* "It's the right school until I was in the tenth grade, but this isn't me."

Frank pulled into the Pancake House and nosed the car up to the large window. "It's not supposed to be you." He reached out and gently pinched away the photo from the young man's fingers. He looked at the boy in the image. The barely controlled mop of hair and delicate-but-severe features bore a strong likeness to the detective. "This is 1998. It's the last known photo taken of the Ax." He reached down between the seats and drew out a large manila envelope.

In the restaurant's large window, Frank watched the reflection of them get out of the Bentley. In the parking lot of the low-priced motel next door, he watched the gray car park. The reflected sun mirrored the windshield.

Mickey finally realized they had left a restaurant for another. He pulled his dark glasses down slightly with his middle finger as if to say, *What the fuck?*

Frank snorted. "I wanted a strawberry waffle instead. Besides, the waitress here is better looking."

The manager led them to the sought booth at the window. On seeing the Bentley with no top, the manager understood but was also confused by the car's weathered condition. The torch-cut convertible top was another story. He watched the two mismatched men as they slid into the booth. The older one stared across the parking lot for a moment and then sat. By far, they weren't the strangest he would seat this morning or any other day.

"Rex will be your waiter today. Can I get either one of you some coffee?"

Mickey held up a "V" of his two fingers as he carefully placed his Ray-Bans upside down on the table. Frank slid the envelope onto Mickey's placemat. "Hand delivered this morning. Danny didn't like seeing a motorcycle rider dressed in all blackout leather first thing this morning. He likes it quiet for the first hour until he opens."

"Who…?"

"Let's just say this came from Mexico. Any more would create questions nobody north or south would want to answer. Or even have to ask."

Mickey drew out the thick stack of photocopied papers. As he started looking at the two-sided copies, he realized single-sided would never fit in the envelope. He looked at the curl of the package and papers. "Someone had this all shoved down their pants under a tight jacket for many miles. This didn't come from Tijuana."

"It didn't come from Rosarito Beach, either." Frank squinted at movement across the parking lots. "Not much between TJ and Mexico City."

Mickey followed his gaze. A female was closing the door to the nondescript gray sedan. She pulled her blue ball cap on over her tightly wrapped French curl bun and dark aviator glasses. Bending, she checked herself in the side mirror, then started their way.

Frank looked back at Mickey. "The city is Culiacán Rosales." He held out his hand for the file and envelope as the aging waiter walked up and set down the large carafe of coffee. Stuffing all the files and the photo into the envelope, Frank watched the coast guard officer stride toward the restaurant's front door. He handed the envelope to the waiter. "Can you stick this somewhere safe, Rex?"

The man glanced out the window with a view of the front door and nodded. He buried the envelope between two menus. "Usual, Frank?"

Mickey held up his two fingers. Rex nodded, turned, and walked off. He nodded at the officer as she passed him while shoving her ball cap into the back of her uniform pants.

Frank thought about the first time he had heard the term for removing your hat and sticking it where the rain doesn't land— stowing your cover. Every navy boot ends up doing it a dozen times a day. *Ten thousand four hundred eighty-seven days.*

"Frank Pounds. You're a difficult man to track down."

Frank looked at the Latina lieutenant. The few pockmarks from childhood acne and a narrow old scar near her left eye didn't detract from her looks. But as Frank studied her face, the word *handsome* more than *pretty* came to mind. Even the voice was more husky than deep. He figured she had probably suffered her share of teasing and harassment in school.

He leaned back along the booth. "The Coasties don't usually try to write me any tickets for driving my long gun too fast."

She blinked a few times. The tips of her right fingers touched gently on the table.

"What can I do for the Coast Guard, Lieutenant..." he squinted at her name tag, "Ramirez?"

"It has come to my attention you somehow have come into possession of a mapping report the coast guard ran a couple of years ago."

Mickey turned with a sour look on his face. His blinking warned Frank there might have been some improper procedures in obtaining the report. Frank leaned back and relaxed in his civilian role of retirement and lack of knowledge. The image and sound of Sergeant Shultz played through his head as he listened to the next generation try on diplomacy.

Mickey reached casually for his coffee mug. "What sort of report?" A trick to out casual the aggressor. His father had built an empire on the art of the Hawaiian shirt and tennis shorts in a boardroom. His boy had paid attention.

The officer's only flinch was a slight change of weight from her left foot to her right foot. "We mapped the continental shelf and secondary shelf from the Mexican border to the L.A. basin. We were hoping to be able to predict where storm surges might be more damaging."

Mickey closed one eye against imaginary steam as he took a slow sip. "So geo-mapping. The same as the mapping the feds have done for the fisheries for the last fifty years. Sounds like a redundant waste of taxpayer's money. I thought you guys were out there saving lives and doing drug interdictions so we can spend our time doing the important work onshore."

The three knew this had rapidly turned into a pissing match. Frank was curious why the officer was stepping so far out of their jurisdiction about a two-year-old mapping. But he knew he would never find out anything if he didn't trot out the fire hose and stop the war before it got worse.

Frank cocked his head and narrowed his eyes. "Who's your commander, Lieutenant?"

"Roberts, sir. Mark Roberts, sir. We're out of San Diego, sir."

Frank could sense the attention creeping into her spine. He cocked his head harder and chewed softly at his lower lip.

"Roberts... Mark 'Mess Hall' Roberts. Yeah, I remember the screw-up. Let him know I'll be paying him a visit here as soon as we have enough time for a dressing-down, maybe a round in the back alley, and a drink for old times' sake."

"Sir... I would—"

Frank growled. "Dismissed, Lieutenant." His eyes were clear and hard as she turned and marched out. He watched through the window as she fluffed, squaring her cover over her bun—twice. She was more upset than she should be about him shutting down her inquiry into the copy of the report.

Mickey cleared his throat as he watched the other detective work on what had just happened. "So, you and her commander go way back...?"

Frank watched as the unmarked gray coast guard motor pool car backed up and drove off. He could have sworn there was a small chirp as it bounced from the driveway to the street under acceleration.

He turned to look at Mickey. "What did you ask?"

"Her commander. You and he have history?"

Frank snorted softly. "Never heard of him."

"But the nickname? *Mess Hall*?"

Frank laced his fingers into a ball at the side of his head. His elbows were spiked on the table. "Your father had almost three hundred people working for him. When it was crunch time, they stayed a little longer, came a little earlier, and I remember times when the weekend looked like any Wednesday."

Mickey thought about his father and the people working for him. He nodded.

"Do you think any of them would have done so for a guy whose nickname was 'Mess Hall'?"

Mickey thought as the waiter placed the dishes on the table.

The smirk grew into a smile as he thought of the battle the old detective had just won before declaring war.

Frank smiled at the heaped helping of strawberry compote covering the waffle. The two eggs were already broken and running yellow into the red juice. The four strips of bacon matched the other four nobody talked about. He looked up.

"Looks perfect, Rex. Thanks. Oh, and I'll take the envelope back."

The man bounced a two-finger salute off his forehead. "On its way, Detective."

Frank waved the extra-crispy bacon at Mickey. "Did you find a brain jock at UCI to put those two reports together?"

Mickey bobbed his head as he swallowed and dabbed at his mouth. "I turned them over to one of my old professors. He said he knew of a couple of kids who were looking for some real-world problems to grind through a computer program they were working on. He sounded confident it was exactly what they needed, and they're what we need."

Frank rocked his head as he cut a bite with his fork. "Sounds like we might need to run by there after breakfast."

The envelope appeared at the corner of the table as he filled his mouth with waffle, berry, and egg. His head softly rocked as his eyes slit shut. The only thing better was a two-mile ride on a smooth, chunky curl with a twelve-foot face in the early morning light.

As he leisurely chewed, he slid the small photo out of the envelope. He studied the usual zits and marks on the young man's slight face. The cut mark under the eye was healing… He wondered how the kid kept from showing up on photo-day without at least one black eye. He remembered how it was the favorite time for the school bullies to leave marks on the lesser classmen.

Eleven thousand four hundred twenty-seven days.

10 MATCHIE, MATCHIE

The room could have passed for a small library used as a dorm room or storage for a dozen kids. The air hung with a mix of popcorn, hormones, stale pizza, testosterone, and fresh nuked Pop-Tarts. The shelves on the wall were a mix of older books, binders, and stored guts of computers. A couple of bulkier hunks of potential sea anchors Frank recognized, or thought he did, from his navy days. The four large windows might have been clean but were hidden behind electronic maps blue-taped to the glass or surrounding trim. Colored markers traced snail tracks wandering from clusters to clusters. Frank knew it meant something to somebody using the room, but not to the two young women working on the program.

Frank checked the duct-tape-patched seat of the old wood swivel chair and sat. He watched Mickey's face slide from a slate of awe to the twist of confusion in as many seconds. The braless blonde in the white tank top was rattling facts and figures like a shifty auctioneer trying to sell swampland to city grifters. Her finger danced from one end of the three monitors to the other in a fraction of a sentence.

Frank's chuckle at Mickey's expense turned to a barking laugh.

The blonde paused and turned. "Do you find this funny?"

Frank softly wagged his head. "Certainly not. But let me ask you a question."

She peeked at her watch in irritation. "Shoot."

"When are you going to have time to explain all of this again, but at a quarter of the speed? Because just listening to you has my pacemaker working overtime. Mickey passed out and went comatose about ten minutes ago."

The even-younger Asian girl, whose T-shirt adorned with a serving of cornbread dripping in butter and honey, giggled. "He's right, you know. You are full-bore quad-shot in a ludicrous mode right now."

The blonde sighed and hung her head. Frank realized she wouldn't suffer being saddled with two older men whose understanding of technology didn't go much past their phones —even if they weren't flip phones.

He watched her neck suddenly flush as she hurriedly crossed her arms over the hard nipples that Frank had noticed as she was explaining the exciting features of their program. She turned her wide eyes at the oldest man in the room.

Frank smiled, held up his hands, and turned them into twin peace signs. "Peace, baby. We come in peace, and we already know we're talking to the leaders."

Her eyes narrowed.

Frank leaned in. "Look, we brought you a couple of huge chunks of data. We asked your teacher if they knew anyone who might help merge the two programs and run an analysis on them. Three days later, here we are. Mickey and I expected some mumblings and grumblings about no time, but you were working on it. But from what I'm seeing, you rocked it down to the beach and took this boogie board out for a high-speed race."

As she finally understood that they were impressed, her shoulders relaxed, and a faint smile pecked at her right cheek.

"Look..." Frank realized he hadn't even asked her name. "You go by...?"

"Tree. Like in the forest." The flash of defensiveness scuttered across her eyes.

Frank leaned back. "I would think you were a little young to be a child of hippies, but I also surf with an old fart named Granite."

"Mom was forty-seven when I came along. Dad refused to let her name me *Surprise*. So they settled on my great-grandmother's name. They thought they'd finished at six kids. My brother was seven when I came along."

Frank's left eyebrow popped up before he could control it. "And the separation between your next...?"

"Midge was in seventh grade when I came along. In many ways, she's more my mother than my mother. Mom died of liver cancer when I was four. Dad just lost it and crawled into work, beer, and sports on the television. Midge got me. We're both Aspies, both nerds, and both have IQs over 160. It's also why we don't associate with normal people."

Frank nodded. "You have to explain yourself to everyone?"

She pointed at his pink toenails and rainbow sandals. "Nah, most people can go fuck themselves. But I figured you might understand about being different."

Mickey snorted. "You've got that right."

Frank snarled a glare. "Don't push it, squirt. I can still find an old Dodge Polara and tie you to a tricycle."

Tree laughed. "This story I've got to hear." She smirked at Mickey.

Frank groaned. "Maybe another time. Maybe over dinner somewhere. But for now, we need to understand what you've done and why." He raised his open hand toward her now demure nipples.

The Asian girl stood and pushed at Tree's shoulder. "You're in my department now. Out of the chair, Stump."

Frank started to intervene but lowered his hand as he saw the smile on Tree's cheek. This was a friendship long before this project.

The young woman turned and stuck out her hand. "I'm Ming, like the vase on my grandmother's dining table."

"Frank and Mickey… just like the mouse."

She smirked and turned back to the computer, typing as she talked. "Yeah, I accessed your dossier." She punched a few more keys. "Top of your class."

Frank frowned as he wondered how this little girl could find any of his records, much less classified documents. "I was fourth from the bottom in school."

She ground her head around with one eye closed and eyed him with the other. Her index finger tapped the enter key. "In a class of five. Don't try to bullshit a bullshitter. You were decorated before you got out of your A-school in the navy. I seem to remember you saving three team members?"

"I had help."

"Yup." She looked at the graphics displayed on the center monitor. Frank recognized the depth charts of the coast off Dana Point. She continued but with a lower voice. "Yeah… help… in a squad of what… four?"

"What's your point?"

"You have a little over four kilograms of metal bracing your spine. Your left hip is a metal silicone ball and socket invented by Doctor Oh up at UCLA. You met him as well as his brother, Soon Tek Oh, the actor. When you're fifty, they will need to replace the joint because of the board you surf on." She spun around in the chair with a serious face. She waved her thumb over her shoulder at Mickey. "His information is only a few pages and boring—except for his father. But then, all this isn't the point."

Frank notched his head to the left. "You do your research."

"When we do, we are thorough. The Stump is seventeen, but I'm only fifteen. What we have can possibly make us million-aires before we can legally drink. I just wanted you to know when I say something, it's the truth as deeply as we can research it. We're not just two silly girls who look cute in wet T-shirts and thongs."

Frank smiled with a slight bob of his head. "Noted." He raised his hand at the monitor. "Dana Point."

She nodded and turned back to the keyboard and mouse. She glanced at Mickey, who nodded.

"Dana Point." She boxed a section of the coastal secondary shelf. "The shelf comes out here and then drops to a narrow second shelf. For most purposes, nobody even cares about the lower shelf. It's narrow and deep." She looked over at Frank. "I believe you crawled along a few miles of this before you got smart and came to us."

Frank breathed a soft chuff and smile.

She clicked on a few items but ignored some of the larger. One looked like what was left of a nineteen-fifties' Cadillac. He remembered the orientation to the small avalanche.

"I'll highlight the car with orange just to give us a marker on this slide." The cursor drew a square, and the white mass turned a soft orange. "These aren't showing white enough to be metal, so I'm going to mark them in light blue for rocks." She clicked on several small blobs, which turned a lavender blue.

Frank leaned in. "Those rocks, as you called them, are almost as large as the old Cadillac you have marked in orange."

She smiled back over her shoulder. "Did you wonder how much they weighed when you were down there?"

He leaned forward and pointed at the one near the car. "I remember this one was at least ten-foot-high and thick. But I have no way of guessing the weight."

Her eyebrows bounced, and she turned back to the screen. The cursor hovered over the boulder. "We designed our program to be used by dredgers for accurately bidding on large jobs. They can troll a usual river like the Sacramento at a little over seven knots and use our overlay on their sonar scans." She pointed to the small white symbol hovering near the cursor. "Says here, your stone is just over seventeen and a half tons."

The blonde smiled at Frank's raised eyebrows and open eyes. "Yeah. Our program says you have some big stones down there, Frank."

He sat back in his chair. It squealed in protest. "I think you're flirting in the deep end."

The two girls laughed. "So, he's quick and has a sense of humor." The Asian winked at him. "We just might take you up on the lunch date when this is all over."

Mickey feigned confusion. "Lunch? There was a lunch in the offering? What lunch is this, Frank?"

Frank leaned back in as he studied the section Ming was outlining. His growl was distracted and distant. "The Sunday brunch you're paying for at the Pelican." He swept his index finger around the area now selected. "What's so special about this section?"

Tree slid off the arm of the barrel chair and into the pocket. Her feet were still on the seat. The limber ability of youth didn't escape Frank's attention.

Tree's arm flopped out as she pointed at the monitor. "I'm impressed. You just made a four-step jump and conclusion about this section."

Ming grabbed a copy of the mile of shelf selected and dragged it onto the right screen. Frank was starting to understand the power of having three forty-inch screens acting as one screen or be three different work zones.

Tree continued as she pointed back and forth between the two monitors. "As we were saying, the program can search for items of specific sizes or larger than a given size. Let's say you're dredging a new river. You want to find every problem larger than say… two tons of stone or a half-ton of metal."

"Why the difference?"

Tree glanced over at Mickey, who was now as curious as Frank. Then she continued. "A half-ton of metal could be a commercial refrigeration unit or half of a Volkswagen. But a couple of tons of rock is about the size of your stove. The metal can be a pain to scoop out if it's our Cadillac here, but a Volkswagen will fit nicely in a thirty-yard clamshell or backhoe." She pointed at the large rock Ming had highlighted. "But a stone of this size needs a drill and blow job."

Frank's head slowly bobbed as he thought. "But we're not dredging…" He deadpanned his side-eye at her joke.

Tree's lips rolled into a closed smile. "No, you're not. But the program did its job anyway. In fact, it found stuff we think it wasn't supposed to find."

Ming expanded the map to cover the center monitor and the left. She reached over and pushed the left to snuggle up to the edge of the center. There was only a narrow black line of the bezels breaking the enlarged map.

"As we ran our program with the older NOAA mapping, it did its job and mapped the run from San Diego to the L.A. basin." She softly spun her chair to face Frank. "There are twenty-seven cars, four trucks, and sixty-seven boats larger than twenty-three feet—nineteen are sailboats. Scuttling is a popular way of getting some money out of a black hole in the water. It doesn't take long for the newness and love to wear thin when the dock fees and maintenance are eating your bank account alive." She turned and called up a dialog box. "Here we also can see there are thirty-two avalanches with drift tails covering more than an acre of the shelf. This is important because every avalanche is as unique as a fingerprint, and our program can geo-tag them." She pulled up a new smaller map over the entire region. Thirty-two red rings glowed among all the faint green lines.

"These give you reference markers?"

Tree shot him with her finger and thumb. "Give the old guy a brownie point." Her head flopped over as she looked at Mickey. "You need to catch up, junior."

Mickey only blushed a tint and waved his finger back and forth at Frank and him. "This is why we're a team. He's the brains, and I'm just the pretty boy."

"Okay, pretty boy, here is the nerf ball question. Of the twenty-seven cars dumped between Dana Point and Seal Beach, how many are Cadillacs?"

"Is this a serious question?"

The blond ponytail wagged. "Nope, we're just playing wild-ass guessing or spitball here."

Mickey's lower lip pushed out as he shrugged. "Maybe three or four...?"

"Final answer?"

Mickey nodded.

She turned to Frank. "You want to guess?"

He drew in a long breath and let it out with a sigh. "I'm thinking until the eighties, the Cadillac was a more dominant car. So maybe five or six."

Ming glanced back at her friend with a smirk. "Let me help you guys out here." She pulled up a dialog box showing the top twenty-five popular cars. "From the sixties to nineteen-ninety, you're right. But it still made up less than three percent of the cars. Statistically, there should only be two down there."

Tree held up both hands. "But when we combined the two mappings, the six-year-old NOAA and the coast guard scans from two years ago, we found nine cars fitting the criteria for Cadillacs. But that wasn't the real stat buster. Seven are the same 1966 Sedan de Ville." She relaxed into the chair with a smile.

Mickey was faster than Frank. "That's impossible."

Frank raised one eyebrow at Tree. "It's impossible, or something is hinky with the data or the scans."

Ming slowly turned her chair. "You're in for a Sunday brunch. Do you want to make a guess on which for dinner at the Pelican?"

"If I'm right...?"

"It's still lunch."

He studied her passive face. There was no tell he could read. "I'll guess it's the scan, but we'll still make it dinner."

"Which scan?"

"The Coastie's."

Tree smiled. "Ding, ding, ding. Chicken dinner."

Frank chuckled. "It's 'winner, winner, chicken dinner.' But there are far better things to eat at the Pelican."

She waved him off. "As I said, the NOAA mapping, seven years ago, came up with boring stuff. But the coast guard came up with too many anomalies. So, when we overlaid the two and reran the program, we got this."

Ming hit a few keys, and all three monitors became a nine-foot-long map of the coast from Dana Point to Seal Beach. The same shape outlined the seven sections of the shelf. In each area was a Cadillac and a large seventeen-and-a-half-ton rock near it. All seven sections were identical.

The four sat quietly, looking at the map from one end to the other.

"How?" Frank turned. His face was ground into itself on the one side.

Ming rotated. "No, the 'how' is the easy part. The coast guard cutter was trolling the mapping sonar sled at five miles each hour. If the ocean weren't smooth, it would be hard to steer and stay on the course moving at dead slow. In some ways, it's easier to copy some of the past scan and just plug it into the section you don't want to bother scanning. Usually, it would still work. But if you're looking for Cadillacs or refrigerators, you're going to be chasing ghosts."

"So why would they do it?" Mickey squirmed in the seat.

Ming rolled her head onto her left shoulder. "Lazy..."

Tree finished. "Or they have something to hide." It was clear the two had practiced their scripts.

Mickey moved to the edge of his seat. "Hide how?"

Ming held up her finger and turned back to the computer with a toss of her chest-length black hair. It fur-balled and then fell back to where it had been all along. "If you're tracking, your computer saves the last few minutes of live track and stuffs it into the saved file as the next segment." She pointed to new green lines marking along the map. She zoomed in, and only five segments filled the center monitor. "Up here in the corner, we see the segment designation. These numbers should show the date first, the laterals next…" She turned her head toward Frank. "Laterals correspond to longitude and latitudes. These run more east and west, so they are laterals." She flipped her hand at the bottom ends of her hair as she turned back. "The last five designate plot mapping within the lateral. As you see on this one, this means it's the second segment on a north-by-northwest lateral."

She glanced over at Mickey and sighed. "It takes a bit to learn to read all this shorthand numbering. But trust me—this is what it means."

Mickey nodded defensively and quipped, "We use the same numbering systems on our case files. It's a government thing."

Ming deadpanned a condescending smile and turned back to the computer, muttering, "Yeah, if the government is England."

Frank snorted softly, and she shot him a wink. Frank slid his feet out of his sandals and got comfortable. He liked this girl.

She tapped the next segment's ID number. "This segment is still in the same lateral, and this should read six four eight zero four, but those numbers have been replaced and reads as the first segment of the lateral at Dana Point—five miles south of this location."

She highlighted the segment and clicked on a small icon. The element changed, and the highlighted Cadillac and boulders disappeared. "Now we are seeing the NOAA scan. The segment numbering is consistent with the rest of the segments in the scan, but what we can now see is the small canyon here." She pointed at a dent in the graph lines."

Frank rolled his body forward, bracing his elbows on his knees. His forehead creased, and his voice was barely more than a whisper. "How large is the canyon?"

Ming smirked at the recruit to her geekdom. The cursor clicked on a scaling icon, and she filled in the canyon from mouth to origin. "About two hundred yards at the mouth and runs a couple of football lengths in at an eight-percent grade most of the way."

"Is all this your program?"

She shrugged as her lips curled. She peeked timidly back at Frank.

Tree snorted. "We lifted many tools from the open-source aspects of the National Oceanic side of NOAA. The atmosphere maps had a few tools, but we created better ones for our purpose. This is an important tool for estimating time and work for the dredgers we want to sell to. We can run it as a macro for, say, two hundred miles of the Columbia River from the bar at the mouth to the first set of locks at the Bonneville Dam. It will be a huge timesaver for them."

Mickey yawned and leaned back in his seat. "What about the Mississippi?"

Tree looked at him with the air of a long-suffering mother. She poked Ming's shoulder. "Show him."

The third monitor lit up with the map of the lower forty-eight states. The Mississippi, Ohio, and Missouri rivers were broken out into twenty segments.

Tree continued her lecture. "When we pushed it to the max, this is what we got. But when we paired it with past dredging contracts, it looked more like this."

Ming clicked to the refined sectioning map, and twenty became closer to five hundred. There were long stretches of open river, but in and near ports, the areas were broken into many sections. Ming zoomed in on the port of St. Louis.

"Ports and the areas around them create jobs depending on what they need in the coming years or what silt has deposited."

She pointed at a curve in the river. "When the river gets full, it gouges out this outside of the curve and deposits it downriver when it slows and eddies in another port." Her finger moved to within the curve. "When the river is low and moving slow, deposits can build in this section as well as in the ports. This impedes traffic, but in a port, what was once a forty-five-foot-deep berth can rapidly become a shallow thirty. Therefore, dredges have been in the San Francisco Bay working nonstop since the late eighteen hundreds. New Orleans employs four companies to vacuum both sides of the river."

Frank rolled his finger. "But getting back to our bogus sections..."

Tree smiled as Ming wiped out everything. A single section filled the entire oversized monitor in the center. What looked like a similar area filled the left monitor, as did the right.

Ming pointed at the first two monitors. "This is the old NOAA scan, and this is the bogus overlay. As you can see, there's not much change."

Frank pointed to the right monitor and a large white square. There was nothing around the area on any of the maps. "And this...?"

Both girls smiled. Tree took the lead. "The university has a fleet of boats. Most are sailboats under twenty-seven feet. But they also have or have access to some research powerboats. We, um, hijacked one of them and went trolling with a commercial sonar mapper."

The right monitor zoomed to the area around the square object. Ming highlighted it and ran the sizing app. Frank leaned in and read the size.

"It looks like two thirty-two-foot containers welded together..."

Tree nodded. "With a large hole cut in the bottom, leaving a small walk space on one side and the two ends with shelves welded in."

Ming added, "And it's on thirty-foot stilts."

"And... an air supply to keep the water out."

Mickey frowned and shifted. "What the hell...?"

Tree turned. "We don't know. We didn't do the dive. It was a couple of guys from the scuba club. They said it was empty but looked like it was used occasionally. One of the four air tanks still had half a load or whatever they call it."

Frank wiped his chin with his hand. The stubble reminded him he hadn't shaved in a couple of days. "Do you have—"

Ming reached out to him. The thumb drive was a squishy pink pig with makeup. The USB stuck out of its butt. "Don't judge. It's all I have at the moment. And… I want Piggy back."

Frank turned it over and over and smiled. He lobbed it over to Mickey. "Piggy, Pinkie… this looks like your department." He winked at Ming. "Don't judge."

As they stood, Frank stretched. "Pick you two up at ten on Sunday?"

Tree pointed at Ming. "I have family duty. You only get Ming this Sunday. If she returns with a good report, you can have both of us the next Sunday."

He looked at Ming. "No family duty?"

"I live in the dorms. I'm from Philadelphia. Keeping the prying family at arm's length is a priority when you're a Chinese lesbian."

Frank smiled and shot her with his finger and thumb. "Well, if I'm schlepping around a princess, I guess I'd better get the Bentley washed."

She snorted with a heavy dose of snark. "Yeah, right."

Mickey raised his eyebrows at Frank and smiled. He shook hands with Tree and Ming. "Great work on the program. I'll give our feedback to your teacher."

11 IT AIN'T ROSES

The sun was right, the surf flat, and the heat was comfortable, but the seagull had a sore throat or had swallowed a vibrator…

"Frank… Frankie, baby."

Pounds could feel the dog curled in behind his knees. *Shit. The bed.*

"Frank… it's your phone. It's the third time it's rung in two minutes."

He yawned and reached up to the small driftwood shelf screwed into the corner of the walls. The wood hid the charger pad for his phone. The phone vibrated in his hand as he rolled over and opened one eye to target the incoming kiss.

He smiled at the dirty blond pixie-cut nurse. The freckles on her nose overflowed across her high cheeks. He thumbed the phone. "Pounds."

"Well, there you are." Danny's voice was quiet but anxious. "The coyote hasn't come for her treat yet, so I know the nurse is there… but you best be humping your lump up here right now. You have visitors."

Frank shifted and sat up. The coyote knew the night with warm legs of the two humans was over. She peeled over the edge and out the door after only a quick pat and kiss from the woman. Frank watched the two as he looked out the open door into the morning wispy fog hanging across the lead-gray cove. It was still early. Someone had disturbed Danny's quiet time before he opened the Shack.

"What visitors?"

Danny now sounded quieter. "The man in black is outside on his motorcycle, waiting. He still has his helmet on, but he's watching me. He occasionally looks up the road like he's expecting someone."

"You said visitors. Plural. As in more than one…"

"Pussy is here with one of her daughters. They showed up about twenty minutes ago, and I had one hell of a time calming them down. They think someone kidnapped the other daughter."

"I'll be right there."

"Oh no, mister. You get a shower first. I don't want the smell of sex stinking up my café, and I'm sure the ladies would smell it too. Just get up here before whoever the black Mandalorian is waiting for gets here."

"Give me five."

Frank leaned across the nurse and set his phone next to his pistol on the nightstand. She snuggled into his chest and kissed the scars. He eased back and ran his fingers through her hair as he looked into her gray pavé eyes. After his accident, they were the first eyes he could focus on. The concussion had blurred everything for the first several weeks. Shapes, pain, and sleep had been the sum of his world. He had seen the photo the *Orange County Register* had run of him in the ICU. It only took one nurse to turn the Stryker bed and Frank over. His body hid the long open section of the mattress that accommodated the stainless steel centipede that held his spine's nine fractures together. The reporter's graphic narration of the dozen tubes and shunts leading into or out of his body had only been cursory of the real extent of the damage or the life support.

"Critical" was a weak word for his condition. His life had been tenuous on the best days—critical on most. In true Disneyland fashion, it was Tinkerbell who saved the day. Or more to the point… Peter Pan. Pan. Short for Penelope.

He kissed her nose. "Sorry."

Her smile was soft. "I heard. You better go before I make you stinky."

He climbed over her. "It's early. You can stay if you want. The door is open, but I doubt if the dog will be back. She's usually up to Danny for a treat and off to whatever coyotes do during the day."

Pan rolled over and straightened out the sheet. "I don't start shift until three, so I'm going to sleep until I wake up. Now don't forget your shower…"

He stretched the nonexistent stiffness she had massaged out of his back and chest in the middle of the night. The massage was much of their relationship. Rock, paper, and scissors decided a great deal of who got the first massage. His to relieve old scar tissue around his metal spine, and hers to reduce the high stress of a day or week in the intensive care unit where they had met.

Two thousand five hundred and thirty-four days.

But most of her days were now spent in the emergency operations trauma center.

Frank wiped the water from his body and reached for the towel. He looked down at the cove and the flat lead ocean. There wouldn't be any surfing on the Orange coast for several days. The weather was all too calm. He looked at the Beachcomber Café buried in the belly of the cove. His voice was more of a gravelly whisper. "Hey, Pan?"

Her body didn't move. "Hmm?"

"When is your next evening off?"

"Friday… why?"

"I was thinking about taking you to dinner in the cove."

"Sea bass sounds good…"

He stepped through the door to dress. Pan's soft snore told him that she was out for the count. It wasn't the first time the two adrift ships found solace in the night or odd hours and then drifted off to their lives again. Friday would be the first time the get-together plan happened more than a few hours in advance. Usually, it was a phone call: *I'm in the area.* Because of his retirement and her working odd as well as long, grueling hours as a nurse, the collection point had become his shanty in the middle of the night.

The coyote liking her was also a bonus for all three. They had grown accustomed to the dog curling up between the hollows of their knees. The occasional shifting of legs could cause a canine groan, but never a growl or an evacuation.

FRANK STOPPED with his hand on the Shack's back screen door. He looked over his right shoulder at the water and low-hanging fog, or what was left of it. Two wet-suited surfers lying side-by-side on their boards just dotted the size of a tick mark. The ocean was barely moving. The waves were only a few inches. He knew the conversation was about anything but surfing. Some days it was more about the water time than catching a wave. These days for Frank, the sleepy conversations with other surfers were better than a six-foot-set with perfect form.

He pulled on the door and walked in.

Even without warning, Frank could see the two were distraught. Pussy's eyes were puffy and red. Tink wasn't far behind but appeared to be holding together better. Frank glanced toward the bathroom and then Danny. Danny didn't even look up but sensed the question and shook his head.

Frank sank in his chair softly. "Where's the other Tink? The Tink with the blue hair."

The pink-haired Tink opened her mouth, but only tears ran from her eyes. Pussy croaked, "She didn't come home last night."

Danny gripped Frank's shoulder hard as he put down the coffee in front of him. Frank noted the coffee was vibrating like a foreboding storm. They waited.

"We've been calling her phone, but it goes straight to voicemail."

Frank held his coffee halfway to his mouth. "Do you have a nanny location app on her phone?"

Tink shook her head, then nodded at Pussy. "She tried—dozens of times. But we just check and remove it about every few weeks. Tink and I are never apart for long. Even at work, I know when she's flying the wire or walking the dog."

Pussy translated at Frank's frown. "They trade off doing the zip line as Tinkerbell. But sometimes, during the early morning, before the park opens, they'll fly the wire and practice new poses."

"Walking the dog?"

The young girl rolled her eyes large and looked at him through her eyebrows and bangs. "Pluto?"

The cast of characters came back to him. Mickey's dog would be sized smaller than Mickey and much smaller than Goofy. People's expectations depended on them suspending disbelief to flower in the park's make-believe.

He pulled out his cell phone and punched through some numbers from memory. He sipped his coffee as he turned in his chair to look out the front window. The motorcycle was a dull matte black. Nothing on the machine was chrome or any other color. Even the large motor was midnight on a foggy night. The rider's leathers were only slightly glossier, but the boots and helmet matched the light-absorbing black. The over-sized gas tank was shaved of any decals or marks. The motor-cycle and rider were designed to blend and disappear like a lost memory.

The phone clicked.

"Dungeon." The voice was curt. Frank had never heard anyone mention the man displaying any signs of casual or niceties. The sign on his workroom door stated simply: *The more I know about humans, the more I love my computers.*

"Dingus, it's Frank Pounds."

"Too long, Frank, too long. I found another long-distance chess player."

"Good. I don't have time to remember a move or two a month with you." Half the game between the two was the lies. Frank's board for Dingus was still nailed to the shack's office wall. It was the centerboard in a cluster of nine.

"Then I'm hanging up. I'm busy. One of us still has a job, you know."

Frank looked hard at the top of the pink hair, now resting on thin crossed arms on the table. The reflection on the old Formica tabletop was only a blush to the faded blue speckles.

"If you do hang up, the next call I make is to your ex-wife." He waited. The man knew Frank had the woman on speed dial. The phone would ring in the next room—his direct supervisor.

The hard-edge dropped. "What do you need, Pounds?"

"I have to go take care of something, but there is a nice mother here who is worried about one of her daughters. I need you to ping her daughter's phone. She's been missing long enough, and I need this expedited. I'm in the middle of a case with an extremely dangerous person who I'm sure would have no merciful feelings about a cute little girl."

"I heard you and Mickey caught the headless case... Put her on."

Frank handed his phone to Pussy. "I'm going to go check on the guy out front. This guy's name is Dingus. He's a dingis, but only to me. But he's no dingus. If it can be done, he can find her phone, and we can take it from there."

She nodded as she put the phone to her ear. "Hello?"

Frank stepped over to Danny at the end of the counter. He could smell the strong South American tea the stringy redhead favored in the morning. As the day progressed or his moods changed, the tea in his bamboo mug would become more exotic or milder. When the Long Gun Surfing Championships were in the area, Danny's mug load never changed. The kick of the tea wasn't the same as caffeine, but after the fifth or eighth mug of the day, Frank knew the young man was wired like a harpsichord or the eighty-seventh line holding up the Golden Gate Bridge in a gale wind.

Danny never moved. Frank wasn't sure the lips even moved. "He hasn't twitched since you walked in. I don't think there's a body or human in the suit."

Frank furled his lips. The skin around faded white. The inner lower lip passed back and forth between his teeth. He blinked as he stepped behind the young man. "This is what happens when you don't go to the leather bar of your choice. It comes to you. Only scarier."

He laid his right forearm flat on the counter as he reached under the edge with his left. Danny watched with his peripheral vision. He wondered about the three-inch-wide centipede lump under the stretched T-shirt the first year he worked for Frank. Then he had seen Frank without the shirt and realized the alien crawling up his back was under the skin. The seven articulations allowed for limited bending but still provided support.

Frank stood and shook his left arm in a single swift up and down. The shaved-down shotgun jacked a shell into the chamber. "If he's looking for a date on Saturday night, he's all yours."

Danny choked and spat his mouthful of tea back into the mug. As Frank silently slipped out the back door, the redhead muttered to himself, "Why do I even work for the man?" His mind never reviewed the cut he got from the house take. There were far cheaper places for people to eat, but the location's solitude justified the popularity and prices. Danny sipped back his tea. For years, he had known his salary could pay for a manager, a cook, and a few waitresses—all of whom he would find annoying. His only nod to other workers was hiring catering workers for the Long Gun days. He paid them triple what they could get catering, and he never asked about their tips. One hustler had told him he always looked forward to working for Danny and the thousand-dollar days. Danny had only smiled and always called the now-lawyer first and let him put his team together. Usually, they were other young lawyers in the public defender's office—always female, good-looking, friendly, and all business.

The leather man's head snapped to the corner of the building as Frank turned the edge. The shotgun was down behind his leg.

"*¿Esperandome?*" Waiting for me?

The helmet didn't move more than an inch either way. The gloved finger barely moved above the leather-clad leg. Frank glanced up the long driveway toward the highway.

"Speak English?"

The helmet dipped slightly.

Like interrogating a corpse.

"Do you want to come in for some food or coffee?"

The helmet moved slightly left and right.

Frank shrugged and stepped to the front door. "Suit yourself." The T-shirt draped casually, but Frank could feel the prickling of sweat as he exposed himself to anything. He let the door close softly.

He put the shotgun back under the counter, the weapon clicking to the magnets. He straightened and locked eyes with Danny.

The young man shied his head away and questioned Frank with side-eyes.

"Live?" He had not seen Frank clear the chamber. The weapon was ready for responsive action—not just a threatening jacking of the noisy pump action.

Frank glanced back out through the large window. The figure still hadn't moved. "For now."

12 ANSWER THE PHONE

Frank sat down and bumped his chin up at Pussy's silence. Pink-haired Tink didn't move. Her arm lay slumped flat on the table with her hand cocked up into her hair. The spray of pink reminded Frank of the cast-off as a large-caliber slug passes out of a body. His eyes diverted back to Pussy.

"I'm just waiting. He's doing something with her phone, but we have to wait." Pussy's chest sighed in on itself. With the masses of silicone, it didn't make much of a difference.

Tink's head rotated. Her eyes were still red, but at least her face was dry. "He finally pinged it, but it was off. He hacked it remotely and turned it back on in silent mode. He opened just the microphone and had it call back to him. There are people in the background, but they aren't talking."

"Did he locate it?"

Pussy glanced over. "Anaheim. In the Ball backlot of Disney. They think it's the big rig barn. They store the night cranes there with other buckets for working on overhead stuff. Think of it like the city or county has rigs to work on tall trees or power lines, only the park is a smaller city." She nodded back into the phone. "Yeah, we're still here. Frank's back. You want to talk to him?"

She listened, snorted, then passed the message to Frank. "He says you owe him two hundred dollars."

Frank crooked his arm along the table and mirrored Tink. "Fuck the asshole. Tell him the *mohel* cut the kid on the bias because Dingus was too cheap to buy him glasses."

The chuckle vibrated through the phone—old joke between old friends. Cops and coroners had a habit of telling old, sick jokes at crime scenes, on stakeouts, or at autopsies to break the seriousness. The thought had always been it was either humor or have a breakdown and check into the looney-bin. Frank had only worked with two old guys who were serious to the end. One never reached retirement. The other collected the first four checks before he ate his service revolver. His widow fought with the county. She said it was their fault. They said he was unstable, to begin with—the county and insurance ended by paying three million to the lawyer, five million to the widow, and all the court fees.

Six months later, she was shacked up with a patrol officer twenty years her junior who moonlighted as a standup comic. When life gives you tragedy—laugh in its face.

Frank fished his left hand in the air. Pussy passed it over.

"Where are we at, Dingus?"

"Two detectives and SWAT just showed up at the back gate to Disney. There was a bit of Mickey Mouse horseshit, but they're combing the barns now."

"Can you narrow down their search a bit?"

"It's better if they just search. I'm still listening, and I have the mobile post patched in. We can't hear the search because they're moving as quietly as possible. But she could have left the phone in one building, and she's in another."

Frank looked over the pink hair. The large window facing northwest toward the cove was one of Frank's few changes to the Shack's outside appearance. Most of the outside remained the same with the look of weathered boards nailed up in the nineteen-forties. The truth about the Shack was a quiet modernization and enlargement from the inside. Only the back of the building was extended the needed twenty feet to hold the kitchen, storage, and a strangely large office. Just like any young boy, Frank had dreamed of a secret tunnel or room. The inherited trust and land with existing buildings gave him both.

The ocean was a grayish-green of stagnant surf. The earlier two surfers lying on their boards were now a cluster of seven. Either school was out, or a few jobs were missing their workers. Frank guessed the former. Surfers don't dump a shift to sit in dead water.

Frank could hear some talking on the other end.

"Dingus?"

"They just found her phone and backpack. They're still searching. The phone was on a work desk near some parked bucket trucks. Is this normal? Does she work in this section?"

"Just a minute. I'll ask." Frank looked at Tink as her head rose. "They found her phone and backpack on a workbench near parked bucket trucks. Is this a normal place for her to be?"

She thought about the placement. Her head drooped, but Frank noticed a side-eye glimpse at Pussy. Tink's eyes closed as she took in a deep breath and sighed. Frank could feel a betrayal of trust and a confession coming.

"Tell them to look for a mechanic named Eric Squirrel. His real name is Errol Swarrelsen, but the name on his jumpsuit will say Eric with a cartoon squirrel over it."

Frank held her stare for a couple of heartbeats and then glanced at Pussy. The twist on her mouth was a torrent of questions bitten back.

Frank raised the phone. "Dingus?"

"Here, Frank."

"Tell the team they're looking for a mechanic named Eric the Squirrel. His mechanic's jumper will have a squirrel over his name."

"Anything else?"

"Just find him first. We'll hash out the relationship later."

"Boss?" Danny's voice was quiet with an edge. Frank spun around and looked. His eyes followed the pointing finger.

"The leather dude just stood up. He's looking up the driveway, but he's texting on a cell phone."

Frank nodded as he stood. "Dingus, I've got a situation here. We'll check in with you in a bit." He didn't wait for an answer. He shoved the dead phone in his pocket and quietly walked toward the counter and Danny.

"He got a text. Then after he read the text, he stood up and has been looking up the road since then." Danny turned and looked at Frank with a questioning face. "Open the wall?"

Frank clutched his lower lip with his teeth. His eyes floated from the dark figure to the floor and finally back at Danny. "Let's wait this out. Is it unlocked?"

Danny nodded. "I unlocked it when the rider showed up."

Frank watched the figure in leather. He was just a black statue. Frank glanced back over at the table and called quietly. "Pussy? Can I see you for a moment?"

The woman glided to his side and watched what they were watching. "The biker was here when we showed up. Never moved from the bike, never looked at us, and never recognized we were even here."

Frank cocked his head. "What do you think? Male or female?"

Pussy curled her lower lip. "When we walked in, Tink commented about it looking like a bad-assed chick." She looked back at her daughter and pumped her head. "Tink?" Nodding toward the front window. "Chick or dude?"

The answer was definitive and immediate. "Chick."

A large car nosed off the highway. The reddish-tan hair and top-down Cadillac Frank would have known almost anywhere. What had once been gold had faded from the Rosarito Beach sun and replaced by years of undisturbed Baja dust. The only thing missing from his friend's car was an early O'Neil 10-6 long gun with hard rails to cut the soft Baja waves.

Danny fidgeted. Frank could almost hear his heart. He knew the young man had sand, but he didn't feel comfortable with just the shotgun. As he pointed out one time, it isn't an aim kind of gun. It's more like a suggested-area kind of gun. The barely one foot of barrel was little more than the chamber with no guidance.

Frank looked at Pussy's arms and tawny body. He had watched Danny get his black belts. But a firefight was something you don't bring a fist to.

"At least bring the AR out. Slip a twenty-by-twenty in it. If we need more, we know where to find it."

The thin man became a soft swirl of air.

The car nosed in next to the motorcycle. The wraith in leather never flinched when the tire rolled past only inches from its toe.

Frank watched as Ralph said a few words to the motorcyclist. The response wasn't what he was expecting. The motorcyclist leaned forward and drew a small pistol from under their jacket. Palming it into their left hand, the right felt higher under the jacket. The hand withdrew a thin manila envelope.

Handing both to Ralph, the leathered wraith mounted the motorcycle, drew in the kickstand, and drove off. The bike made extraordinarily little dust. Frank guessed the wraith rode on many dirt roads in Mexico or wherever he or she lived.

Frank took the coffee mug from Danny and looked down at the AR-15 with a large-capacity clip strapped to two others. He snorted softly. "Don't get a hard-on carrying the weapon around—it's just Ralph now."

Not to be let down, Danny shaded his eyelids and looked sideways at the older man. "You never know. He might be hiding a whole squadron of berserker midget clowns in the trunk."

Frank's hand and mug paused at his mouth. "In that case, and only in that case, you have free rein at target practice. Just be deadly accurate. One to the joke case and two to the laugh center. When wounded, they become zombie mimes."

"Got it. One to the crotch and two to the throat."

Frank, getting into the spirit of making fun of killing, turned in horror. "Oh, for cripes sake. Haven't I taught you anything? Never get near the voice box. A zillameter to either side, and they become zombie talk show hosts. Go for the lungs."

Ralph, oblivious to being evaluated as to what he may or may not be hiding in his trunk, finished reading the documents. He flipped through the few pages and opened his door.

With his foot half out of the car, he stopped to look at the window. The men leaning against the counter knew they were invisible in the morning light and darker interior. The reflection of the eastern light made the window a mirror.

Caustic surfer humor for a friend bubbled up. "He's checking to make sure his toupee is on straight."

Danny snickered.

Frank turned and slid onto one of the counter stools. "Danny, how about breakfast. See what the girls want. Ralph and I will just eat whatever lands in front of us. But I know he's partial to pancakes."

At the sound of the door, Frank didn't even turn around. "Over here, Ralph."

The man from Mexico straightened his shirt, licked his palm, and patted down his hair. It didn't help. He still looked like the aftermath of a bad night.

He dropped the envelope and documents in front of Frank as he pulled out the next low stool. His thumb smoothed along the upholstered leather seat. He remembered when Frank had driven down to Rosarito to have them all upholstered. The surf ran high all week, and every night was two beers, exhaustion, and a quick dinner before sleeping like the dead. The open-faced cabana supplied an early wake-up. The days started with an hour of surf before breakfast. Good times.

Frank studied his coffee as the man sat. "You look like the

ass-end of a two-month bender. Or is it the mop rag on the floor of a Tijuana whore's room?"

The bloodshot eyes were only slightly darker than the man's hair. His eyelids were fighting with morning and the need for death.

"I don't remember. It's been too long since I've engaged in either one." He looked up as a large mug of coffee appeared. "*Muchas gracias*, Poco."

"*De nada, señor*. Omelet, bacon, and pancakes?"

The man smiled broadly to be remembered so well. He leaned back on the stool and lightly backslapped his hand on Frank's arm. "I like your boy's style. You raised him well. His mother would be proud."

Danny rolled his eyes and turned back to the grill. There was a lighter step to his feet. The assault rifle under the counter was forgotten—for now. The trunk of the car was still closed.

13 THE LAST GOOD DAY WAS YESTERDAY

R alph pulled hard on the coffee in his mug. As he thought about the information in the packet, he wished it were something stronger—much more potent.

Through connections far beyond his longtime relationship with Frank, he knew he could get a foreign resident visa in a heartbeat. He had been thinking about it more and more lately. The times were changing, and keeping Rosarito Beach a quiet, sleepy town safe enough to bring a family and relax at the beach was becoming more of a challenge every day. Some days like today, it was by touch from hour to hour.

He glanced over at the stack of paper and photos facedown. The pile face-up was thinner. He had forgotten how fast the detective in his friend could process information. He looked up as Danny placed the pancakes and bacon in front of him. From his hip pocket, the young man produced a bottle of sugar-free syrup. Ralph smiled up at the tall man. It was truly grand to be remembered.

"*Estes perfecto, mijo. Gracias.*"

"*De nada, señor.*"

Frank reached out for his mug. Ralph knew he never looked up from reading. Ralph knew he would only occasionally pause, searching his memory for the right translation of a difficult word. This report was typed *rapido*. The words were simple and straightforward. It had been for Ralph. But the sender knew it would probably be read by the man north of the border. The man snooping around in important doings south of the border, but now had importance to the man's life and home.

Frank sipped and then held the mug in midair. "Is this right? The mayor and all his council? *En totas*, not *en total?*"

"*Si. Si.* Is what it says. The person is being formal and using Catalan. They may even be from Spain itself. One never knows these days. We are as much a mixing cauldron as you *Norte Americanos.*"

"Any of them missing their heads?"

"No. From what the report said, it was a bloodbath in the city hall. The cartel soldiers came in and blocked all the exits, and then systematically searched the entire building. The obvious workers could leave, but the council and mayor…" He gently shook his head. "This is the kind of garbage I have worked hard to keep out of Rosey. I want families to spend their honest-earned money to relax and play in our ocean. Not the tainted money of the cartels."

Frank started to answer and then looked up at the two large plates of food. He moved the stacks of information into one. Shoving the whole to his right, he made room for the soft omelet over a waffle. The one-egg omelet was only to hold the chorizo, onions, and jalapeños together. The waffle was what they sold as a chaffle. The batter was made with only two eggs and a cup of mixed cheeses—no flour. The cayenne pepper, cumin, and cinnamon were there only to give it a kick. It was as close to vegetarian and keto as Frank wanted to let Danny take him. His heart and liver would last for as long as he needed them.

The two men leaned into their breakfasts. Only the occasional slurp of coffee broke the sound of chewing. Neither was racing, but old habits tainted how they ate. Both had lived in worlds dictated by the need for speed. The early years of surfing had made chorizo burritos the quick breakfast of choice, mostly washed down with strong coffee.

Ralph sipped on his coffee and then leaned back to look past Frank. His mug was still in the air as he studied Danny sitting at the table with the two women. As he watched, Pussy raised her cup to her mouth. Ralph's left eye ticked open larger. He had thought the sleeve of the woman's T-shirt was just large but now knew it was filled with muscle. He could tell even at a distance that the smaller woman with the colorful hair had been crying.

He leaned forward. His voice was as soft as the Mexican afternoon. "What's with *dos niñas?* Especially the one with the arms like...?"

Frank shot him a stern look. The man froze midsentence. Frank cleared his throat as he chewed and thought about what to share. Of all people, he understood privacy surpassed most needs to know.

He washed his mouth with coffee and slowly patted his lips. "One of the twins went missing last night. They pinged her phone, but it was at her work. Not where she normally was, but then Disneyland is a big place to work. We're waiting to hear back from the local officers."

"But they're from down here?"

Frank thought about the man's world. Rosarito Beach had grown to a population of only fifty or sixty thousand people. The nearest city was Tijuana, with over two million. Although his city was small, his café also had a California 800 phone-number. The man's world was small but also large and not so local.

"They live closer to Disneyland, but they didn't know who else to call." He looked with one eye over the coffee mug. "It's... complicated."

Ralph peeked a short glimpse over Frank's shoulder. "*Si.*"

And slowly bobbing his head at the sight of the rigid chest and more hardened arms, "*Si*… I can see that."

Frank pushed the empty plate forward. Taking up his coffee mug, he stood. "More coffee?"

As Ralph pushed his forward, Frank stepped to the carafe sitting half-full on the heater. He filled his mug and set it back on the counter as he filled Ralph's. "The biker in all black…?"

The left of the man's face pulled his one eye wider open. He leaned back on the stool as he thought. The motorcycle had changed a few times, always newer and faster. The color and gear had remained the same. "The man is a mystery. Nobody knows where he is from. He crosses the border with seeming total impunity. I was at the border once. The *Americano* guard was questioning me, and I was in my official car. It was early morning, and I had an appointment in Los Angeles at the City Hall. Suddenly *El Noche* comes flying through the checkpoint. Nobody even looked up. It was as if he was the invisible man. I have seen him wind through traffic backed up for a mile, and he gets nothing more than waved through."

Frank turned on the short stool and leaned against the counter. His elbows lay cocked back on the counter, relaxed. "Danny thinks it's a woman."

Ralph turned on his stool. He sipped on his coffee and scanned the southern view out of the window. Neither man was looking at the seagrass or cars washing past. "It could be. Nobody has ever seen them without the leathers and helmet. Even when the temperatures are over one hundred, it is always with the black."

"But you were talking with them just now…"

Ralph's short breath was a soft snort. "You never talk *with* them. You talk, they nod or shake their head. The conversation is one-way. They deliver. If they are still standing there, they are waiting for a reply."

"You asked them something about the packet, and they gave you a pistol… care to share?"

Ralph gave his old friend a slow-eyed glance. "Someone thought I needed some protection. They must not know me well." He smiled. Frank smiled back. He remembered the two dive knives mounted on the nose of Ralph's longboard. A slip of the thumb and the blades would slide out of their scabbards cast into the fiberglass. "I asked *El Noche* if they would be okay with what was going on. They shuffled their hand at the dirt here. I think they meant they would be staying here."

Frank pushed his lower lip out. "Or they live here, which brings up the question of why you're here. It's not like the midnight rider couldn't just drop off the packet to me like they did the last time."

"Last time?" Ralph's face screwed up into confusion as his head slowly cocked to one side.

"When you sent up the info on the Hachet—"

"Frank?"

He looked over to see Danny approaching, holding out his phone.

He pushed the green icon. "Pounds." His eyes slid shut as he listened. "Okay. Thanks. I'll call you when we get up there." He hung up the phone and turned to Ralph. "Give me a minute, but I also need to go to work."

Ralph snorted. "Nice uniform."

"Yeah, maybe I should change to my formal uniform."

"The one with only one hole in the shirt?"

Frank looked down and stuck his finger through one of the holes in his shirt with the Ramones' first album cover. Johnny's head was just a hole, as was Tommy's crotch. The neck cuff had long turned to granular fray. His baggies were only a few years fresher. The rainbow painting on his huaraches was scuffed and worn, as was the pink nail polish on his toes.

He rolled his lips into a drawn smile and wiggled his eyebrows. Turning, he approached Pussy and Tink. Danny pulled the black thermos mug from under the counter. The skull and crossed long-gun surfboards didn't escape Ralph's eyes. The logo went back to their surfing days: *surf or Die.*

You can take the sixteen-year-old out of the surf, but you can't take the surf out of the man.

Ralph watched the real man he knew as he spoke to the woman and girl. The man's left hand was out and only lightly resting on the woman's forearm. The two females' rigidness told him the news wasn't what they wanted to hear, but it wasn't as bad as they feared.

The three rose as the girl wiped at her eyes and face. Frank pointed at the door to the back. Danny waved Tink over and guided her to the toilets.

Frank's grip changed as the girl left. He gripped the woman's bicep in support. Their heads were close. The woman was stiff, but her face was askance. Ralph waited. His turn at the information would come.

Frank turned and came back. Folding the information envelope, he exchanged it with Danny for the thermos. He held up the flask with the surf slogan and thought.

Danny stumbled. "Wha…? Wrong thermos?"

Frank's lower lip furled white as he watched Tink come out of the back. She shyly nodded and kept going. "No, Danny, it's fine. Just the wrong day for it." He looked up at Danny's outheld hand and shook his head. "Nah, it's fine. It's just a thermos and coffee."

He looked at Ralph and sighed. His head fell slightly back as he looked over at Danny. "Don't wait up. And don't wake me in the morning." Indicating the envelope, he added, "And put this in the safe. I'll come get it when I wake up."

He reached out and turned to Ralph. "I need to get my car. Walk with me."

Ralph looked him up and down with one squinted eye.

"And change into something more fitting for a hospital."

As they stepped out, they watched the two women climb onto a red Harley. The lavender pin-striping was old-school.

The low rise of the front forks and short sissy bar matched the paint. The men admired the subtleness of the chopper.

Ralph scratched at his red hair. "Back in the sixties and early seventies, there were a bunch of bikers who would show up in Rosy every Friday night. They hung around in a cabana they had built on the sand across from the Pig Cantina. They were quiet and stuck to themselves. Their choppers were more like this—built for long comfort. Not so much whore…"

Frank nodded. "Flash. I think the word you're looking for is flash."

"*Si.*"

As the motorcycle raised only a small dust cloud, the men turned and walked around the building.

They were halfway to his shack before Frank cleared his throat and looked across the headlands at the ocean. "They found her twin hiding in a dumpster. She was severely beaten. She couldn't talk to them. When they touched her, she only shook and whimpered. They figured she was underage, so they took her to the children's hospital. They will probably move her as soon as possible once they find out she's in her twenties. But at least they can get some x-rays and patch her up."

"Wait," Ralph stopped and faced Frank. "The girl in there was her twin?"

Frank nodded.

"She looked maybe only fourteen…"

Frank smiled and resumed walking. "You're getting old, Ralph. You're getting old."

As they approached the shack, a gray blur slithered down off the porch and into the low brush. Ralph waved his hand out. "Is that…?"

"Coyote. *Si.*" Frank smiled with a forced, broad smile. "She likes sleeping with me."

Ralph thought a moment and then started to snicker. "*Amigo,* I told you years ago you'd go to the dogs."

Frank nodded his head as he winked. "*Si*, but this one is mutual."

As Frank changed his shorts and into a fresh, almost-new shirt, Ralph looked around the sparse interior. He wondered at the box under the small table with only two chairs. He could tell the three windows were all aligned to allow a view of the ocean. The door faced toward the cove. His trained eye counted the five tiny black dots bobbing on the swells. "Does the surf ever come in enough for a long gun?"

Frank turned and held out the front of the shirt. The darker blues and reds were subtle on the black shirt, but the lighter blues of the letters *ELO* echoed the five doves flying over the spaceship. Ralph remembered the small concert for the dead musicians. It had been a sad year. The concert was a private affair, and the T-shirt was bootleg at best.

Frank looked up and frowned.

Ralph knew the man had just gone to the day, or somewhere else. "The surf in the cove."

Frank blinked a few times as he looked out the door. His angle was wrong, but he could see the blue water. "Sure. But some of the better days are just sitting or lying out on the swells."

Ralph glanced out the door. "*Si. Camaradería.*"

Frank shuffled his chin in agreement as he slid his feet back into the huaraches. "Yeah… hanging out with the brothers."

Ralph looked around at the shack and sea brush as they climbed into the Bentley. "Why did you move out here anyway? It seems so…"

"Deserted?"

"*Si*. No peoples."

Frank smirked as he started the car. "Just the coyote and me. One less person to fuck up my sleep."

The redhead spread out both arms and hands. "But… but, here?"

Frank shrugged his shoulder and face. "It's been in the

family for about nine generations. It was a land grant from *El Presidente de Mexico.* The original Pounds was made an honorary *Californio* and married a Mexican girl nobody else would have. She was a half-breed by a drunken sailor. Her mother was from a good family but couldn't endure the shame, so she threw herself off the cliff at Dana Point. Off the same cliff that her family threw the cattle's skins off to the waiting boats below.

"When the girl was twenty, everyone knew she would never marry. The family wanted her to become a nun, but she only wanted to teach the children to read and write. Even the Indian children sat under her oak tree and learned.

"One day, a young trader from Pueblo de Los Angeles came to trade for leather. He sat nearby and eventually asked her father if it would be okay if he learned how to read and write from the daughter. The man said only if he married her. The young man had no land and told the father sadly of such.

"The father saw the young man also liked his daughter and said he would let the boy know when he came next. The father petitioned for a land grant from the president. Only to make the young man respectable enough to marry his daughter." Frank sowed his hand at the land. "So, this is it."

"So what happens to it all when you're gone?"

Frank nosed the Bentley next to Ralph's car. "Nothing. The state gets it all. They will bulldoze the two buildings and annex it all into the existing state park of the cove. The grass and sea brush will remain the same, and the antelope, red deer, coyotes, and many other animals will continue to live as they have for thousands of years. I'm only a short-term tenant."

Ralph continued thinking as he got out. "Just like the other tenants."

Frank grabbed the polarized dark aviator glasses from the holder. Putting them on, he could see the ghost of Danny at the counter. "Every life is a ring or circle. Some of us are lucky enough to see how those rings interlock and circle with others."

He looked over at Ralph. "You didn't tell me why you came all this way."

The man waved it down. "It's nothing. Go take care of the ladies. I think they are more *familia* than you say. And *la familia siempre es la primera*. We talk later."

Frank's eyebrows jumped behind the aviators. But he knew he needed to get to the hospital. He waved as he backed out. Turning, he nosed the tank of a car up the driveway.

14 STERILE ENVIRONMENT

Frank eased the Bentley off the street and pulled under the large apron. The building had once been a busy gas station when attendants wore bow ties, hats and checked your oil. A single gas pump with a mechanical lever and a twenty-gallon glass bottle on top stood sentinel on the outer island.

"*Amigo,* I don't think they still serve gas anymore." Frank chuckled as he realized it was his old partner's voice he had heard in his head. It was a standing joke about the single gas pump from some time before they were born. Frank's eyes slid shut as he breathed in through his nose. The mass of cut and potted flowers in the outside racks were almost enough to induce a rapture or happy coma.

"Hey. I charge double for you freeloading pansy sniffers."

Frank's face broke into a smile and a silent laugh. He didn't want to open his eyes. *Shit.* He still couldn't remember her name—only that it was either deep south or maybe Indian Mexican.

He rolled his head toward the voice before opening his eyes. "You're a cruel, cruel woman, Cruella de flower on de windowsill."

Aola's snorted laugh was snotty enough to make even a pig

blush. "You are a piss-poor suck-up, Frank Pounds. Come on in. I just made a fresh pot."

He remained motionless. The dark aviators reflected her taking a double-take and then throwing her hip out into her fist. "Coffee, asshole. I don't do the hippie shit… until Saturday night."

He pushed the door open. "French roast or just hard-scorched black?"

She looked down at his toenails and then turned in a huff. "You still need to take the time to do your nails. Their condition is downright disrespectful. If you're lucky, I'll find some chicory to put some hair on your balls."

He looked at the cracked and scuffed pink enamel. She was right. He didn't like it, but she was right. The tribute to his partner wasn't about him sleeping or doing work or surfing. It was about the ritual of mindfulness. It was about whom his partner had been and the space he held in their lives. It was the small thing he could do for the man who had been his mentor and saved his life a couple of times, and helped him live with his mistakes. He shrugged in resolution and stepped into the jungle of the woman's amazing flower shop. The high ceiling of what used to be the repair bays of the gas station allowed for the light from the skylights to filter through a floating jungle of hanging baskets. Some of the tendrils hung low enough to mingle with the tall plants from the jungle on the floor. Frank had always marveled at the curated plants from every end of the planet. Orchids hung next to draping ropes of what looked like cactus but were a hairy something-or-other from China. He gently ran his hand down the hairy spines.

"Don't be stroking my hairy monkey dicks." The voice seemingly floated from the jungle itself. "I work hard to make them limp. You stroke them, and they get an erection. Then I can't sell them to the bored housewives of Orange County."

He passed his hand down more of the long tendrils. "No ma'am, don't want no sixth-grade erections." He smirked as he guiltily wished to see just a twitch of what his touching was accused of. He wondered if it were true.

He turned the corner into the small office lacking in plants—except the single large flower on the monitor. Frank recognized it as a famous painting by Georgia O'Keefe.

A large white mug sat on the desk corner across from the crossed boots. The rainbow on the cup framed a unicorn farting. Frank's smile pulled up into his right cheek. He recognized the unicorn as a bastardized version of My Little Pony. It had been Kahuna's favorite T-shirt. The powder pink one with the hole in the side, or the soft faded blue one turning to granular dust with each last wearing. Someone had thought it fitting he be wearing it when they ran him into the oven. Frank wasn't asked, but he agreed—it was the right thing to do.

Frank silently took up the mug and sat. He looked back out at the jungle as he sipped. Taking it all in. *Two thousand eight hundred ninety-four days.* The view never seemed to change.

"You forgot again."

"What?" He turned to look at the woman almost laid back in her chair.

"My name."

Frank sipped. Busted chops, twice in a handful of minutes. This wasn't turning out to be his most winning day or endeavor. "Does anyone remember?"

"Everyone who counts. My mother, my sister… 'Book 'em Danno.'"

Frank looked at her out of the side of his eye with a raised eyebrow. He waited.

The small laugh was almost a snort. "I have thousands of customers. Even more I deliver to. You seriously thought I'd forget a name like Kahuna Kalani Paniolo Parker the third and a half?"

Frank almost spit his coffee back into the mug. "The fuck…? You lie about the half?"

The two laughed. The joke was that he was the third son by

the second wife but born before they could marry. His father was named Hank or Jake or something nobody who knew Kahuna cared about. The man had thrown him off the ranch the day he caught him with one of the ranch hands. The fifteen-year-old Kahuna begged his way to Oahu where his older sister took him in. It was the way of the beach people. They lived on the beach free and only had to move every three weeks—usually to another beach for the compulsory three days. His education had come at the hands of diversity in teachings as well as cultures. When he was eighteen and applying to the Hawaii State Sheriff Division, he was fluent in the five most common languages spoken in Hawaii—English, Pidgin, Mandarin, Cantonese, and Japanese. Or, as Kahuna would flip, Island and tourist. The pure Hawaiian he worked to master beyond singing.

Frank wiped at his eyes with his thumb and forefinger. "Fuck it. I'm just going to call you whatever flower I think of first."

The woman smashed her lips flat as she leaned back in the chair. The boots only shifted slightly. "Works for me. Aola means flower of the south in Choctaw or Muskogee or some other fart in the road Mother fell in love with."

The boots moved off the desk as the woman rocked forward. Her hand dusted aside her coffee mug as she leaned in and looked hard at Frank. "This isn't about remembering my name, is it?"

His lips rolled, and then just the tip of his tongue peeked out along the edge. The moistening was still dry. He slow-blinked as he leaned his head forward. The shake of his head was small and slow. He looked up at her in a side look. "No. No it's not." He put the mug down and reached in his pocket. The wad of folded bills was close to an inch thick. He pushed them across the desk. "I want you to add another hospital to your schedule."

The woman swallowed gently. Her eyes were frozen. "Which one?"

"Children's Hospital of Orange County."

The breath through her nose was noisy, the weight of it heavy. "Who's the kid?"

He looked at the cracks in the concrete floor. They wandered crazy and with no meaning. He bit at his lower lip and thought how crazy the world could be at times. Just like cracks crazing across an old floor.

"Her name is Tink. I don't know what last name they have her under. To get close to her, you'll have to use my name. I told them you'd be around, but even so…"

"They know me at CHOC…"

His face shrugged as he looked up. "Not like this, you haven't. There will be an undercover cop in scrubs wandering around. Once word gets around, you'll be fine, but at first, you can just drop them at the nurse's station on four north."

Her left hand scratched her chest where a bra strap may or might not be. "Can I ask…"

Frank thought about Kalani, his boyfriend, and everything else this woman probably knew. "She's not a kid. But when they found her, the EMTs thought she was. She's small. But they couldn't ask her. Somebody had beat her badly. Maybe they thought they had killed her—we don't know. A busboy or someone found her in a dumpster behind a restaurant early this morning. They thought she was a body dump, but she was still breathing. We only found out about her because I was pushing for a missing person. They found her phone abandoned back in the shops behind Disneyland. She's one of the Tinkerbells who ziplines from the Matterhorn."

"Is she awake now?"

He shook his head. "When I left, they were wheeling her into surgery. They had to wait for a team to come over from UCI Medical Center. One of the broken ribs had punctured a lung, and there were some possible cracks in her spine. It's going to be a long day."

Aola rocked gently in her chair as she thought. "I'll get some arrangements up there this evening, so she has something nice to wake up to. Any idea about flowers?"

He snorted softly. "When you see her and her twin, you'll know. I'd say anything close to neon pink and blue should work."

She scrunched her face and turned it sideways. "Neon?"

"Yup. Just like the kids dye their hair nowadays."

Her eyes went wide as her mouth shrunk into a dot. "Oh…"

Frank stood and turned at the door. "Let me know when this runs low. I'll drop off more."

She picked up the pile of money and turned it over. Thinking. "Yeah… I'll let you know."

His eyebrow raised as he suspected she wouldn't. "Daily. I want her world filled with beauty. They aren't going to move her. It's easier to protect her where others wouldn't think to look. I would think when she starts running out of the room, the overflow can brighten other rooms, as well."

Aola smiled. "Now you're starting to think like a blooming idiot."

He wiggled his eyebrows once and left. The warm glow would carry him to his next appointment.

He never really liked the Orange County Sheriff's Department headquarters on North Flower. The neighborhood was called the Flower District. The only thing growing was over-fertilized grass and anemic trees. Everything else was asphalt and raw concrete. The building always reminded him of a bunch of packing boxes jammed into one another. There was nothing smooth or design-worthy about the large, chunky building.

The man behind the desk had been a lot slimmer and less

chunky when Frank and Kalani reported to him. The years and the job were working their magic to an early grave.

The sheriff looked Frank up and down. "I don't even have to see your feet to know you're wearing huaraches with pink nail polish. Take a seat, Pounds."

Frank felt every bit of the weight he hadn't had on him since the accident. *Two thousand five hundred and sixty-five days.*

The sheriff turned a page in the file prepared far down the command staff. "It's been a couple of weeks since—"

"Thirteen days."

The man looked up. "Thirteen days… what?"

"Thirteen days since they found Mary's body."

The sheriff turned to the front page that he was no longer used to perusing for pertinent information. He checked the date. Frank waited while the man tried to do the math. He lowered the file and looked up. His face cleared from scowl to passive. When the sheriff ran the detectives, Pounds hadn't been his favorite detective, but he did have one of the best clear rates.

The man ran his left hand through his thinning hair. The long shallow sigh complemented the soft squeak of the chair's springs.

"Okay, let's start with the young girl."

"Woman."

The man's eyes became cold and hard around the edges.

Frank leaned in slightly. "The young woman is twenty-six."

"Then why is she at CHOC? It's a hospital for children who can't pay…"

"And the best place to leave her in hiding." His index finger tapped down on the edge of the large desk. "Look, when they found her, she was unconscious. She didn't have any identification on her and couldn't tell the paramedics how old she was. They saw what looked like a beaten young teen—she's only about four-foot maybe nine or ten. She has dyed neon-blue hair. Her body is more ten-year-old than woman. By the time they knew how old she was, I was there. She still wasn't awake, but they talked to her twin."

"She has a twin?"

"Yeah, but her hair is pink. Anyway, we have someone seriously beat up. Whether it's attempted homicide or just a beating, we need her in hiding and in a care facility. Now, unless you want to go down and arrest her for impersonating a little girl so you can throw her in county lockup…"

The man held up his palms and then laid his one index finger over the other. "Peace. I'm just trying to get a grasp of what she has to do with you and the case we're paying a lot of money for you to work."

Frank's lips furled. His gaze slid off to one side as he thought. "Stick with me on this…" He rolled his finger in the air. The sheriff nodded.

"The mother of the twins, for no better identifier, is the manager and bartender at Mary's bar."

The man closed his eyes as his brow pulled the one eye open. He looked at his former detective. "There are several qualifiers in your statement. Care to explain?"

Frank focused out the window. The short drop descended to a flat rooftop filled with satellite dishes and repeater antennas. It was commonly referred to as 'the forest.' He watched two maintenance workers massage the electronics blister on one of the dishes.

Finally, he pointed out at the forest. "There are two guys out there working on one of the dishes. From here, can you tell me what sex they are?"

The man glanced at the workers over a hundred feet away. Turning back, his face was bored. "Who cares?"

Frank nodded back out the window. "Because the woman is about to shoot the man."

The sheriff's head snapped back around. He studied the two workers. "Which one is the female?" He looked back at Frank.

Frank shrugged, feigning boredom. "Who cares… as long as they get the job done?"

"And this has to do with the woman being the mother of the other two women… how?"

"Having not done a full medical exam of Pussy, but for the girl's sake, she is woman enough for them to call mother. As for the two girls, they have budding breasts making little balloons under their T-shirts. Facially, they are androgynous enough to pass for whatever they say they are. Disneyland identifies them as fairies or pixies. It works for me."

The man squinted his left eye as his face pulled. "Whose pussy are you examining?"

Frank snorted. "I'm not. Pussy is the mother's name. But if you ever see the hard steel of her body and large biceps, you wouldn't question what she says her name is."

The sheriff's brows extended high above his rolling eyes. "Let's see if I've got this straight. The mother may or may not be female, and her name is Pussy."

"Correct."

"The young twins aren't really hers, but they view the relationship as family."

"Correct… but they aren't actually twins, either. They just work hard at looking the same."

The man rolled his eyes and head back toward the large window looking out over the forest and greater Santa Ana. His body gently followed the eyes and head. Frank counted three deep breaths ending in sighs.

"Anything else I want to know about this clusterfuck?"

"We're not sure if this is connected to Mary's murder."

The sheriff looked back over his shoulder. His eyes examined Frank through four slow blinks.

He looked back out the large window. The workers in the blue jumpsuits and white helmets had moved to another antenna. He pointed at them and snorted. "She still hasn't killed him yet."

Frank watched the two. "He just hasn't cracked one of the old misogynist locker-room jokes... yet."

The sheriff steepled his fingers in front of his chest as he watched a helicopter transition across the sky. Frank thought it was about halfway toward the Pacific Coast Highway. "How much do we owe you so far?"

Frank could hear the irritated edge in the man's voice. It was the same old chief of detectives. Pushing for closure by pointing out how much an investigation was costing the taxpayers. "Twenty-six thousand."

"Does that include your little swimming date?"

Frank snapped his fingers. "Thirty-two thousand and forty-seven-cents." If the man were going to play the nickel-and-dime game, Frank would lean back as hard. They both knew Frank was in this with a personal edge, and the sheriff had inserted himself in a low-profile murder because of Frank. The money just a whip to goad the progress and work. The roles had changed, but the interaction was the same.

The sheriff choked on his snort. "What's the forty-seven-cents for?"

"Taxes."

The man's finger pointed at the sky in an *ah-ha*.

"So, you've cost me more than a rookie's annual salary. But have you learned anything we can use?"

"We think a cartel enforcer called the *Ax* killed Mary and the guy out in Orange."

"Wasn't the guy in Orange connected to a cartel?" The man rolled his head to look at Frank.

"Yes, he was. It appears he was a highly placed front guy here in Orange County, but he lost his head."

The groan was low as the sheriff turned his head and pinched the bridge of his nose. The silence bumped over the silent laughter the two gelded war horses shared. Crime scene humor was gallows humor, but homicide took it far past anything near the executioner's noose. The sheriff thought about the last homicide the three had worked together.

The lieutenant had been in the neighborhood. Or more expressly, having dinner with his wife's parents, four doors away. The sound of a pump shotgun is distinct. It had stopped every other sound on a warm evening. He had called it in. The first responders were a beat patrol—a training officer with his brand-new trainee. The trainee made it two feet into the door and puked on the front sidewalk. Every other deputy, detective, and the coroner had to step around it.

Nine hours later, the lead detective, Kalani, suggested a small café for breakfast. Five men sat around the table in civilian clothes from their disrupted evening. Cataloging the seven bodies had turned into sorting out the mixed-up scattered body parts. The two killers had used high-powered automatic shotguns, which separated limbs from bodies. The high-capacity clips had made the sorting tedious, strenuous, and exhausting.

Even sitting around the large circular table, the enormity of the scene still hadn't broken through the shock. Each of the five minds ground through what they had processed in its own way. The oldest victim had been in his sixties; the youngest girl was fifteen. Once they found the three safes, the family had appeared to be in the middle of the cocaine trade.

None of the deputies had spoken a word since they left the scene. None had said a word when the manager led them toward the back to the large table. Everyone was sorting what they would need to put in their report—all had filled their hip books with notes.

The perky waitress, who they all would have carded, walked up as she popped her gum in her mouth. The snap was louder than she had thought it would be. Ten eyes burned at her.

She slumped on one hip. "Well, aren't we a mess of doom

and gloom this fine Sunday morning. Someone die?" Still met with silence, she soldiered on. "Who's up for a Bloody Mary?"

The hesitation was followed by four hands. She looked at Kalani in expectation.

He sighed deeply. "I need a Dirty Beach Fuck."

She squinted as she cocked her head. "What's that?"

"Start with a double Sex on the Beach and add a double Up Against the Wall Muthafucker. Throw in a handful of green olives, some onions, anchovies if you have them, and a pineapple spear. And I'll take the Loco Moco."

All five had watched the little girl... She finally tapped the point of her pen on her pad and looked up. "Half the bar, anything I can grab, and one Hawaiian locomotive. Got it." She looked around the table. "Anyone else want food?"

The sheriff's head rolled over toward Frank. The two nodded and snickered. "Bloody Marys."

15 HOW'S THE WATER

Frank had always loved the tall lacey eucalyptus trees scattered through the University of California. When the city of Irvine anointed the college to be built, a sister city in Australia volunteered hundreds of almost full-grown trees. As Frank slowed for the turn, the air was full of the pungent smell of the sunbaked leaves.

Frank nosed the Bentley into the narrow driveway and pulled to a stop at the guard shack. As the security guard—with a cluster of zits and a futile attempt at a brush cut—leaned out, Frank held up his out-of-date sheriff's wallet. The kid was still confused by the Bentley-turned-convertible with a blowtorch.

"I need a parking pass for the computer labs."

The kid blinked a dozen times in the two seconds it took for him to engage his mouth. "We don't have passes for convertibles." His mind stumbled on what he had said. "And you can't park in the labs anyway, sir."

Frank looked over as the passenger door opened. The faded rusty hair was still crinkled even with the tight pull-back into a large bun. The leathered face behind the mirrored aviator dark glasses looked a dozen years older than he guessed was her actual age. The guard slid in and sat. She pulled the door almost closed and then snugged it with a proper British pull for a fine car.

She looked up at the kid, and his mouth hanging open. "I've got this, Erik."

"It's Paul, ma'am."

"Okay, Herman." She looked at Frank and nodded forward. "Let's go. Turn left at the street."

The car glided down onto the street and turned left. Frank peered over. "Care to tell me what's going on?"

"Do you know where you're going?" Her smile was playful.

"Not really. I know it's one of the tall, white concrete buildings."

She laid her head back, facing the sun. Frank could tell her eyes were closed. He guessed she also knew her way around the beach if not a surfboard, but he had never seen a redhead on a long gun.

Her smile cracked. "We have several of those. Turn down the next utility access on your right." She waved with her right hand.

Frank looked. Her eyes were still closed.

He snorted as they eased around a small curve, and the one-lane access road appeared. "Come here often, sailor?"

She sat up and pointed. "Park in the slot on the left."

Frank smiled at the sign. *Reserved for Security Only.* "Are you sure I won't get a ticket here?"

She smiled and opened the door. "Do you know where you're going, Pounds?"

"Do I know you?" He raised his aviators and squinted.

"Not unless you have started paying attention to the short-board rippers on the point. You bus drivers only see us as obstacles to hit or dodge."

A flash of a bright yellow wet suit flashed in his memory. The coiled snake was distinctive and custom sewed in. Frank didn't need to ever read the words. The flag and sentiment had been around since the colonies fought to become a nation.

Frank smiled. "I don't think I ever tread on you." He put his hand out. "Frank Pounds… but then, you already knew that."

A single eyebrow crested over the glasses. "A distinct car. I almost missed it. What with no long gun strapped to the back rack. Betsy Rotroff, but they call me—"

"Snake?"

She chuckled. "Close. The kids call me Betty." She stood and gently closed the door. "You're good here for a few hours. Where are you going?"

Frank stood. "Somewhere on the fourth floor. It's a work lab. I think I can find it again."

"There's a couple of interesting labs on the fourth. Rumor has it some of the kids have hacked the system. They get solid four-ohs and above."

Frank snorted as he lowered his glasses. "I've seen some of the work. I don't think they need to shake the gutter for those kinds of scraps."

"Well, I hope you find who you're looking for." She waved and turned.

Frank turned and looked up at the tall building. "Thanks again, Betty."

The freckled fingers wiggled over her tight military bun.

FRANK STOPPED and leaned against the doorjamb. There were five large television screens around the room—any sports bar would be jealous. But what made him stop were the dozens of whiteboards with multicolored mathematical formulas jamming the white space. One board was marked up with blue, one red, one green, and seven in black with notes in different colors. The two guys in what looked like pajamas and T-shirts stood watching a dark young woman scribble out a new equation on a fresh board. As she started to stoop, she grabbed the lower part of the large board and lifted. The whole moved upward.

She resumed pounding and swirling the black marker.

The male with the rats-nest of curly hair turned. His eyes filled his large, thick glasses. He blinked as if he wasn't sure he saw a person standing in the doorway or if it was a hallucination. He elbowed his buddy, who turned whiter and wide-eyed.

The ghost child stepped over to the woman, leaned in, and whispered.

She looked at him for a few seconds and then turned to see Frank.

Slowly capping the dry marker, she studied the man leaning in their door. Frank studied her back. From the features, she could have been from a few countries that Uncle Sam had sent Frank.

She walked about half the distance and then spoke. It confirmed his guess of Pakistan or Indian.

"Can I help?" The harder British clip moved his guess to a better neighborhood of New Delhi.

Frank smirked gently. "I was just stunned by the solid use of old school technology. New Delhi?"

She smiled. "About an hour on the train out of Mumbai. Have you been to India?"

He nodded. "I did a two-week tour once with a friend. We were on R&R, and he had family spread around the country. We rented motorcycles. Remarkable countryside, but the cities almost killed us."

She stepped closer. Her right cheek pulled at her mouth. "How did you like the food?"

Frank smiled and chuffed softly at the memories of nan and tandoori cooked meals. "I could have stayed longer with street food. The restaurants seemed to cook for the tourists—Russian and Americans. I think the English stayed sheltered in the Ibis hotels with paste for food."

"My aunt and uncle run a small restaurant up in Orange. They learned how to cook on the streets. It hasn't changed."

"I'll get their address sometime. But"—he glanced at his watch—"I need to get to a meeting I'm already late for."

She gave him a small bow that he returned with a nod. He wasn't sure what was about to start happening, but he knew the last thing he needed was any relationship with a college student, even if she did look about thirty.

But the address of a great restaurant was worth the scary territory.

He opened a door. Six La-Z-Boys and six giant screens filled the lab with a military killing game. The room had no other illumination. Blackboards of some kind covered the windows.

As a wave of what looked like giant spiders swept over the crumbled ruins, and the six guns started shooting, a disconnected voice barked from the dark. "Shut the fucking door."

Frank snorted and backed out. He didn't even want to know what research was being conducted—if any…

The next door was open, and he was reasonably confident he recognized the small rear-end and legs encased in black leggings with pink and lavender skulls and unicorns dancing in the dark. The black ponytail hung over the one ear and down from her neck. The sports bra was dark blue with gold trim. Frank guessed it had an anteater on the front—the school mascot, the much-loved Peter Anteater.

The blonde bent over a laptop, typing at a blurring speed. She looked up at his soft knock. "Ming?" Tree looked down at her laptop and back at Frank. "This paper is due in less than an hour. You two talk somewhere else."

Ming stood and turned. Frank smiled. The sports bra read *Eater* in a gold-embroidered script. She blinked and then grabbed her large thermos mug. Stepping out into the hall, she quietly closed the door. "Roof. I need the sunshine."

Frank chuckled at the several scattered chairs on the roof, not designed as a veranda. He remembered several buildings overrun by the hijinks of testosterone-jacked SEALs. He had the right to judge. He had led the mattress assault on the roof in

Qatar. The air-conditioning ran a constant sixty-six. The daytime temperature was well over one-ten. The swing could cause colds or just sinus problems. You couldn't legally take any medication and remain on duty. Sleeping naked on the roof made sense. *Eleven thousand three hundred and forty-eight days.*

Ming slipped on her gold-mirrored aviator sunglasses and sat. "We call it the beach. For many nerds, it's the closest they'll ever get to the real beach, about a mile and a half over there." Her hand waved a pointing middle finger. Frank understood. He could never imagine living anywhere other than near water. Even in the sandbox, water was only a helicopter jump away.

He slipped into one of the chairs nearby. "I was wondering if you had any more ideas on the anomalies on the scans?"

Her head rolled over. "Anomalies as in general, or are you asking about what we're calling 'the bus'?

"The bus?"

"It has about the same shape as a larger bus or RV. The shell was two shipping containers welded together. Eight-foot wide, eight and a half high, and twenty long. They were medium containers, which are the most common for shipping out of China."

Frank leaned back. "And being welded together, you get a forty-foot city bus." His head rolled over. "Do we know anything else about it? Like shipper markings?"

The girl jerked and spat her drink back into her flask. "What's this *we*, Padawan? You got a mouse in your pocket?"

The two laughed. "You're too young to know such a smartass line."

"So is Mickey, but he said he got it from his father." She looked over. "Is it true his father was your partner?"

Frank nodded. "In a way. He was my T.O.—Training Officer." Frank's chest gave a small hiccup of a laugh. "He took it further than most. I live in a shack on the south coast. Randy figured there was no way I was eating right, so he used to bring me home all the time. I think Mickey was about five or six. He was smaller than the other kids, so he kept riding his Big Wheel when his friends had moved on to bicycles."

"Big Wheel?" She reached for her phone but only found her butt in her leggings. No pockets.

Frank laughed. He could only guess how defenseless she must feel without her instant connection to the world's knowledge. "It's okay. We'll do this the old-fashioned way. You sit and listen while I tell you a fact about the world. All you have to do is accept it as gospel truth."

She hesitated halfway out of the chair. Gently, she eased down. "Gospel…?"

Frank rolled his eyes. For a genius with a smart mouth, sometimes she was just a little too literal. "Okay, but not in the sense of going to church—unless it's the Church of Mattel Toys."

"Like Barbie?"

He nodded. "Like Barbie. But they also make other stuff, as well. One was a tricycle with a big front wheel and tiny back wheels. The kid sits with his butt a few inches above the asphalt. Most kids can barely see over the handlebars and front wheel, and it was all made from plastic. I think they only cost about twenty or thirty bucks back then."

She nodded. "They have a red frame with yellow handles. I think there's a blue part somewhere."

"Then why did you ask what it was?"

"I didn't know what it was. But down in San Clemente, every year, they have a downhill race with office chairs. Well, it started with office chairs. Anyway, people race all sorts of stuff. What you describe, I've seen. Think of guys bigger than Mickey or you, riding one of those down a hill at fifty miles an hour…" Her smile was infectious. For several years, Frank had watched firsthand what she described.

"Ever gone down to watch?"

She shook her head. "Like I told you when we went to

brunch, I don't get out much. School takes up much of our lives. But YouTube is a great stress breaker."

He rocked his head back and gently let it fall. "Hmm…"

She sat in silence, remembering how her grandmother used to sit for hours, never moving, never making a sound. The little girl would slowly get up from the bed to see if the woman was asleep.

The woman's mouth never seemed to open or even move. "*Xiǎo nǚhái yīnggāi biǎoxiàn chūlái.*" *Little girls should behave.*

When Ming turned ten, she was fluent in both dialects that the Chinese household spoke. Her kanji perfected enough to have her grandmother stop twisting her ear for sloppy brush-strokes. Many in the community paid her to write letters home to China. Her time growing up was spent with older grownups instead of children her own age. She soon discovered how rare it was for her parents to still speak their native dialects, if they speak any Chinese at all.

"How tall did you say the standoffs were?"

She startled. "I did?"

"Hmm, when we first met. You or Tree were rattling off many figures and information… but I remember you saying something about the bus being up on tall legs. At the time, I had a picture of a Daddy Long Legs spider."

Ming's face and mouth screwed up in thought. "The divers said they seemed about thirty feet. About the peak of a two-story house. But then, they're frat boys." She held up her thumb and finger about three inches apart.

Frank smiled and snorted softly about the abused six-inch joke and Ming being a lesbian. "So even for a Chinese lesbian, size matters?"

She rolled her head his way and smiled. "More than you can imagine."

Frank's eyes grew as he drew in a large breath through his nose. "I'm certain I don't want to know."

Frank slow-blinked as he thought. Across the campus's Central Park, some other tall white buildings stood on an even taller rise. A falcon danced in the thermals between the buildings. Something was there as the bird swooped down and shot through the narrow canyon between the buildings. Suddenly, it nosed up and shot out from the canyon, still between the walls. The small bird above never stood a chance. It had not seen the dark-mottled predator in the shadows of the buildings. The claws closed as the falcon pitched over backward, carrying the now-dead prey to be lunch.

Frank's one finger rose. "Do you remember if the legs were straight up and down or splayed?"

The access door slammed shut. Frank's head turned at the sound. Ming's chair sat slightly turned, but empty.

He turned back to face the sun. The air was clear of birds. The sky had only a few puffy white clouds hanging. It was the sort of day when lying on the longboard could lead to a sunburn.

The steel access door slammed open against the wall. Ming marched across the white gravel roof. "I'll let you talk to him. But if you fuck this up, your chances of getting a date with the math queen are so over." She handed the phone out. "His name is Dawson, as in Jack Dawson from a stupid movie where he drowns."

Frank took the phone. "Hello, Jack?"

There was a soft growl. "She's wrong. But it's worse. I was named after Dawson's Creek. A truly droll little series, but Mom was smitten—her words, not mine—by the main character Dawson Leery, sir."

"Oh. Okay." Frank looked up at a young woman having pure fun. An imp from the guy's hell. "My name is Frank. Frank Pounds. I'm working on an investigation… Well, let's just say I'm interested in what you found when you dove off Dana Point."

"Yes, sir. The bus. Well, it's not a bus, we just…"

"Call it that because of its size. Ming told me. What I want to know about are the support legs."

"Yes, sir. As I told Ming, the height was about four of my height, and I'm six-foot-six."

Frank looked at the small pixie in front of him and smiled. She must have heard and figured out what he was imagining. She flipped him two birds, sat down in her chair, and pulled long on her thermos.

"Describe the legs. I mean, were they straight up and down? Splayed out like an A-frame? Tied in a knot like a pair of rabbit's ears?"

The joking passed right over the kid's head. "Yes, sir, they were bowed out, like arches, or a small person trying to ride a large horse."

"As if they designed them for something large to pass between them?"

"Now that you put it like… yes. Maybe like a small submarine could get in and raise its tower into the cutout in the floor. Yes, sir."

Frank worried his upper lip with his teeth. "Hmm… the interior. I'm assuming you had a light?"

"Yes, sir. All three of us had lights. The interior was almost empty except for the walls. There were heavy-duty shelves welded onto the walls. At one end, they were only deep enough to fit a closed Mac Air Pro. But at the other end, they were almost as deep as my arm. They looked like you could put bales of hay on them. They looked strong enough too."

Frank closed his eyes. "Go back to fitting a closed laptop. Did you mean only a couple of inches between the shelves…?"

"No, sir. There was maybe a good foot or so between the shelves. But the depth was only about fourteen or sixteen inches."

"So you could stack five or six laptops on the shelf…?"

"Yes, sir."

"Ming said there were some air tanks there…"

"Yes, sir. A double row along the one end. I would say about a dozen four-foot-tall tanks. One had a regulator on it. It was reading about half-full. But it was set on a slow bleed to pressurize the bus. That's how we found it. There was a small trail of bubbles leading down to the bus. They were large up near the top but got smaller as we got deeper. But we just followed them down... and bingo. There was the bus."

"But then someone would occasionally need to come service the bus and swap out the tanks..."

"Yes, sir. That was our thinking too. So we didn't hang around. Whoever was using it probably wouldn't like us being there."

Frank's head rocked gently. "Smart move. Well, you've been a great help, Jack."

"Dawson, sir."

"Yes. Dawson. Thanks."

"So you'll put in a good word with Ming...?"

Frank looked over at the young girl absently winding her long hair in and out of her fingers. "Kid, if she doesn't owe ya, then I do. So, yeah. I'll put in a good word for ya. Thanks again."

Ming's head rocked forward. She held her hand out, and he handed the phone back.

She slid the phone down the back of her leggings. "Well?"

"Whatever he wants you to do, I think you should do your best to do."

She waved her hand. "Pfft. The math queen already has the hots for him. She just doesn't know he has the hots for her. It's a done deal. No. I mean the bus?"

Frank thought about his SEAL training. "I think it's a drug drop for a submarine. It sounds like it's rigged for marijuana as well as hard drugs like coke, heroin, or fentanyl."

Her face contorted. "Shit. Fentanyl is some scary hell. Just a pound of it in the wrong place could wipe out half of Orange or L.A. County."

Frank lowered his eyelids as he took a breath through his nose and nodded in agreement.

Both were thinking as they walked down the stairs. Frank stopped her at the door to the fourth floor by putting his hand on the top of the door.

"This program of yours…"

"What about it?"

"Who all is involved in developing it?"

"Just us two. It's our master's research project."

"Master's?"

"Well, it started as just some weekend fun in the dorm, but once we saw the real potential, we spun it up into a master's thesis project."

"Why not go for the full boat and a Ph.D.?"

She smiled. "Because as a lowly masters, the research stays ours. The rights to the program are ours. But if we open it out to a Ph.D…."

Frank smiled and spread his hands. "They take it."

She drilled her right finger into her left palm. "Nailed it in one."

Frank pulled open the door. "Don't screw with a Chinese lesbian."

"Or her wing girl." She slugged him softly on the shoulder.

"So how close are you to finishing it?"

She turned into the empty lab. "Oh, it's finished. We're just applying it and polishing how it works. We want to get it so someone with little or no knowledge of computers can run the program. We also want to get some of the other programs in the dredging world, like Depth Vision and Dredge Sight, and have ours work seamlessly together."

"So are you…?"

"That was what Tree was working on. We asked for access to their code so we can cross code. This way, they'll bundle into a single program. Start with scans, build your quotes, and do the dredging. All in one program."

"So you're close?"

She shrugged her face. "Close enough. School isn't done for a while."

Frank squeezed her shoulder with his hand. "Keep me posted."

As he reached the elevator, she called out, "Hey, Frank?"

He turned with his dark glasses in his hand.

"The metal in your back. It sounded like a lot of metal and moving parts… How stiff does it make you?"

He thought. "I still surf… so, not much restriction."

"Does it hurt?"

"Everything is perspective. I get headaches that hurt worse. And a stubbed toe in the night…"

She winced. "Yeah, a motherfucker."

He bobbed his head as he slid his dark glasses on.

"I just wondered. I hope I wasn't out of line."

He swung his head once. "Just keep asking questions instead of hacking into classified government personal files. Who knows, maybe one day, I'll want to know the difference between a Chinese lesbian and a regular lesbian…"

She blushed at being caught with a snoopy computer, but laughing, she wound her hand through her long straight hair. "We have better hair."

As he stepped into the elevator, he heard her parting shot.

"Stop by sometime when you have time for us to paint each other's toenails and talk silly girl talk."

The elevator engaged quietly. He scowled at his toes.

16 CHOP-CHOP

The drawer's large rollers were almost silent, except in the still of the morgue. The door clicked with a snap of metallic finality. She hung on the handle. Children were always the hardest.

Her eyes opened as she looked at her fogged reflection in the stainless steel. The last vestiges of any color hid in the tight curls of white. She didn't mind the gray hair; she had only wished it hadn't arrived until she was in her sixties instead of searing its way across her head for her fortieth birthday. The first path painted its way after the cracked skull—courtesy of a drunk finding their way home much later than most.

The brain damage had been almost unnoticeable to the untrained eye. Her occupational therapist, on the other hand, was her instructor. The motor skills of her right leg were those of a one-year-old. She had worked hard at getting the brain to rewire into some form of control.

The strength to stand all day at the autopsy table had come in the gym as she focused on leg presses multiple times her body weight. The control she finally accepted came with some form of a third leg. Her right hand found the carved lion's head of her cane. She found it in Tanzania. Handle to tip were carved animals the Maasai tribes told world-building folklore about. It had been love at first sight. The wife of the carver had admired her diamond stud earrings. The trade, and their hug, was an exchange of sisterhood.

She rolled her head and shoulders along the wall of cool stainless steel doors to the cadaver drawers. She looked at the chart of work to do, written on a dry-erase board across the room. The words were in black ink. In her early years, she had nightmares of wiping off a case number, only to have the board add three more. The faster she wiped off cases, the faster the board added them. Some weeks, it just seemed like dreams.

She sighed and returned to her desk to finish the report. The release of the child was a rush. She was Jewish, and tonight would be the third day—the religiously dictated day for burial.

She turned at the sound of the outer door opening. She stood with her backside braced against the first autopsy table, her hands stacked on the cane, her face impassive. Anyone using the front door was business. Only the back door with its chime was more work. Some days, the difference between the two worlds was only slight and a small bit of sweat.

The tall man appeared in the half-door of glass. She smiled. Only her voice command could open the door. Sealing for an autopsy was regulation. "Open the door."

The click was audible, and the door slid open.

"Frank Pounds, as I live and breathe." Her smile was broad and warm—and then it was not. She turned with a sour look on her face and worked her way toward a large computer screen. "You're a week late."

"I love you too, Dee Dee." He strode in but knew the frost wouldn't melt until they finished the business—the screen filled with a close-up of a beheaded neck.

"Hypoxia is what killed him." She clicked a few keys. Half a monitor large enough to make most sports bars jealous tumbled with four new documents and a graph. She waved a clicker at the monitor. The graph grew. "The gas in his tanks wasn't what he paid for. Someone gave him a hotshot of nitrogen." She looked at his stony face. "It's no laughing matter, Frank. The shit will kill you."

He nodded and pointed to the other spikes on the graph. He had seen enough mass spectrometer readings to know how they worked.

"He was dealing with severe pain lately. This is the residue of hydromorphone, your old friend Dilaudid. This spike is cyclobenzaprine, or what I can only assume was Flexeril. Those would probably explain this... which is benzodiazepine. It's quite common in you vets..."

He nodded. "For panic and anxiety attacks..."

She turned. "Yes, Frank. Other than the hypoxia from the nitrogen, I would say our man was the same as sixty percent of all the vets I get through here."

"Only sixty?"

She turned back to the screen. "Maybe not so high." She clicked the handheld wand, and the graph returned to its smaller size. "What's missing in Mr. Shores was large doses of alcohol. In fact, what was missing in the man's liver and kidneys was any alcohol. Or hard drug abuse. Other than his being murdered, he stood to live a long healthy life."

Her hand jerked, and the image of the neck filled the screen. "The removal of his head was almost surgically clean. There were no hack marks of the first attempts we normally see with most horrific severances. This was one swift movement. If this were the early eighteen-hundreds in France, I would say it was a well-maintained and sharpened guillotine. But this is Orange County and the twenty-first century, and so... I'm at a mystified loss." She turned to him and stood silent.

Frank's eyes grew as he looked at the neck. "So, surgically removed is out?"

Her finger circled the bone. "If a surgeon had done the work, this bone would have shown striations of a bone saw. What you see is the lower half of the C-5 cervical vertebrae.

"On someone the size and mass of Mr. Shores, the C-4 is the narrowest section of the neck. So, it would also be the most logical target for severing the head from the body. The result of the cut having bifurcated the C-5 tells me, us, the cutting blow was educated, but swift."

Frank cleared his throat. "So the instrument was swung handheld… like a machete."

"That would be my guess." She pointed again at the two outer edges of the neck. "The neckline is almost the same length on both sides. This, and the lack of a large pool of blood at the dumpsite, leads me to believe, one, he wasn't killed there, and two, he was erect, possibly in a kneeling position when he was struck."

"Like he was kneeling on a surfboard—paddling."

"Yes. That would fit the criteria." She smiled. "And if he were out on the water, it would explain the lack of blood in the sand."

Frank's face screwed up as he clamped down his left eye in thought. "How much force does it take to cut off a head? And can you apply enough force while standing or sitting on a surfboard?"

She rolled her lips with a deep sigh flaring her nose. "I called my friend back east at the Body Farm."

"FBI…"

She nodded. "He said if sitting or standing on a surfboard, you would have to work out. But he sent me this clip of the official executioner for the royal family of Saudi Arabia."

She typed and hit return. A small screen filled only a portion of it. The clip was only a few seconds. The sword swung from over the executioner's head and effortlessly down. The body and head separated.

"He explained the man is large, well-trained, and the sword is surgically sharp."

Frank rolled his finger in the air. The clip repeated. It was like watching a train wreck—gruesome but fascinating.

She moved her weight from one hip to the other. "Evidently, Anne Boleyn, Henry's second wife, thought the ax to be beneath her. It was crude and dirty. The back of the ax head was a hammer. The royal would bribe the executioner to first hit them with the hammer to knock them out, so they weren't conscious during the many hacks of the small ax."

Frank frowned at her. "But she still…"

She rolled her eyes. "I had to look it up to confirm what he said. But yes, Henry did send for a special swordsman from the north of France. The sword was weighted but extremely sharp. He took her money, but also took her head in one clean move."

"But it still puts us back to the question of who was big enough to take Mary's head off while he's on a surfboard."

Dee Dee typed some more. "The surfboard is on you. But first"—she hit enter and stood, then the image and documents changed. "meet Hector Pedro Chavez."

She clicked the handheld and pointed to the spikes one by one. "Cocaine, Quaaludes, tequila, and Rohypnol."

"Some party."

"Yes, Frank. You might say it was a party to end all parties." She rolled her eyes from being dragged into another detective's crime scene humor. She clicked the wand, and the image filled the screen. "It would appear our executioner is an automatic."

"Automatic?"

"Like the placekicker who keeps kicking the ball through the uprights but always three feet above the crossbar and in the left half of the uprights. It's an autonomic assessment and response. If you put a patch over their weaker eye, they still kick the same with an eighty percent accuracy."

Frank smiled coyly. "What if you put a patch on the other eye?"

"Then, they can't see the ball and kick the holder instead."

Frank groaned. "No, I mean putting the patch on their dominant eye instead."

"They lose depth perception and alignment. They're lucky to boot it through the goalposts, even one out of ten."

"So blind their dominant eye, and they swing wild."

"In football, they kick. Baseball, they swing. Golf, they swing. Football is kicked. That's why they call it football."

Frank remembered seeing the medical examiner at a picnic a few times. The Jets jersey was always the same—Namath.

She cleared her throat and continued the lecture. "What you're looking at is the lower half of the C-5 vertebrae." She pointed at the two sides of the neck. "But there is about an inch difference in the neck."

"So he was falling over?"

"At an estimated five-foot-four and only a hundred twenty... more than likely, he was being pushed over by the blow."

Frank pointed at the lower half of the vertebrae. "But his swing and aim were the same."

She nodded. "Swing and aim were consistent. Same killer."

17 IS SHE AWAKE

The glass door whooshed open. Frank's toes stopped just over the threshold. He knew it wasn't a regular hospital, but then, the smell stopped him none the same. *Two thousand five hundred and thirty-six days.*

The sharp smell of cleaner was weaker—smaller patients, smaller lungs, smaller damaged goods. The childhood graphics on the walls were meant to be happy and friendly, but the concern on families' faces said otherwise. The children's hospital got some of the worst cases in the Southland. Because it was a no-charge hospital, they got the patients who had little or no insurance or money. Poverty can rob the souls of parents and steal the health of the most vulnerable. This hospital was just for such patients and their families.

As part of his rehabilitation after the accident, Pan had brought him here to read to children. Even the simplest stories were appreciated. Sometimes Frank would ask the kids to read to him. They wanted to see his back—the cause of his searing headaches. It was a trade. He would take a handful of aspirin and close his eyes while they read. Almost all of them would try to make up stuff to see if he was listening. They all learned he was focusing on their every word and knew most of the books by heart. The ones who struggled, he helped. The ones who struggled even to read, he schooled for hours. For him, it was focusing on something other than the pain. For them, it was the one-on-one they had never had. For others, it showed them a white cop not only wasn't scary but could also care about them. No matter why they were in the hospital, they would return to school with a new skill and a love for reading. As Frank knew and taught, reading can take you anywhere in the world and beyond.

He took a deep breath and stepped in before the doors tried to close on him. The receptionist looked up. It had been a while. Her smile was slow but warmed. Her hand raised, and the fingers wiggled. The evening shift had been Frank's favorite time to visit. After the pain of physical therapy. After the pain of chemotherapy. After the traumas of surgeries, probes from doctors, pokes from nurses, and every mind-numbing experience a kid had to endure, but never imagined it could happen to them. This was Frank's time. A soothing voice. A favorite story. A friendly face to tuck them in. They never knew he had had a similar day and needed the quiet time just as much as they did —or even more.

"Hello, Jan. How's the family?"

She smiled. Nobody asked about her family. Everyone knew she was alone. She had grown up less than a mile away. The orphanage was long gone. The mental hospital was also gone. The electroshock therapy was now only a faded memory of an ugly past. She was still, technically, a ward of the state. Orange County, to be more exact. She lived most of her free life in a group home. But when she was awarded a judgment for her past treatments, she moved into a small cottage. The woman next door had been the only nurse who cared for her with compassion. The woman lived with her daughter, who looked after her day and night. Jan sat with the nurse in the afternoon to give her daughter time to run errands. The daughter only thought Jan was a caring neighbor. She never knew why Jan had bought the small house next door.

But her *family* was the miniature statues she loved to enamel paint. Most of the painting was with a magnifying glass and a one-haired or three-haired brush. Most of the statues stood less than one inch tall. Frank knew she gave them away. If not, the small house would be wallpapered with tiny figures.

She smiled and turned the small statue on the counter around for him to see. The Down's Syndrome was only a hint in her flattened speech. Only the eyes were a giveaway. "I started painting the Marvel people. Some of the kids li…"—she took a short breath and smiled—"really like them." She turned the statue so she could see the face. "I was painting just the men… because the boys like them. But this is Wonder Woman. I like her."

Frank nodded. "She looks like you."

She blushed. The flush hit the white hair at her temples. "I… I miss you, Frank."

His lips rolled, and he bit at his lower lip. "I miss you too, Jan. But I don't need the therapy anymore."

She slumped and looked around the desk before looking back up. "But the kids do."

He lightly touched the top of Wonder Woman's head with his finger. "True." He looked up at the round face. There was no hidden motive, no self-serving, no guile, just the way she saw the world. "Let's see how I do with this one, and then we'll see, okay?"

"Okay, Frank. I'll be here."

He smiled. "It's what I count on, Jan. It's what I count on."

The man in the all-dark-blue scrubs stood out at the nurses' station. The other three wore scrub tops with dogs or kittens. Frank leaned over the counter. "Serraveno, you really need to lighten up on those steroids." The young man held weightlifting records in the department and the state. The arms and shoulders strained the usually baggy sleeves and top.

The man looked up with a start. "Jeez, Pounds, what are you doing here?"

The older nurse next to him snorted and backslapped his arm. "He's logged more time here than you've been on the force." She smiled and jerked her head. "How ya doin', Frankie?"

He pushed his lower lip out and bobbed his head in a bad imitation of her Bronx accent. "How youz doin', Holz?"

She pointed her finger at him, laughing. "Don't getz me started."

Frank chuckled. "Books in the same place?"

"Same room, but we got a bigger shelf. They moved it across to the other wall."

Frank bounced his fist on the counter and turned. "Thanks, Holly. And Holly?"

"Yeah, Frankie?"

"Get the meatball a decent shirt. He looks like a bite-in-the-ass cop with all the dark blue."

The deputy's face flashed with offense. "I wore one with dogs on it…"

The nurse breathed dramatically and rolled her eyes. "K-9s. Drugs, takedowns, arms in their teeth—funny at a cop picnic… but here?"

Frank pointed at the deputy. "Behave, Serraveno, or they get to have their way with you."

Frank went to the break and storage room. It only took him a few minutes to find the right book.

The room was dim. The bed seemed too large for the small body. The head end of the bed tilted up. The blue hair was almost black in the dim light. The ventilator tubes obscured half of her face. If it wasn't for the intubation, one could almost believe she was asleep.

Frank checked the monitors. His long recovery had taught him how to read all the monitors and what they meant. The sedation drip was light, but the weight on the dry-erase board read ninety-one pounds. Her breathing was weak—only four pounds of pressure. The oxygen saturation flickered between ninety-four and ninety-five. The morphine drip was a dose he would expect for a toy poodle, but it made sense with her under sedation.

He turned on the small reading light attached to the low table next to the chair. The ventilator's rhythmic soft wind, only interrupted by the steady soft beep marking the end of each cycle of recording the heart rate, hardly filled the room.

Frank sat. The small nose was about all he could see from the low chair. His right hand slid over the cover of the book. It wasn't the classic large book, but it would do for now.

"In a quiet street in London lived the Darling family. There were Father and Mother Darling, Wendy, Michael, and John, as well as the children's nursemaid, Nana—a Saint Bernard."

The sound of his reading was soft but carried across the hall to the nurses' station. The nurses all leaned back in their chairs. Serraveno turned his head to look at the head nurse. She glared at him but nodded her head for him to mind his own business. He resumed studying the woodworking magazine but stopped turning the pages.

18 WET CONNECTIONS

The finger was light on his skin. In the dark, everything was more sensitive. His skin tingled. He had heard the car door close softly up at the Shack. He could almost count the number of steps taken around the Shack and down the old, shorter driveway. The trench would not be a problem for her current orthopedic shoes. The old Dansko clogs she wore on the ward weren't made for all-terrain.

When she opted for surgery, the first day, they caught an attempted suicide. The young man had decided to take a high dive off an overpass for what he thought would be head-on with a truck. He hesitated a split-second. Instead of hitting the nose of the truck, his knees hit the windshield. His face and shoulders left a large dent in the top of the cab. The momentum of the truck turned his flat dive into a spinning tumble. The top edge of the trailer caught his second rotation high on the hips. Both shattered as the body folded in the wrong place. The T-3 and T-4 vertebrae were ejected in four pieces.

The second faceplant punched a deep hole in the thin roof of the trailer. The body stuck.

California has a rule about surgery. If a patient needs a unit of blood, you give them a unit. If they need thirty-two units, you keep pumping it in as fast as it keeps running out. The average hundred and eighty-pound man contains only ten units. The rule says if the patient needs a thirty-third unit—no.

Most trauma doctors in a major metropolitan hospital have access to a few other tricks. A couple of units of platelets can slow the bleeding through small punctures. Extra plasma can extend time while you keep looking for and patching all the leaks.

When the surgical team looked up and called the time of death, the table, crew, and floor were awash with over forty units of red, white, platelets, and plasma. The suction machine had choked with overflow three times. In the crisis, the head nurse had cleared the machine by dumping the contents on the floor.

Pan's clogs never stood a chance. When you stand in one place for three straight hours, your knees lock, the nervous system goes to sleep, and you can't feel where your feet are. What is traction on a clean, waxed linoleum floor might as well be roller skates when the footing is slippery blood.

She had twisted her ankle and blew her right patella going down. After her surgery, she had spent her recovery in Frank's shack. Her physical therapy was to climb up to the Shack for three meals a day and then walk down to the cove for a swim twice a day.

"You still need to get your front-left wheel bearing looked at."

She reached between his legs and clutched firmly. He didn't even twitch. She leaned down to his ear. "You know how I know you're lying?" He grunted with a small laugh. "Because, asshole, I bought a new car."

He rolled over and frowned in the dim moonlight. "New car?"

"I took in the bearing like you said. The bearing, brakes, crack in the engine, new radiator, tires, and a new radio were going to cost me more than a large chunk down on a brand-new car."

He glimpsed his watch as he sat up and leaned against the wall. "What did you get?"

She shrugged her shoulder and face with flattened lips. "A thirty-eight woody."

He laughed and poked her in the armpit. She giggled and folded into his lap. "You know the penalty for lying to me…"

"Roll over, or I'll just start here." She grabbed his cock.

The dog had heard enough. She rolled over the end of the bed and padded to the door. One back glance of disgust and she was so much fog.

"See, now you scared the dog."

"She went to go hunt."

"She ate a couple of leftover burgers when Danny was leaving."

"She needs more. She's eating for more than a few now."

Frank feigned shocked horror. "She… she wouldn't do that to her daddy. She's just a kid."

Pan pushed him over onto his face. "The term is kit, and yes, she's old enough to date other boys."

He pushed up and looked over his shoulder. His voice was his detective voice. "Do you really think she's knocked up?"

She pushed his head around and his face into the pillow. "Men." She started pushing on places she knew were always tight. "They never notice when the rows of nipples turn from dots to teats. I'll bet she's been hanging out here all night lately, too."

Frank thought about what the coyote would need to be eating and what she would need for a den. He'd have Danny order more meat for her. Fried burgers weren't what a young mother needed.

Hours later, Frank took a break outside. Pan had drifted off to sleep during the second hour of the massages. Whatever had happened at work had her wound up. The slip of moon was sinking into the cold black water, and the silhouette of the south end of Catalina Island was a black lump on the glimmering flat. Only a few streetlights of Avalon glowed softly. There wouldn't be any surf for the next week.

Frank settled down into the gray Adirondack chair. The pair of chairs came from an old friend. The man had been a mentor to him as a young deputy. At his funeral, his widow cornered Frank and told him to come get the chairs. Frank never asked. She had opened the door, pointed at the back yard, and headed for the back bedroom. Frank could hear her crying.

The soft sound of Pan's foot on the doorstep was all he heard. The last of the moon glittered in her wet eyes. She had a thousand-mile look.

He looked back at the sea. "I thought you would be out for the count until noon."

Her voice was only half there. "Surgery starts at oh-four-thirty."

"I thought the game-planning was only for the docs."

The pair of light blue, little boy panties flickered through his sight. He hadn't remembered her taking them off earlier. But then, clothing came and went with her as easy as taking a breath.

She stepped into the second chair and corkscrewed down into it. "I would have slept, but I could hear you thinking out here."

His head rolled as he looked at her. Her eyes were drier but still halfway to Hawaii. "The noise of what you were working on was too much to concentrate in there."

"You first."

The smile tugged at his mouth as his vision returned to the black lump he knew was out there in the dark. She always won.

~

THE WATER WAS ALMOST LUKEWARM, and the swells rode under the board without notice. Frank had the hood on his summer sunscreen skins up. He never knew if it might take a while before the right person showed up.

The ocean soaked up any noise the land produced. It was as if the sand where it touched the water was a magical sound wall. Cars and trucks, less than a half mile away, may as well be miles away. Only someone paddling a few yards away made any noise.

His mind churned over what Pan had said. The surgeries needed for incursions of stupidity on the day-to-day were bad enough. But working one of the leading trauma hospitals for Orange County also meant they were the county morgue. Especially for the indigent, the Jane and John Does of the world, and the too-near-the-edge to have insurance or arrangements for funerals.

Indigent deaths went jointly with the ever-expanding homeless population, many who never had any or forgot to care about carrying identification. Some had long ago forgotten who they once were or stopped caring enough to forget who they were beyond the street name in the ever-changing camps.

The rise in deaths due to drugs, especially fentanyl and opioids, caused concern for anyone paying attention. Pan paid chronic attention. Her uncle had died during a drug bust. The baggie they thought was coke burst open. Her uncle was the one who administered the NARCAN to the three other officers. All three needed a double dose. The pouches they carried only held six nasal injectors. He thought he could hold his breath long enough to get them and him out of the building. He tripped.

Frank attended the double funeral before he had met Pan.

He heard the small splash of a hand paddling slowly. The right hand was a larger splash. The stroke had curled the left, and it didn't open enough to make a full stroke. He also knew the former FBI agent would never stand on his board again. The flats were his surfing days.

"I figured you were hanging south for a reason."

Frank lazily rolled his head to the other direction. The neon yellow surf skin with the red racing stripe down the left side, front and back, was the man's trademark. Frank didn't know if the man still owned the Mazda Miata with the blown Chevy big-block or not. He had gone out and watched the man race at Riverside and Fontana a few times. He had been competitive. Now, he was just a stroked-out surfer.

"You need a haircut, Granite."

The man snorted at the old joke. Neither one was getting a job any time soon. "You keep wearing the hoodie, and some old biddy in the squatter shacks is going to call in a sighting of the Unabomber."

They relaxed with their eyes closed. They were fading in and out with the heat of the sun.

Granite opened his eyes and shook his head. He pushed on the longboard and sat up. Watching the shoreline and the other bodies lying on softly bobbing boards, he looked down at Frank.

"What did you need?"

"Fentanyl."

"To buy?"

Frank pushed himself up. The cooler water on his feet felt good. "Information."

"How specific?"

"When did the traffic bounce in the OC?"

The former agent squinted. "Define 'bounce.'"

Frank looked at him as if he were a misbehaving dog. "Five percent over a couple of months is a ramp-up. A one-week jump of ten percent is a spike. I'm guessing a while back the street started seeing a doubling or more. That's a bounce."

The man's squint ground around to study the people and buildings in the cove. "From what I heard, it was more like four times, and the ramp was only over last June till September. The hospitals are running out of NARCAN and switching to bottles of naloxone. Same stuff, but the dose isn't metered so they can shoot the higher dose needed." He stretched and swung his cocked arms around. "That shit is one of the only reasons I'm glad I'm out of the shit stream these days. It was bad enough ten years ago, but now... no fucking way. DEA catches most of the shitstorm, but the Bureau still gets dragged in."

Frank furled his lips and nodded his head in an upward jerk. He didn't miss the horror show Orange County was becoming.

"Any of your buddies have ideas on where the flow might be coming from?"

"From or how?"

"Okay. Both or either."

The man wove his hands together and folded the left hand open. From the way he did it, Frank could tell it was no longer an exercise. It had become a habit or a nervous twitch.

"Where is somewhere down in the center of Mexico. How is still a mystery." The man turned his head to look at Frank. "Got any ideas?"

Frank chewed on the side of his lower lip. "Working on it. If I find anything, I'll find you."

The man nodded as Frank began to paddle toward the cove. "Let me know if there's anything else I can help with. You've got my number."

Frank straightened and pushed his hood back to his neck. "There are a couple of heads missing..."

The man's head wagged gently. "I never did body parts. But I'm assuming you're talking about Mary Shores?"

"And another. The guy up in Orange. If your old buddies could shed some light on the guy..."

"I'll ask. You still living in the old shack?"

Frank nodded. "You can get ahold of me through Danny at the café. Or you can call my cell number if it's time-sensitive."

"I thought you retired…"

"It's just a consult gig. Randy's boy roped me in." He laid down and started paddling. "I had an opening in my busy schedule."

The man nodded and muttered to himself, *"For a fellow surfer."* He laid back down on the board and was soon fast asleep.

19 CATCH UP

Mickey glanced irritated out the copy store's front windows as he shoved the stack of papers in his briefcase.

"Sir, I do have bags…"

Mickey's face rose. He took in the young woman. He wondered if she was as young as she made him feel old. At thirty-one, he would have liked to think he could still ask someone like her out to a nice dinner. But now he felt like he would be viewed as a lecherous old man if he did. He swore he would never poke at Frank's age again. He knew Frank wasn't old, but he was gray when he didn't shave, and retired didn't help.

His sarcasm bit more of his tongue than her understanding. "It's okay, miss. I'm used to old-school. It's more ecofriendly like your millennial friends keep harping about." He had no idea if he fell in the millennial bracket, but he would never admit such a square peg fitting in a wonky hole.

He pulled his case off the counter and turned to punctuate his point. The young woman seemed to wait until the glass doors swooshed open. "Sir, you might need your credit card." She held it aloft.

He turned. The flush was burning at his collar. But he knew even a thousand dollars of custom tailoring couldn't hide his being caught as an asshole.

She held it out for him to take. "You might need it this afternoon for the senior special." She gripped it hard as he tried to take it. "I'll turn twenty-eight next month. Next time don't be an asshat. And before you ask, I *am* the manager." She released the card.

Mickey steamed his way to the tan-turd Taurus the motor pool had issued him. The radio didn't work, the front end had a shimmy over sixty, and there was a growling rumble in the rear they told him not to worry about. The day started shitty and was smelling more like a cesspool every hour.

The folder was a joint project on drug dealers, transporters, and major players in Orange County and its international connections. Juanito Pedro Garcia y Espinoza had started as the file's focus, but it had led to other names. One of them was Maximillian Cortège, the Ax. What had surprised Mickey was most of the report had not come from Orange County or even the United States. Much of the report was on Interpol forms. Over half was in French.

He backed out of the parking slot and headed for the street. The traffic was heavy on Beach, and he sat waiting. He watched north at the light. He was kicking himself for using the copy center on Beach, as it was always a pain to get out of the parking lot.

The woman in the copy center started to insert the next customer's thumb drive in the slot. The lucky rabbit's foot drive was still in the slot. She thought about the dashing asshat. *He'll be back.* She pulled the drive and slipped it into her back pocket.

Mickey's phone chirped. As he watched the light a block away change to red, he thumbed it open. The traffic made its last scurry through the red light.

"Yeah, Frank."

"Where are you? I'm at your office."

"I scored some information from Interpol on Pedro. I'm at the copy center on Beach. I just printed it out—"

The garbage truck skidded around the older Volkswagen with the surf rack. It was already going faster than it should with the garbage bin lowered in front. The tan unmarked car sat on the apron. Only at the last second did the man on the phone see the truck bearing down on him.

The garbage bin crushed the trunk of the car as the truck's weight pushed the lightweight vehicle into the mass of speeding traffic. The contractor's truck in the fast lane drove the car's engine sideways. The minivan, which had been trying to speed up enough to get around the large tool-laden truck, crushed the driver's door and seat until the passenger area was a single seat between two doors. The seven cars behind only added small insults and confusion to the mess.

The driver of the garbage truck jumped out and rushed into the mass of wreckage with others. They smashed the passenger-side window and reached into Mickey's car like they were checking on him. Withdrawing the brown briefcase, they looked about, then continued to calmly walk across the other lanes and away, disappearing behind the back of Norm's restaurant. Nobody thought to remember what they looked like.

"Mickey? Mickey? What just happened? Mickey?" The phone in Frank's hand turned dead, then only a dial tone.

20 WREAKING HAVOC

Frank had the technician at the sheriff's department ping Mickey's phone as he rushed out of the building. He told her to send the location to his phone. As he backed out of his parking spot, patrol pulled up alongside.

"Pounds, we have your partner on Beach. They'll be clearing the accident for hours."

Frank put the Bentley in drive. "Get me there." He didn't want to be stopped by some dickwad cop from Santa Ana looking to make a name for himself.

He knew the modified Chevy engine under the hood could outrun any car the sheriff had bought in the last ten years. Keeping up was no problem, even if it became a high-speed run. His custom speedometer was out of a Lamborghini that lost a race with a freight train.

The race to the wreck was a slow crawl because of the warm weather and school being out. Frank chewed on the inside of his cheek, thinking about the day and how it was also senior discount day, and everyone had gotten their social security and unemployment checks the day before.

They were held back two blocks from the scene, so Frank skirted the area and came to the parking lot from a back street.

He parked in front of the copy center. Most of the employees were trying to see what was going on, even though it was over a block away. He slid up next to the two dressed in the center's uniform.

"What happened?"

The blonde turned. "The garbage truck hit a car and knocked it out into the heavy traffic."

Frank thought about information. "Have any ambulances left yet?"

"One, but I think it was more up this way." She pointed to the back end of the clusterfuck. "I think the guy in the tan car is still in there. I recognized the truck they use for the jaws of life. It just showed up."

Frank turned. "The guy in the tan car, was he just here? A snappy dresser."

She thought about the question and studied Frank. She looked down from the Nine-Inch Nails T-shirt to the surf baggies and the sandals with the beat-up pink toenails. "And you are?"

Frank sighed as he drew out his old badge wallet. "Frank Pounds, Orange County Sheriff's detective. If it was Mickey, he's my partner."

She nodded. "The Odd Couple. Yeah, it was him."

"He was copying off a case file for me…" He hoped his face was asking, and he didn't have to ask verbally. He knew copy machines cached the last few hundred documents they printed. He had broken cases with just this little bit of knowledge.

Her face lit up as she reached into her back pocket and held out a rabbit's foot. He hesitated and then took it. Obviously, there was some meaning in the good-luck charm.

"It's a USB thumb drive." She took it and exposed the plug. "He forgot it. I figured he'd come back for it. I knew whatever was so important, he'd be back. He had me run the print with the cache turned off."

"Did you see what was on it?"

She shook her head. "Not really. Most of the stuff we get is boring enough to put you to sleep. Some of the stuff you wish you never would have seen and could forget. But this was just documents. A lot was in French, but mostly English. There were some photos, like mug shots, and then some other pictures like on the street, but mostly just documents."

Frank cocked his head. "Sounds like you saw more than a little."

She shrugged. "In this business, your eyes and mind work at the same hundred-sheets-a-minute the machines run at, but he made me stand over the machine so that nobody else got near the copies. The printing ran fine. Just basically another boring bunch of documents."

Frank looked over his mirrored aviators. "Basically…?"

Her eyes twinkled as she flattened her lips. She thought about what to tell him, but he wasn't being an asshole. "It's kind of hard to miss watermarks stamped *Secret*, even if they are in French."

Frank held up the rabbit's foot and studied it.

"You want me to print another copy?" She turned toward the open door and started inside.

"No." Frank thought as he looked back toward the accident. Following her inside, he thought about other options. "Yes, but can you make a couple of copies of the thumb drive?"

She followed his line of sight. "You don't think it was an accident, do you?"

He pushed his glasses back up his nose and shook his head. "I've got an address. Could you also email a copy to it?"

"We can FedEx a thumb drive to anywhere you want also."

His head rocked as he chewed on his lower lip.

She glanced back toward the wreck. "I'm curious."

"About?"

"When you found out your partner was still out there…you didn't even twitch to rush there."

"And?"

"My dad is a cop in Inglewood. Up in Los Angeles. He got shot once. His partner showed up at the hospital the next day…" She took the thumb drive and inserted it in the central computer hub. "He said something about the first twenty-four."

"Was his partner involved in the shooting?"

She stood next to the large high-speed printer. "No. Dad had stopped to get some beer. A kid was holding up the store. The kid was nervous and just randomly shot the place up."

Frank nodded. "In the first twenty-four hours, the only people you want to see are the only people who can make a difference. This starts with the emergency medicals and ambulance. It's their job and training to save you and transport you. The next up is the emergency doctors and nurses. It's their training to get you to surgery. The next people you never see. Those are the ones who give you the best chance to make it to the bell. After that, it's the Intensive Care Unit who will watch over you until the clock strikes midnight or the twenty-fourth hour." He leafed through the large document. She had been right. It was all top secret and a lot from France. He looked up. "If you ring the twenty-four, you have a good chance of walking out of the hospital."

"It sounds like you've rung the bell before." She tore open a blister pack of three thumb drives.

Two thousand five hundred and forty-seven days.

He nodded. "It took me twenty-nine days to ring the bell. I keep waiting to walk out of the hospital."

She set the third drive down next to the rabbit's foot. Frank thought about the wreck and the foot. He had never seen Mickey display any form of superstition. He glanced toward the window at the sound of an ambulance's squawking horn, and then the warble siren ramped up. He leaned his hip softly but harder against the counter for support. He looked at his watch.

Looking up at her blue eyes, Frank could see the darkness of worry ringing the light. He wondered if children and spouses of cops everywhere were born with the marker or grew into it.

"And so it begins."

Her face was stone. She had been there. She slid the over-sized envelope across the counter. "Address it to wherever you want it to go. I'll double wrap it all, so it's at least semi-legal, but there won't be a record of it. This one is on the house."

He filled in the address for the café. He put a note at the bottom. *Atten: Janitor. Replacement part for microwave.* When he first hired Danny, he found the microwave on his bed. The explanation was the offender was only used by those who didn't know how to prepare proper food. It was still on the small table—unplugged.

Three thousand seven hundred and twenty-one days.

He reached for his wallet. "I can pay."

She froze. "No, you can't." If she had had an Adam's apple, Frank could see it would have bounced off the top of her throat. "Your partner was having a bad day. I guess I called him 'sir' when he needed to be flirted with. It's my training." She waved her hand as she shooed the thought away. "He went butthead, and I responded like an asshole..." Her eyes drooped shut as her head volleyed back and forth. Frank knew how it went.

He held out his credit card. "I've been there. He's been there... too many times. But he's only a kid." His eyes rolled. "Well, thirty-two going on fifty going on three."

Her eyes opened wide. "He's only four years older than me?" Her mouth said *Fuck.* "The 'sir' must have really stung. I remember when I made manager here, and one of the kids called me 'ma'am.' I wanted to backhand them."

She pushed at the credit card. "Seriously, this one is on the house, Detective." She presumed.

"Frank. Frank Pounds."

"Frank." She reached for the stack of business cards. "Here's my card. Call me when he can see visitors. I'll bring him some flowers or something."

Frank looked at the card. Los Van Niewenhuize. "You pronounce it like Los Angeles or lost?"

She laughed. "Loose like goose. Dad had a sense of humor. He figured a cop's daughter would be running loose in the street. It's Dutch. I'm named after his father's mother." She smiled largely. "You weren't even going to try the last name. Chicken."

Frank rasp berried his lips lightly. "It's 'Van New in House.'" He smiled at her shocked look. "I had a SEAL buddy with the same last name." Frank smiled at the now twinkling blue eyes and blond hair. "So, whose smile did you get?"

The smile pulled back on the left. "I got Mom's lips but my father's mouth."

He laughed as he turned with his thumb drives of information. "Yeah, cop brats have potty mouths. But deputy's kids are saints."

She chuckled at the old departmental jab. "Yeah, you mispronounced 'shits.'"

21 ICU AND THERAPY

There's a package coming today or tomorrow—however long it takes FedEx to get here from Santa Ana. Bury it in the safe where I can't find it."

Danny poured the fresh coffee. "There's a bunch of shit in the hole. You really need to spend a week and sort it out." He put down the carafe and leaned on it. "Just because it's the size of a deep freeze doesn't mean it will continue to hold more and more shit you drag home."

Frank grumped as he turned the page over and looked at the crime scene photos from somewhere in France. Or he assumed they were in France. The writing was all French.

Danny leaned over a bit to see what had Frank so distracted. Color would have been upsetting. The black-and-white copies he saw as more artistic. "*C'est sûr. La vie de guerre.*"

Frank looked up, squinting. "You speak frog?"

"*Non.* I parley vu food."

"But you just said something about war."

"*Guerre? Oui.* It's what getting you to order every morning is —a war."

Frank leaned back against the chair. "Is that why you're

always pissy in the morning? Because I don't order fast enough?"

Danny rolled his eyes large in exasperation. "Well, duh?"

Frank waved his finger at Danny's face. "Don't do that. It's not a good look on you." He shoved the stack of photocopies around. "So do you read enough to know where in France this is and who they're talking about?"

The redhead raised the stack and stood to his full six-foot-six. He mumbled as he examined a few pages, turning them over and laying them face down on the table. Finally, he carefully took up the read pages and laid them back on top of the stack. He held it all to his chest and looked at Frank.

Frank had waited almost five minutes, but his bark was still soft. "What?"

Danny's eyes bounced and blinked. "What are you having for breakfast?"

"Fuck you. Food. Whatever the fucking cookie wants to slap down in front of me. Today, tomorrow, any fucking day I eat here. Now, what the fuck does the report say, froggy?"

Danny gently placed the report on the table. "Somebody really wound the bitch up this morning." He turned as he swiped the carafe off the table and walked away. "Page three. If you weren't so fucking *vago*." Danny placed the carafe back in the machine. "Something, something, something, Juarez, something, Sinaloa cartel."

Frank turned the papers over. "Lazybones has nothing to do with it, asshole." He found the passage, picking the words out of the text. The report was about the cartel wars in Mexico. But if he was working out the information correctly, this report was about stuff ten years ago that he never heard of—even though it was his job to hear. The news got laundered in either Mexico or here.

Another report showed a grainy image of four young workers, stripped to the waist, leaning on shovels in a tunnel. The tunnel could have been a mine: the miners and an ore cart. But

Frank could tell the cart was the body of a large contractor's wheelbarrow only temporarily attached. Once the tunnel could run, the cart would be a train of flatbeds stacked with drugs.

He looked at the worker closest to the photographer. The tattoos of twin bluebirds on the front shoulders matched another photo he had seen last week.

The plate was placed on top of the report. The two poached eggs sat on two triangles of burned toast. Gravy that Frank didn't think they offered was drizzled over the whole. Enough black pepper to choke a jalapeno laced the entire thing. This was the test.

Frank lifted the plate and slid the report to one side. He looked down the café at Danny, the consummate host. "I'll be your waiter today." The young couple wasn't surfers. Frank's guess at this early hour was that they were lost.

He looked at the eggs and burned toast. *Nine thousand two hundred thirty-nine-days.* The cook was prickly. The sub had been scheduled for five days of liberty at the tip of Italy. Instead, they picked up the SEAL team in the middle of the night, four miles south of Sidonia, Crete, in the middle of the Libyan Sea. The Mediterranean was hitting force-four gale winds and seas. The crew was not happy. Used to calm, deep in the water, they were tossed about on the surface. The six-man team was silent. The crew took their silence as unfriendly or just rude.

The sub made its way slowly toward the Strait of Gibraltar. Even the team didn't know the drop point—the target could be Tripoli, Tunis, or somewhere near Algiers. The ship's slow pace left it open to the rough seas. But orders were orders. And waiting was part of the team's life.

The team was served leftovers. Pancakes cooked hours before were griddled and topped with barely edible snotty eggs. Dinners were reheating of the same charred SOS, making MREs sound like fine dining. The cooks were only showing what the crew was feeling. None of the SEALs blamed them. The sub had been at sea for seven months.

One breakfast, the team as one, ate and cleaned their plates. Then stood, held out their trays, and asked for seconds. The cooks and others were still mulling over the reaction of the worst they could dish out when the executive officer came in and slipped Frank their assignment. They had thirty minutes to gear up.

Sunrise was three short hours away. Because of listening posts, they couldn't use motorized zodiacs closer than three miles from shore. The long swim was expected. But they thought about the last meal for the next ninety-six hours of nothing but protein bars laced with speed.

Pick-up night, the cook cleared away the chicken he had been serving. Six trays hit the table with rare steaks and two lobster tails each. Cookie's only question was who wanted a baked potato with all the trimmings. The next morning, as they hustled off the ship before breakfast, they laughed about finally getting adopted.

Frank cut up all the food and dug in. He struggled not to sneeze or throw up.

Danny refilled the mug and took the plate. He checked on the customers and returned, then pulling out one of the chairs, he sat. His elbow spiked the table as his chin rested on his flopped hand.

Frank tried to ignore him. But the freckled elbow was all but touching his mug. Frank sipped and put the cup down. "What?"

Danny sighed. "If you don't talk to me, I can't help you."

Frank spread his hands across the reports. "This is all cop shit. You're not a cop."

"Where's Mickey? Your partner."

Frank lowered his head and focused on the sentence he had already read four times. It still didn't make sense. Nothing was making sense.

"Frank...?"

"What?" He didn't want to look at the man. The bell hadn't

rung yet, but his phone hadn't, either. The most useless a cop could feel was when his partner was in the hands of those other professionals.

"Where's Mickey?" Steel was hardening the man's usually gentle edge.

Frank leaned over, left elbow on the table. He rested his head against the knife-edge of his hand. Eyes closed. The finger gently sawed across the bridge of his nose. "In the ICU. Someone tried to kill him yesterday."

Danny sat, stunned.

He knew about the twenty-four-hour rule. His voice was soft. "When did the clock start?"

Frank straightened enough to look at the second set of numbers on his watch. "Nine fifty-four."

Danny looked around at the large Billabong clock over the cook's station. "You have two hours to get to…?"

"UCI Medical."

Frank gathered the reports and shoved them back in the copy center bag. "Put these,"—he reached in his pocket and separated the new thumb drive from the rabbit's foot—"and this in the safe." He stood, thinking. Numb.

Danny paused. "Frank?" The man looked up. "You need a shower."

He nodded and headed for the door. "Thanks."

Transitioning from the parking lot to the door was always the hard part. The only time it wasn't was arriving unconscious in the back of a fire truck. They knew they couldn't wait for the amateurs.

The droning *whoop, whoop, whoop* of an incoming medivac helicopter woke him from dead thoughts. The hospital was the epicenter for most traumas in the Orange County basin. Beach and boat went to Hoag Hospital on the land's edge, where the money meets the sea. But for everything from the tiny broken finger, to gunshots, to creatively rearranged vehicles, UCI caught it all.

In the big county to the northwest, L.A. was split up. East and south went to the L.A. County Medical Center. It also had a medical lockup on the fourth floor. The center and money had their choice of Cedars Sinai or Hollywood General. The Westside clustered to Westwood and UCLA unless you graduated from the other school, and then you took your chances at County Medical.

In the Orange, UCI did the job of all of them. Transients to wealthy, the school took them all. Kids went to Children's Hospital of Orange County, usually just called CHOC.

Frank walked a familiar path through the emergency room. The usual suspects lined the waiting rooms. He nodded a greeting to the receptionist dealing in two languages; the head tick was mutual with the security guard. The man was the "old guard" when Frank was in-residence.

He turned at the attending station and headed for the ICU. The splayed hand was a bit more forceful than he was used to. The blue scrubs were covered with a yellow surgical gown. The long gloves were doubled over the gown. The surgical mask covered most of the face left exposed by the double head-drape and bandana-hat. The face shield gave the appearance of the whole head frowning. Only the pale blue-gray eyes were recognizable.

"He's not here, Frank. They took him back into surgery early this morning. The word is, it's going well. But he will be in lockdown for at least a full seventy-two. He kept crashing. The forensics lab called yesterday evening. They found fentanyl blown all over inside the car."

"Why surgery now?"

"They needed to stint his aorta and a few other complications. It's a good thing he's in such great shape. He'll be fine, but eventually, he'll get more metal than you."

"Metal?"

Pan nodded. "Both hips, a knee, his left shoulder, and his jaw's wired shut around the intubation. They pulled a broken tooth for the tube. It was either that or stick a tube in his throat. They still might have to. That's all I know for now. But I need to go. He's not the only crisis at the moment."

Frank nodded and lightly tapped the face shield. She nodded.

~

THE PHARMACY HAD what he needed. The small bag had felt so tiny and yet so important as it swung in his hand.

Leaving the hospital, he placed a phone call. The order and directions were easy enough to remember. The little bag had become three stops, a couple of twenties, and four larger bags.

He told the guard where he was parking and drove in.

"I've got to know. Did you think of the toe spreaders, or did some woman help you?"

Frank laughed at the man-jab. "Look, I've been painting my toes for…" He was going to tell her the days… but for some reason, it seemed wrong because he would have to explain about the accident and his partner. "Since before you found out about french fries and ranch dressing. This is not my first rodeo." He wasn't going to talk about Pan finally taking pity on him and teaching him the right way to do his own nails a few years ago.

Ming swallowed. "What do you call this again?" She pointed at the strange burrito.

Frank smiled. "It's a North Shore. My old partner turned me on to them. His niece or cousin or somebody up in Orange has a cart. It's shrimp sautéed in rooster sauce, sprouts, avocado, and pickled ginger, wrapped in rice-paper, then flash deep-fried just to get it crispy."

"So Hawaiian, Mexican, Vietnamese, and Chinese. United

Nations. I likie." The young Chinese bit into another chunk. Her eyes closed around the flavors and textures.

Frank laughed. "You said only a healthy snack. So that's what they made." He looked down at his feet in the lap of her partner.

Tree grumped. "I just think they should make the brushes longer. Imagine the laminar flow you could get with, say, a two-inch-long brush." Frank could tell she didn't know if she was talking to anyone or just herself. She was geeking out in the way only engineers can. She leaned in and filed a couple of sharp edges.

Frank flinched. She looked up. "I'm sorry. Did I hurt you?"

Frank smirked. "Just remember, I get to do your toes next." He smiled in a way he hoped look maniacally goofy.

She went back to filing. "Don't quit your day job."

He chuckled. "Speaking of day jobs… The other day you were typing like mad. Something about getting some of the dredging companies to give you access to their coding or something?"

"We asked to have access to their program coding to make ours blend seamlessly."

"How did it go?"

"I got invited to a videoconference over at World Dredging —it's local. I thought I was going to have a war with only one or two companies. There were nine of the biggest players tied in. Four were some of the largest dredging companies. They did all the talking for me. One was a crusty old guy from Amsterdam. He said if the others didn't give us access and support, he would back us to write all new software to make their stuff obsolete."

Frank harrumphed with a smirk. "So they're going to give you access?"

She snorted as she turned his foot back and forth. "They had emailed the access codes to their servers before I got back here. Ming was already going through one of them. They have some seriously old programs. We might have to clean up their programs before we can marry them."

"How much can you make reworking their programs?"

She leaned back in an arch. Frank wondered if his back ever had that much flexibility. She looked over at Ming. The one dark eyebrow went up.

Tree sat up straight and frowned at Frank. "You think they would pay us to write new code?"

"How old is it?"

The girls snorted in unison. "Remember a Windows version called "Vista"?

Frank cocked his head in a corkscrew and slowly pronounced "Yessss…?"

Ming poked the air with her middle finger. "Older."

Frank closed his eyes as he worked at remembering old systems. "Wasn't there something with an X in the name?"

Ming laughed as she waved her empty hand in the air and imitated Gollum from The Lord of the Rings. "That was XP. Extra Precious."

Tree jumped him with a snicker. "This guy is running a kludged version of a program based in Windows 98. It barely runs on a machine running Windows 7. He can't upgrade it to 10 because the housekeeping protocols will see it as a virus and wipe it out."

Frank's face scrunched on one side. "Can you save it?"

Ming lowered her head and looked evilly out of the tops of her eyes. Her voice was low and gravelly. "We have a few people we could bribe to help. It would take a week or so, but it would be so clean it would be ready for the next great operating system from Seattle."

Frank chuckled. He liked hanging out with these two. They were playful and evil at the same time. "How much bribing are we talking about?"

Ming slumped down in her chair. Her thumb and cocked finger stroked her chin. Frank was getting the feeling she was the one who knew everyone's weak spots. "Probably a few cases of Monster, half-dozen pizzas, a hospital-sized box of pull-ups, and a few hundred dollars of trinkets. Maybe a water-cooled gaming tower or two."

"Pull-ups?"

Tree tweaked her cheek and left eye. "Adult diapers. The boys down the hall get into some intense gaming when they're beta-crashing new games. I think they also have been sniffing around for faster machines."

"The towers."

She nodded. "Maybe even a server."

"Are they really water-cooled?"

Ming leaned forward. "The harder you push a chip, the hotter it gets. Most office drones push a heat-sink block on top of the chip. The fan blows over it, and the world is good."

Tree kicked in. "A heavy stockbroker is crunching numbers. But the second you jump into pushing graphics—shit heats up fast. A single graphics card can crunch more calculations in a millisecond than the stockbroker's tower will do all day."

Ming's hand flopped out, and her middle finger was stabbing and pointing at the roof. "Every tower those guys own is loaded with quad-bridged cards. Those fuckers are in a cabinet with some serious chilling going on. The only way to step it up is water."

"But water and electronics…"

"We're not talking about dropping the motherboard into a bathtub while it's still plugged in. We're talking about running a micro radiator for a heat-sink on the chips, cards, and anything getting warm. The cooling runs to a large water tank and the recycling radiator."

Tree leaned over. "The one in the biolab…" They both started laughing hard.

Frank waited it out. "Biolab?"

"Two years ago, we built a hidden tower. The system was

broken into pieces. But the cooling sink was the genetics freezer."

Ming had her arms wrapped around her body. "We were all clueless. The guy strapped on diapers for a four-day weekend gaming competition. He came in third but couldn't hear the alarm going off as the freezer temperature ballooned over the minus thirty threshold and baked off all the bunny sperm in the petri dishes. The whole year's trials were toast."

Tree's eyebrows were wiggling wildly. "But we got the reputation for building killer towers."

Ming's face was magenta as she laughed. "Yeah. Bunny Killer Towers."

The three laughing on top of the tower was good for Frank. He hadn't relaxed just for fun since the early days in the navy—before everything in the world became serious. Even as a rookie in the sheriffs, there was always the part working.

His gut tightened as his phone vibrated. No matter how bucolic it was with the new friends, the real world was only a phone call or text away. He fished it out and swiped it open to read the text. The girls froze in silence.

"He's out of recovery. Doing well. Vitals strong. Will keep posted."

Frank texted back a thumbs-up. He silently slid the phone back in his pocket and then thought of something else. He left the phone out so he wouldn't forget.

He motioned for Tree's feet. She traded seat and roof with him. He started with the emery board.

As the sun got lower, they laid on their backs. The six feet flattened on the wall of the stairwell. The sun glistened off the sparkles in the clear coats over the pink. The smaller, more tender pink feet bracketed Frank's twisted surfer feet.

The photo got a laughing face, a purple heart, and two pink hearts from Pan. Frank wondered if it would earn him a back rub.

Ming hugged his shoulder and arm as she looked at the reply. "How's the boy doing?"

"She said the surgery went well."

Tree finished picking up the trash and pedicure supplies. "When we first met you… there was something about tying him to a tricycle and a car or something? You were threatening him or something. What was that all about?"

Frank stumbled back with wide eyes. "The telling of those days would require dinner. Maybe even a stroll on the beach."

Ming perked up. "More North Shore?"

Frank laughed. "I said dinner." He fished his finger back and forth between the two. "Who do I have to get a note from to release you two from this hellhole?"

Tree stood. "Nobody. And you promised a walk on a real beach."

He jacked his head sideways. "Done and done. We will dine forty feet from the water. And the stroll will probably be before dinner, and maybe after as well."

"Is it on the dive charts?"

"Sure is. Crystal Cove."

22 I'M HERE

The slender waves barely rumpled the sheets. The body was shallow in the bed. The monitors still stood watch— soft beeps and ticks. Every twenty minutes, the soft muted drumming of the air pump filled the cuff. The numbers blurred, stabilized, ticked smaller, and replaced by the sum.

The lizard brain remembers. Frank knew the second before every beep, tick, bump, burp, or wheeze to fill a hospital room.

He returned to the book. "Where was I...?" His finger moved down the page. "Well, a mother, a real mother, is the most wonderful person in the world. She's the angel voice that bids you goodnight, kisses your cheek, and whispers 'sleep tight.'"

"Define 'real mother.'"

Frank looked up with a smile. Pink Tink stood in the door. "I just did."

"Even if she's not what society thinks a mother is?"

"Does she kiss your cheek, tell you good night, and... something, something, something?"

"Yeah... kind of..." Tink slumped into the other chair. "We call her and check in."

Frank smiled. He had guessed it was in their nature. "She

wouldn't be your mother if you didn't have anyone to care about you checking in. No matter what she looks like, would you have it any other way?"

Her lower lip furled in and bulged. "Nah. We had it the other way far too long."

Frank nodded his head in acknowledgment. He slipped the thin green-leather frog bookmark into the book and closed it. Pink Tink had her hand out, so he handed over the book.

She looked at the worn leather binding. Opening the book, she fluffed a few pages to the copyright page. Frank knew the signature by heart. The young girl had gone to the play. She loved it so much that she wanted her mother to get the book for her for Christmas. She had signed it so everyone would know it was hers.

Tink looked up. "Olivia Peaches Saulsberry?"

"My grandmother. I think she was eight or nine at the time."

Two more pages back, and she smiled. "First edition and dedicated by the author. I'm impressed." She softly closed the book and returned it.

Frank looked at Blue Tink. "I think Peaches would be, in her words, 'all atwitter' if she knew who I was reading it to."

Pink smiled and snuggled deeper into the chair. "I think Blue will be all atwitter when she hears which book she is hearing."

Frank shrugged minutely. "How are you holding up?"

"Disney told me to go home until she's okay. They frown on the cast moping around the park—even if we're in a costume and aren't speaking. Kids know when you're not excited to be there." She inclined her head toward her twin. "Any word?"

"The head nurse was in about an hour ago. They're weighing bringing her out of the coma in a couple of days. The downside will be brutal pain. The upside is she can hear me read and talk to you."

Pink sighed, and her head flopped over. Frank could see the

dark circles of pain around her eyes. "And you need to question her…"

Frank held out his palm.

~

"So how is she, Pounds?" The sound over the phone was tinny, but he could still hear her deep concern. A mother is still a mother—no matter who they are.

Frank stepped into the hall but still spoke quietly. "They're thinking about bringing her out of the induced coma on Friday. They're worried about how much pain she'll be in. But they can't bring her out without extubating her. Taking the ventilation tube out. But if they can't control the pain, they will have to reintubate."

"And you understand all this stuff?" Pussy sounded worn out at only minutes into the afternoon. Frank worried about her working the bar alone.

"Yeah. I went through most of it and probably more. I was on the ventilator for fifty-eight days and nine surgeries. But what about you? You sound like your last leg was yesterday."

"I'll survive. I just worry about the girls. We're all we have, and Pink's not handling it well. They were never separated for more than a shift or something, and then they would talk or just puddle like a batch of puppies."

Frank leaned back and checked the chair. One bare foot hung out of a mass of board shorts, a T-shirt, and pink hair. It looked more like the blob of a dog or cat than a human. He moved away from the door.

"Yeah, Pink is here but curled into a chair. I don't think she lasted a whole page while I read to them."

"What are you reading?"

"The 1929 first edition. They need to know their history."

"Edition of what?"

Frank snorted. "What else would I read to a Tink?"

A finger poked at his back. He turned. "Just a minute…" He held out the phone and mouthed *your mom*.

As she took the phone, her voice had a catch in it. "M… mom?"

She walked down the hall. Frank returned to the book. Some medicines are selective.

~

THE ROOM WAS ONLY HALF AS CLUTTERED as the ICU had been. The head of Mickey's bed was raised. It helped the tubes running through the tracheostomy, in his throat, suction the lungs. The stitches and bruising on his head were only the preview. Frank had seen the list of his injuries.

HeRtz showed on the pad.

Frank nodded. He pointed at the small plunger near Mickey's hip. "Don't try to tough it out. There's no help or cure in being the tough guy. Press the plunger every time it hurts. It might be too soon to release any more morphine, but the machine does count the times you push it. It gives them a better scale of your pain than drawing the frowny face."

Mickey had an iPad and a stylus. What he wrote showed up on the pad Frank held. With a sweep of Mickey's hand, the pad would clear for the next message.

"1-10" appeared on the pad.

Frank nodded. "My three might be someone else's eight or nine. But it's better than nothing."

Mickey slumped in the pillow. Frank knew that after only a few minutes, he was already getting tired.

"Do you remember anything about the accident?"

"GARbAge Trk"

Frank rocked. "Yes. Pushed you out into the traffic. Anything else?"

"WomAN"

"What about the woman?"

"TOOk cAse"

"Took your briefcase…" Frank knew the information was in there. It would just take a while to bring it out. "Do you remember what she looked like?"

"DARk h…" His eyes flickered in confusion.

"Dark hair?" He got the back of the stylus pointed at him. "Dark brown, black, straight, or curly?"

"Blk… stRAt"

"The woman—black, white, Asian, or Latina?"

"L"

"Would you maybe remember her in a lineup?"

Mickey nodded slightly. "MeT BeFR"

His eyes closed as he thought.

His eyes fluttered.

"Navy"

Then he shook his head.

"BRAkFAst"

Frank thought back over the last couple of weeks. It felt like a lifetime. *Fifteen days.* He looked up. "The coast guard chick who followed us? Are you sure?"

"Y"

"They found fentanyl trace in the car and on you…"

"PuFF FRom HAnD"

The pad slid flat, and the stylus hung loose in his hand. His eyes rolled into the eyelids. He was done.

Frank checked the monitors. The blood pressure ticked down. The respiration was only constant because of the ventilator. The pulse was under the man's usual. He rolled his head to look at the whiteboard. The regular stats were posted. Mickey was done for the day.

Frank closed his eyes and worked through the accident. He imagined the crash, and then the driver rushing to the passenger side of the car. She opened the door. Reaching in, she stole Mickey's briefcase and the information he had. If he hadn't forgotten the rabbit's foot in the copy center, he might have lost it as well.

The "puff from her hand" had him stumped. The real garbage collector they found knocked out in the back of the strip mall. The truck had been a weapon of opportunity. The traffic was just the bullet in the gun. If the construction truck had been in the middle lane instead of the fast lane, Frank understood he would be at a funeral. Now, it was only a game of waiting for Mickey.

He called the only person he knew who could help.

He explained the conversation and about the morning at breakfast. "I need someone I can trust when I go down to the Coast Guard Station in Corona del Mar. If she's there, I need a deputy who can arrest her, or at least haul her in for questioning."

"I'll clear my book. But I think we need to take my vehicle. Even a siren wouldn't get us there fast enough."

23 COASTING

As the sheriff and Frank rode in the Huey, Frank pointed out points of surfing interest. The helicopter slid along only a few hundred feet above the modest surf. Too much to sleep on, but not enough for the longboards Frank and his friends used.

As they approached Dana Point, Frank asked the pilot to stand off the north cove by a mile. The chopper hovered as Frank pointed out the darker blue of the underwater valley.

"Have we sent deputies down yet?"

Frank shook his head. "I want to know where all the buses are parked. If they have one, they'll have at least a handful."

"Do you think this is what the surfer found?"

Frank furled his lips and vibrated his head. "I never heard Mary talk about surfing here. This surf, if there is any, is too chopped for a long gun. It's only good for all the small boards we've been seeing. For us old guys, this is flat surf. We need at least a consistent three-foot to six to get going. A short run of a hundred yards is just exhausting to paddle hard, catch the wave, get up, and kick right back out. I'll show you down the way here what we look for."

He tapped the pilot on the shoulder. "The point just south of Cristianitos Road."

The pilot nodded and nosed the helicopter forward. As they cleared the Dana Point Marina, a three-mast, square-rigged ship sailed in. The sheriff smiled and quietly pointed. Whether they sailed or not, it didn't matter. The ship was worth the admiration.

The helicopter swung around in the air. Seven surfers looked up and recognized the sheriff badge on the side. Most of them put their arms up. The two men laughed. Kids were always doing the 'I give up' for cops and deputies alike. The officers all wished the real bad guys were as compliant.

Frank pointed at a darker section further offshore. "If the surf is running for long guns, this dark hole is where we sit. You can catch a twenty-footer here and ride her the mile to the San Onofre Nuclear Reserve boundary. It makes the day worth the work to walk down and paddle out."

"Where do you park?"

Frank pointed. "They line the street around the Carl's Junior."

"Long walk."

Frank snorted. "The mile is what bicycles and skateboards are for."

"You pack a hundred-pound board the size of a barn door and then jump a skateboard? No thanks."

Frank tapped the pilot and chopped the air with his flattened hand. The helicopter headed south. He turned back to the sheriff. "Most of the kids started on skateboards. Adding a surfboard was just second nature."

The helicopter put them down next to the building where they needed to be. A seaman with only one stripe on his sleeve met them on the side of the helipad.

Frank yelled over the sound of the spooling-down rotors. "We're here to see Commander Mark Roberts."

The seaman frowned as he opened the access door. "No such person, sir."

Frank looked back at the sheriff. "Strike one."

As they walked down the hall, Frank thought. "Is there one in San Pedro?"

"I wouldn't know, sir. I've only been here for six months since boot camp, sir."

The sheriff, frustrated with being the silent extra—after all, it was his helicopter. "Who's the commanding officer?"

"Dingerman, sir. Captain Jake Dingerman, sir."

They turned left, and a couple of offices down, they walked into the one with the captain's name on the glass door.

The slender man stood and stepped around the desk. "I heard the chopper come in. Knew right away it wasn't one of ours. When the Blackhawks squat, the building groans. I'd hate to have been here when the old Sikorsky Seahorses set down." He stuck his hand out. "Dingerman. Jake Dingerman. How can I help the Orange County Sheriff Department?" His eyes were on Frank's America, Ventura Highway Tour T-shirt, board shorts, huaraches, and fresh pink toenails with sprinkles.

The sheriff shook and nodded at Frank. "Frank is the investigator. We're just following a lead on his murder case."

The commander shoved his hand at the two seats. "Get you fellas something to drink?" The seaman stood ready.

"Nah, we're good. It was a short ride down. But before everyone goes off shift, we need to talk to a Lieutenant Ramirez. Female."

The commander pushed a button on the phone.

"Sir?"

"Shelton, find Lieutenant Ramirez and get her in here ASAP."

"Sir." The connection snapped.

He leaned back in his large chair. The way his hands ran over the leather, Frank guessed it was new, or the man rarely got to sit at his desk.

"You fellas sure you don't need anything? Water, soda, beer, or some tacos? This might take a while. She's on the *Edisto*, the second cutter down."

Frank and the sheriff held up their hands.

"Murder. Serious charge. Can I ask what my lieutenant has to do with this?"

Frank looked at the sheriff. The man nodded. His tongue paused, wetting his lips. The whole investigation was a basket of disjointed chicken parts. But he decided to focus on one piece.

"Four days ago, there was an attempted murder of a deputy. Eyewitnesses saw a woman ram a stolen garbage truck into the back of an unmarked car driven by the detective. She rammed the car into heavy traffic for the kill. The perp jumped out of the garbage truck, breached the unmarked, stole a briefcase full of evidence in another matter, and dusted the detective with fentanyl before escaping."

"Did the detective die?"

The sheriff shifted. "No. But this attempted murder, mayhem, destroying public property, stealing public property, obstructing justice—"

The captain held up his hands. "Okay… I get it." He shifted and leaned forward. Elbows on the desk, he wove his hands and rested his chin. "This, I take it, is only part of a larger investigation…"

Frank nodded. "We have a brutal assault on a young woman we believe is part of this, as well as two headless bodies."

The man's blink was uneven. "How do you cut off…"

"We're trying to find out."

The knock on the door was soft. They turned to find the yeoman. "Lieutenant Ramirez is here, sir."

The commander fished his hand. "Show her in, Rick."

The woman stepped in and saluted. Frank rolled his eyes and looked at the sheriff as they stood. "Strike two."

"You asked to see me, sir?"

The commander pointed at a side chair. "These men are from Orange County. This is Sheriff Roberts and Detective Pounds. Gentlemen, this is Lieutenant Maris Ramirez."

They all nodded. "How can I help?" The young woman was what Frank's mother had always called peaches and sunshine. The rounded cheeks may be rosy but blended in the dark walnut skin. Her eyes were a matching black for the closely cropped tight curls. Excluding the crisp iron on the dungarees, she looked like she could play rough rugby with older brothers.

Frank took in a long, slow breath through his nose. She wasn't the person they were looking for, but she was part of the puzzle. Or, at least her name was. "Ramirez? Father or husband?"

"Neither and both. My father was Spanish Cajun. Born in Puerto Rico but came here in the first wave of family to southern Louisiana. Plaquemines Parish. The other Ramirez was the guy I married for twenty-seven days."

Frank mussed at the probable sting. "Not even a full month..." She sighed. It sounded like old news she had moved far beyond. "The only things my ex wasn't was blond, a surfer, and honest. I went to the priest who married us. He already had the paperwork for the annulment filled out. It turned out he heard confessions for three of my bridesmaids and my maid of honor. I left those four at the church door and in his bed. I done got shat and ran to college."

After the answers, Frank was almost afraid to ask. "Where was college?"

"I got a scholarship for Cal Maritime in Vallejo."

"So you knew you wanted to join the coast guard."

"I knew I wanted to go to sea. I just didn't know how far."

The sheriff squirmed. "I'm sorry... but Cal what?"

Frank chuckled and held up his hand to stop her. "It's okay. He was born and raised in Orange County but never so much as laid on a beach." He turned to his friend. "California State

University Maritime Academy. Think of it as the Quantico of everything about ships and shipping."

The lieutenant laughed. "Except, I'm no spy."

"What do you do on the…"

"*Edisto*, sir. It's a WPB or coastal patrol boat, sir. She's one-ten of twisted steel and sex appeal. Sir. We are the Swiss Army Knife of the fleet. We can be doing rescue in the morning and interdiction after lunch. If we have extra time on our hands, we can be scaring the board shorts off the stubbies trying to steal a long gun."

Frank snorted with a smile. He glanced at the confused sheriff. He smiled at her. "Do you surf?"

"Never had the time to learn. Besides, with this figure, ain't nobody wants to see me in a bikini. My toes also cut me out. I'm missing the left big toe. I had a bout of Charcot. So I can't hang ten. It also took some of the nerves. Without my shoes, I can barely get up off the floor."

The sheriff frowned and raised his finger. "Shark-O…?"

Frank reached out and covered the sheriff's raised finger. He patted it as it came back to rest. "Your duties?"

She pointed at Frank. "Navy, if my radar is right." He nodded. "You would think of me as First Mate or the XO." She caught the question on the sheriff's face. "Executive Officer. I oversee electronics and security."

Frank nodded. "A few years back, the Coasties mapped the shoulder from Mexico to L.A. Would this be in your wheelhouse?"

"It didn't go down to Mexico. From just south of here, the shoulder peters out. They say it has something to do with the plate tectonics. I think it just wore off. The shoulder survey ran all the way to San Nicol Island. North of there is just an undersea FUBAR. Everything is crumpled and jumbled, so there is no real shoulder. The rumples cause their own disturbances and flatten the surf. It's why the long guns grab the point at Rincon. Mugu has potential, but you can go gray waiting for any real surf."

Frank smirked. "Because of the rumples. Were you on the mapping?"

She crossed her leg. "Only the part we had to redo. There was some computer glitch a few years back and the mapping corrupted. We reshot about a hundred miles of it. The jarhead beach to Long Beach."

"Who has access to the mapping?"

"To the mapping or our computers?"

Frank sat up and looked at the floor with wide eyes. He grunted through a blink as he thought. He felt like he was poking her with a needle and kept getting a fire hose of information back. "Let's start with the mapping."

"Do you have a fishing boat?"

"No, but I have friends…"

She smiled. "They have access. Anyone with the right equipment or program has access. What we do is for and in the public interest—and for national security."

"And the computers?"

Her finger pointed at the floor. "Here on base… maybe six or eight, but our computers are tied to the national protection network. So if some weenie in Washington wants to know the slope ratio of the shoulder north of Irishman's Gulch versus the south, they just open their access, show their need to know, and bam, they are dancing on the digitals."

"So it's not secure and privileged information?"

"No more than the forty-dollar streetwalker on Broadway is a monogamous girlfriend."

Frank shifted, and he could tell the sheriff was getting antsy. "One last question, and then we'll let you two go to chow. How would someone find out you were involved with the mapping enough to impersonate you?"

She snorted with underlying anger. "Easy. Before we got

Dinger here, we had a CO who hated the media. He hated them almost as much as he hated women and color. So, when the news crews found out about the mapping, it was a slow news day. The crews could shoot a bunch of B-roll at the beach with surfers and sailboats in the background and then come over here and interview me. For about six months, my face, name, and rank were on the news until people wrote in for them to interview anyone but me."

Frank nodded as he stood. "And the internet didn't help."

"Oh lord, don't even get me started about the internet."

They exchanged handshakes.

The captain stood silent and then spoke softly. "So obviously, she wasn't the one you're looking for..."

Frank wagged his head. "No. The Latina we met was a good fifty pounds smaller, fifteen shades lighter, and had the personality of a freshly castrated pit bull."

The man winced. "Well, if you ever need to take a ride with some strong backup, give her a call. Someday she is going to be one hell of a captain. Just don't tell her I said so."

Frank gave him a two-finger salute and wiped it across his lips.

The ride home was mostly quiet. Frank watched the ocean.

The sheriff, true to his nature, watched the coast traffic. California had frozen hiring the week he applied for the Highway Patrol. The sheriff's department was his second choice, but it had served him well.

Finally, the sheriff became bored with watching the slow traffic from a distance. He sat watching Frank for several minutes. The man didn't even twitch. He was busy being the ocean, and the ocean was consuming the man. The sheriff wondered if the job had ever been as consuming. And then he glanced down at the toes.

Everyone knew about the toes. Only Frank had known about his partner's toes. The man wasn't openly gay but was openly Hawaiian. His background was Samoan Polynesian. He always had a smile and an open hug for anyone who was in need. More than a few deputies were over to the man's apartment for needed food and even a couch. The friendly ear to just sit and listen was a given. Only those who visited him at home saw his toes with pink polish. It was his only nod to whom he was deep inside.

During Frank's long recovery, he became bored and had another patient paint his toes. She had been doing her own, except for the foot at the end of a full leg cast. They made a deal. She showed up for weeks after she was discharged—for toes and talk.

The sheriff shifted in his seat. He didn't know if it was untouchable territory or not. "You finally got your toes done."

Frank wasn't sure if he wanted to talk about it or not. But he fished out his phone and pulled up the photo of the six feet in the late afternoon light.

As he put the phone away, he leaned toward the sheriff. "It was an investment in the investigation and my sanity. Those are the toes of the ones who are going to take down the drug smuggling ring."

"They look young."

Frank smiled as the helicopter put down on the helipad. "It's not the years that count but the miles in those years."

As they entered the quiet of the sheriff's office, the sheriff walked to his side cabinet. He pulled out a bottle of scotch and two glasses. "Sorry, I don't keep ice around."

Frank smiled gently. "It bruises the single malt." He took the offered glass.

The sheriff offered out his glass. "Here's to only two strikes."

"Here's to knowing who our support ship will be for raiding a few buses."

"Buses?"

Frank pointed at a chair. The two sat and sipped while Frank explained about the bus, the depth, and what it was rigged for.

"And you think there are more?"

Frank closed his eyes as he cocked his head. "It makes sense. A single sub capable of diving to that depth could service a few at a time. You wouldn't need a safe house. The bus is safe enough. As long as the air maintains the pocket and the drugs are sealed tight, they can sit for months. Only move what you need when you need it."

"But you said the bus you found was empty."

"Sure. No drugs, but the air tanks had been used for a few weeks, maybe. Check it out and make sure it works before you stuff it full of a million dollars in dope."

The sheriff leaned back in the chair. He looked over at the large desk chair in yearning. Frank laughed.

"You can go sit in your big chair."

The sheriff snorted. "I was thinking about it down in Diego. I don't think Dinger gets to sit much."

"Or it was a new chair."

"It was nice."

Frank nodded and then resumed serious. "Back to the bus or buses."

"What about them?"

"Well, I've been thinking about investing in the two gals who built the program that found them. They have the backing from the dredging industry but not money. The people they talked to showed support and agreed there was a need for their software."

The sheriff cleared his throat and took another sip. "I don't see the problem. It sounds like a good investment. But do you have funds you can invest?"

Frank nodded with a short snort. "More than enough. I could probably buy them out and just retain them as goof-off employees. But there is the problem. These two work hard. I want them to see where their work got them and where they will be soon. Not some broken-down old detective surf-bum with money who comes along and saves them."

The sheriff looked at his empty glass. He rested it in his lap. "Where do you want to go with this?"

Frank leaned in. "I seem to remember a statute about turning in some criminal and a portion of the recovered goods..."

The sheriff smiled with a low growl. "Good night, Frank."

24 OUT OF UNIFORM

The bar, in general, was quiet. Only a few small groups or couples were quietly drinking. The jukebox was playing Donna Summer. Frank had only to listen for two lines to realize it was always the closing song during the disco era. Forty years and still going strong in the gay bars.

Pussy set down a mug of coffee as he sat at the stool. Frank looked at her. "Do I look that bad?"

"Honey, your eyes are bleeding. Who were you reading to?"

Frank sipped. "I stopped in to check on Mickey. He was out. His stats were up enough for them to go in and replace the hips. Knowing him, he also had them install a pneumatic pecker while they were down there."

"I thought I recognized the voice. How's it hanging, Pounds?"

Frank and Pussy looked over at the two LAPD officers in uniform. Both had a fruit drink in front of them. Frank frowned, but something was familiar, and something more was off.

Pussy leaned forward and growled in Frank's ear. "Deputies Taylor and Garcia."

Clarity flashed across Frank's face. The two deputies in

costume laughed. "Jeezus, guys. What's with the Blue Meanie nut suits?"

The blond smirked. "It was either this or the leather, but my chaps are out for cleaning, and his jacket has a rip in it."

Garcia laughed and backhanded his shoulder. "But man, was it a great party."

Frank studied the uniforms. Most of the detail was dead-on, but the pouches on the Sam Brown belt were wrong. The cuff pocket held a double set. There was no weapon or taser. But the billy club was old-school—or looked real.

Another uniform came to mind. "Where do you get the uniforms?"

Both men's eyebrows rose. "You thinking about…?"

"Nope. But I have a suspect who had a very real Coastie uniform."

"How real?" The L.A. cops were gone, and the Orange County sheriffs were at full alert.

"Right down to the gray motor pool car."

Taylor spun his drink around with his right hand as he thought. "Most of this gear came from the internet or supply house up in the big city. But a motor pool car… That's a whole different layer of fetish."

Garcia nodded. "It's above my paygrade too."

"Thanks, guys. Have a great night."

"You too. We thought you were retired. Are you private-eying now?"

Frank vibrated his head. "Consulting on the headless case."

The two cringed and shook. "Scary shit there."

Frank agreed and turned back to Pussy. "How about you?"

She rolled her eyes and let her eyelids droop. The shrug in her head and shoulder said it all. She was beat.

"Nothing has really changed. Pink talked the hospital into not kicking her out. She just snuggles in with Blue. They never did sleep in separate beds. The nurses told me they can tell when she sneaks into the bed. Blue's pulse drops, the blood pressure drops, and everything turns to what might pass for normal. Because they aren't home, I just bunk in here like old times."

"Yeah, I checked in for a little bit. Pink was reading the last of *Peter Pan* to Blue. She was already in the bed. I don't know if Blue was even still awake."

Pussy stretched her arms across her chest and massaged the large, chiseled biceps. "I don't know if they will ever try dating, but I pity anyone who tries to get in the middle of them. Even when they're studying on opposite sides of the dining table, their feet are touching. They're just like puppies or kittens. They don't even comb or brush their own hair. They just dry it off and wait. The other will finger it into shape or pick up a comb."

"Has she said anything about—"

Pussy shook her head. "I think when she's ready, she'll only talk to you. But it will help if Pink is there."

Frank ran his fingers through his hair as he leaned into his braced elbow and hand. "We're pretty sure we know who the person is for her and Mary, but we need to catch them."

Pussy pointed at the two deputies standing up. Frank nodded.

The blond came over and put his hand on Frank's back. "It was good to see a friendly face in here. You ought to come in more often."

Garcia joined in. "Pussy is a friendly face… but, well…"

Pussy growled. "You want to get it cut off, Garcia?"

The two deputies backed up with hands held up. "Really, Frank. Good to see ya. We'd stick around and chat, but we both have first-watch." They turned and laughed their way out the door.

Pussy studied Frank.

"What?"

"Just figuring you out. You were friends with Mary. You know some of the regulars. You paint your toenails pink. You charm my daughters like no man has before…"

"Are you saying these as a bad thing?"

"Nope." She held up her hands. "Just taking count." She peeked in his mug. "You want some more, or you going to make it home with that?"

"I'll be fine. I have some thinking to do. It'll keep me awake."

"Well, thanks for checking in on us. Some days it seems like we're all alone. The reach-out is bigger than you think."

Frank winked and pushed up and back. "The girls are safe. Maybe you should think about closing early."

She snorted as she looked at her watch. "You're kidding. This place is about to make rent. We're still about ten minutes shy of the front door opening and not closing. Our clientele is at parties right now, and then they come here to pair off."

He pointed at her. "I'm just saying. You need some sleep yourself."

Frank shouldered his way out of the door as his phone barked. He hadn't heard from the old dog in months. He swiped the phone open as he leaned on the windshield of the Bentley. "What's shakin', boss?"

The voice was quiet. "I'm sitting watching my boy sleep."

Frank knew what was next. "Norm's on Beach or Sarah's?"

"Better make it Norm's. The other is buried in the past."

Frank opened the car door. "I'll see ya in about thirty. I'm up at the top of Orange."

"Mary's?"

"Yeah. I'll explain when we're face-to-face."

"Thirty, boot."

THE BLUE-WHITE GLARE of florescent was almost painful on Frank's eyes. He decided to wear his mirrored glasses into the twenty-four-hour diner. He was surprised there was only one Huntington Beach cop car in the back.

His head ground around the large room until he found his old training officer. The booth fit his criteria—window onto the street and a wall behind him.

"Boss?" Frank slid into the booth. His back to the room.

"You want me to wear those mirrors for you, rookie? It's fucking night out there." Frank pulled them down. "Oh, fuck no. Put them back before you give some vampire a hard-on."

"Nice to see you, too, asshole."

Randy leaned in. "What the hell have you been doing the last few days? You look like shit."

Frank pointed at the ceiling. "It's been a long couple of days. But these lights are simply hard on the eyes right now. What did they say about the kid? When I stopped in, he was still down in surgery."

"I got there just as the knife was about to leave. He said it was a little longer because the thigh bone was crushed on the door side."

"Femur. The bone is called the femur."

The older man's hand rolled over with the middle finger growing proud. "So they took out the whole thing and put in a transplant. He still ends up with metal hips and stuff, but his bone would have never been right. He also got a bulletproof kneecap."

Frank started to tell him the bone name, but the finger grew back.

Mickey's father sat back. "What's the prognosis? Is he going to have more metal in him than you or not?"

"Probably." Frank looked up at the waitress. "We'll have two coffees to start." He looked at Randy. The man shook his head. Frank looked at his watch. "Better add a short stack sandwich."

The older waitress had been working the graveyard shift for as long as Randy and his rookie had been coming in there. "Eggs and meat?"

Frank looked at Randy and thought about the old-school order. "On vacation with roadkill."

She took the menus off the table. "Over easy and bacon. I'll be right back with more coffee. If you're hiding them eyes, I know you're needin' more coffee."

Frank looked down at his empty mug. "Thanks, Loretta."

Randy yawned. "You think I need to start making room in the company?"

Frank's eyes bounced all over the table and then looked up. "Mickey? I wouldn't bet on it. He's got a long road to drive down. Hell, just the new shoulder and both hips will have him in rehab for the next few months. You'll know about Christmas. But with him, I'm betting on the badge."

Randy blinked a few times with his whole face as the waitress poured more coffee. "If Mickey took after anybody, he took after you more than me. I got passed over and looked for the door. You… Hell, look at you. You never have to work again. But here you are."

"Mickey asked. And if he hadn't, I would have stuck my nose in it anyway."

Randy rocked as he rolled the coffee mug back and forth in his hands. "Yeah, Mick told me." He looked up. "Fellow SEAL?"

"Mary was the Big Red One. But we surfed together—same board shaper. The guy grew up in the Cove, shaping boards with his dad or some older guy. I never asked." He sipped on the coffee. "They lived in the old garages."

"What's going on with the case? You two making any headway?" The man smiled at the pun.

Frank was too worn out to respond. "Some. We thought we had a lead on the killer, but it turned out to be a dead chicken."

Randy smiled at their old term for leads with short lives. He watched as the plate of food arrived. He looked up. Loretta knew her cops. The second plate was in her hand behind her back.

They smiled.

The two ate in silence like old times.

Randy gathered his fork and knife at the five o'clock and pushed the plate forward an inch. He stared out the window, thinking about the street. "He said it was the one you two met, but she's not the Coastie down in Dego…?"

Frank wiped his lips and pushed his plate toward the middle. "Not by at least fifty pounds and a lot of shades darker."

"But the name and duty were right?"

"And there is the scariest part. I might run back down and go through mug shots, but there's also a small unit out here at Corona del Mar. It sits at the mouth of the Newport harbor."

Randy rocked his head. "A friend had a house there on the tip of Balboa Island. It looked right at the small cutter they keep there. Yeah, they probably could pull up mug shots of all the Coasties in Southern Cal. Computers are a lot more powerful than the mill in your Bentley will ever be."

"I was thinking the same."

Randy snorted. "How many gallons to the mile do you get out of that beast of yours?"

Frank smiled. It was an old barb. "Probably better than you get out of the tank of yours."

"Oh no. I traded the Hummer in for a Prius." His voice dripped with sarcasm.

"Bullshit. I saw the Escalade when I pulled in. It looks like it's bulletproofed too." The dick-measuring never stops.

The man's eyes and eyebrows rose in a no-comment admittance. Frank knew how close to the border the man lived. His leather factory was across the border. The Speed Belt had all but replaced the old Sam Brown made in Texas. Frank liked the tuck-away holster he always wore in the back of his pants. No bulge under the T-shirts—just security.

25 CLOSING OUT

The most impressive picture hanging in the Shack was taken from water level. The mystery rider was only hinted at in the dark, murky steam of the closing wave. Only the tip of the long gun is in daylight. It was one of the early shots taken with a water camera during a North Shore Giant Wave competition. The tiny print on the image only reads, *Fifty-foot Banzai Pipeline closes out on competitor.*

To Frank, it was an analogy for much of life. Even when sunlight is showing only a foot away, you can still get drilled.

Frank was hyperaware of the grainy black-and-white photo behind him. It was why he kept it there. On days like this, it made the skin crawl over his metal spine.

His right foot was in the pool of sunlight as he dialed the phone.

"San Diego Station Coast Guard."

"This is Frank Pounds. I was down a couple of days ago. I'd like to talk to Captain Jake Dingerman, please."

"Yes, sir. Hang on, please."

"Dingerman."

"Frank Pounds, Jake. I need a favor."

The man laughed. "You want a date with the Lieutenant and her cutter already?"

Frank smiled. "Not just yet. But if this goes in the direction I think it will, I'll need more help than just her cutter. I might need your whole fleet to be limos for a bunch of divers."

There was silence on the other end. "Sorry. The chill down my spine needed some coffee. What can we do for you now?"

"I'm about twenty minutes from your auxiliary station at Corona del Mar. I need to look at all the mug shots of all your personnel in Southern Cal. Is there a way I can do that?"

"I'll make the call. What time were you thinking?"

"Probably around ten."

Frank could hear the distant pen on paper.

"Anything else?"

Frank furled his lips. He wasn't sure he was walking up a gangway or out on a plank. "A few years back, the Coasties conducted an extensive mapping of the outer shoulder. Is it possible to get access to the raw daily mapping? Would you guys keep it once it was all consolidated?"

"For that, you need to talk to your future date. She's the one." The smile shone through the phone. "Let me get you transferred. She just went on watch."

The phone snipped in his ear. Danny hovered with fresh coffee. Frank nodded thanks.

The phone clicked with the wet metal sound common with all phones on military ships. Frank wasn't sure it was because the phone seemed to predate the Korean War or just designed to be a modern tin can on a string.

"Bridge."

"Detective Frank Pounds to talk to the Lieutenant, please."

"Sir."

He could hear the phone being passed with his name mumbled in the background.

"I'm flattered, Detective. I thought I was the only one-and-out when I didn't get a text the next morning. Where are we going?"

"Lieutenant, when we bust this one, I'll come take your whole crew out to dinner."

"My complement is eighty-seven, including the support. And, as you know, the shop is never closed."

"How about I throw the base a luau? Spouses and family included."

He could hear her shift the phone to the other ear. "Okay, now you have my attention."

"The mapping we spoke about."

"The shoulder. Yes? What about it?"

"Would the daily mapping be stored somewhere as the raw data? Even after it was all stitched together?"

The soft scratching across the hole-drilled metal told him she was using both hands to do something. It was the number one advantage of old-school over cell phones. The modern flat piece of liver usually hung up.

"Okay, I've got it. What do you need to know?"

"How can I access it?"

"We could start with lunch…"

"If I need to come down, I'd be bringing a couple of nerds with laptops."

She chuckled. "Now I know you're serious. Do you have an email for the nerds? I can send them a link with access."

"I'll call you later with it. They're students. I'm not sure when they wake up or if they even sleep."

"But they know how to crunch these raw files?"

"Trust me. These two live for raw data files."

"Then I look forward to talking with them. I'll give you the direct line."

He scribbled the number on the back of a photo of seven dead bodies. Only one had a head.

"Thanks. We'll talk after lunch."

"I'm at chow from eleven hundred to twelve hundred, but they can transfer the call to my cell."

"It will probably be about thirteen or fourteen-hundred."

"Done."

Frank started to put the phone down but dialed another number instead. He had known the number since he was a teenager.

The tone was flat. "Murphy."

Frank smirked. His least favorite 'money uncle.' "Mr. Murphy, Frank Pounds."

"Yes, Mr. Pounds, what can we do for you?"

"I need someone who can put together a corporation start to finish."

"Anything else?"

Frank looked out the window at the flat tide. His smile was pure mischief. "Yes. Yes, there is. If you have one who is a lesbian, it would be best."

The older man was more old-school than his grandfather. The tone chilled to subarctic. "I'll check with HR and have them get back to you." The disconnect was sharp. Frank rolled his eyes at the Faustian yoke he bore with his inheritance.

Danny slid the edge of the plate across the table. "Don't even think about going to work without at least breakfast."

Frank smiled at his mother hen and stood.

The man's eyes rounded with a threat.

"Chill. I just need to pee."

Frank watched the calculations of the coffee consumed. There was a curt nod, and the man twirled on his toes like only a drama queen could. "My job is done here." The sashay was even more exaggerated by the height of the slender queen. Frank shook his head at his closest gathered family as he headed for the toilet.

The phone rang halfway through the waffle stacked with eggs, chopped ham, and Ortega chilis. Whoever it was, wasn't listed in his phone. He let it go to voicemail. A moment later, the readout was for the law firm.

He smiled as he filled his mouth with food. "Whaabow?"

The voice wasn't bubbly, but there was a slight husky giggle. "You thought it was the Smurf calling, didn't you?"

As he swallowed, he thought about the voice. He knew he had heard it before. "Keep talking." He snuck a sip of coffee to clear his throat but forgot Danny had warmed it up. It was steaming hot and dead black. The sip turned into a slurping spit.

Danny's tuned ears snapped his head around. Customers or no customers, there were a few things he couldn't stand. He snap-rolled out his finger of accusation.

"There will be no spitting in my parlor. I don't care who you are. I will eighty-six your boney old ass for thirty days."

Frank's finger rose as the voice on the phone started to talk and then started laughing. "Are you at the Shack?"

"Yes'm."

"Is the coffee as good as the mouthful of food sounded?"

Frank cocked his head and squinted. "Who is this again?"

"Jasmin. Jasmin Perlmutter. But call me Jazz—your HR-appointed, U-Haul-card-carrying dyke."

Frank almost spit his coffee again. He planted the mug and backwashed the sip of hot coffee.

Out of the corner of his eye, he could see Danny V-fingering his eyes and then him. His mouth was saying *I'm watching you.*

Frank turned to look out the window. "Excuse me."

"No excuses, Pounds. I'm halfway to the parking lot. Just sit back and relax. I'm at Fashion Island, so I'll be there in about fifteen minutes."

Frank chuckled. "This I've gotta see. Fifteen won't even get you out of Corona del Mar."

"Shit. Okay, I need to change my shoes. Make it twenty." The snap sounded like an old flip phone.

Frank studied the black dots lying on the flat surf like fly droppings on a nice silver picture frame. He squinted his eyes to desaturate the color until it was almost a faded silver-plate photo. He wondered if any of the bohemians in the cove, back in the twenties, ever surfed.

He looked up at the closing curl. He loved the analogy for life. But he spun around and really studied the interior of the café. Picturing antique surfboards hanging from the ceiling. Paintings of the cove in the early days. Nudists, striped-singlet swimming trunks, women with parasols, and old cars.

"We have a newspaper, Danny?"

Danny looked from around the half-wall. He blinked. He pointed toward the front door.

Frank blinked. *We have a newsstand?*

He walked out the front door. Taking one look at the prices, he walked back in. He passed the cash register and into the backroom. Finding the toolbox, he removed the large hammer.

"What do you think you're doing?"

Frank smiled. "Tomorrow, when they ask, tell them to install a freebie stand or leave ten papers on the counter."

Danny stood, watching his boss having fun with his temper. Three large *bangs* and a *boing* later, Frank returned with a paper. He stuck the hammer in Danny's hand. "Oh, and by the way. I have company coming. She'll want coffee and what I just had."

"When?"

"She said she'd be just in time."

A few minutes later, Danny slid the platter across the table. The rumbling rattle made Frank peel down one corner of the paper and look up at the full six and a half feet of redhead. Danny rolled his eyes as he poured the coffee. "It wasn't me. I think a coven of bikers just rode up."

The paper flipped back. Frank growled. "It's a gang. Coven is for witches."

The door swung open. The short spikey hair did nothing to smooth the rough edges of the woman. Height-wise, she could almost give Danny a run for his money. The custom leathers added nothing to the brawny body. The woman looked around. Danny stepped aside to reveal the man reading the newspaper.

She smiled and removed her gloves as she walked. When she got to the table, her jacket oozed from her shoulders, and she caught the collar in her one hand. The coat made one flip in the air and slid to a stop under the window as she slid onto the chair.

She turned the plate a quarter turn and then attacked with a knife and fork. She forked in one bite and picked up the mug of coffee. She was reading about the armed holdup at the jewelry store in Seal Beach when the corner of the paper curled down. The eye studied her.

She rearranged the food and forked another bite into her mouth. Still chewing. "Good morning, Pounds."

The top of the paper rolled to meet the bottom. The frown was consistent across both sides. "You…" He was at a loss for words.

She took another bite. Her head and eyes tossed the attempt aside. "Was the night dispatcher at the SO. Yeah. I graduated from law school while you were still in UCI Medical Center." She slurped more coffee. "I graduated the next year with my master's in business administration, focusing on small businesses and entrepreneurs. I'm your dyke on a bike who knows starting a business from start to bankruptcy—as you requested." She shoveled another large load of waffle, egg, and ham into her mouth and chewed as she watched him.

He gathered his hand in a pinch at his mouth as he quietly considered her.

Danny couldn't stand it anymore and brought the carafe over. Quietly, he refilled Frank's mug. He looked over at the Amazon-tall, raven-haired, leather-clad woman—his sexuality was having an internal war.

Frank turned his chair sideways and looked at the café again. "Danny, I've been thinking. What about finding some old balsa boards from the turn of the twentieth century and hanging them from the ceiling? Then we can get someone to paint pictures like they were old sepia photos of people in the cove."

Danny kept looking at the woman. His snarl was wispier than snarky. "They were nasty nudists."

Frank looked at the man. "Yes… and artists, writers, actors, and just down on their luck bohemians. What's your point?"

"Is this your decorator?" His tone turned more catty than usual.

Jasmin almost spat her coffee back in her mug.

"No spitting."

She looked up at the tall man. Few men were taller than her. Truly taller. "Sweetie. Don't sweat it. My taste would have this barn stripped down and refinished in leather. I'd have pussy whips hanging from the ceiling. Ball gags would be issued to all the wait staff as would the leather maid's outfits." She calmly took another sip of coffee. "So chill. I'm just a lawyer."

Danny's eyes rolled as he turned and walked away. "Scary. I don't know which is to be feared most."

She looked at Frank. Her voice was calm and quiet. "What?"

Frank put up his hands. He wasn't going to get into his employees' fantasies with someone he didn't know.

She pointed her fork at the now empty plate. "Does he serve this every day?"

"There is a whole menu last time I looked."

"Yeah, but the chilies and chopped ham… Only thing better would be a bed of strawberry compo on the waffle first."

"Tell him. I'm sure we have it—or will."

She dabbed at her mouth and pushed the empty plate away. Crossing her arms on the table, she leaned in. "What do you need done?"

Frank smiled in a mew. "What do you bill?"

"Four-seventy-five an hour plus expenses."

"When does the clock start ticking?"

"For you? When I actually know what the hell I'm going

to do."

Frank chuckled. "It's going to take a few hours to explain."

Her head cocked as the upper eyebrow drew back. "I had a busy schedule today. I think I was going to get a pedicure or something."

"What color?" His smile was almost human instead of predatory. "If you're going to work for me, there's only one color."

"Which is?"

He held up his hand. "First, I need a shower and a fresh shirt. Then I need to go up to the Coast Guard Station for a couple of hours to look at mug shots. And then, and only then, it's going to be up to my partners."

"Let me get this straight. You need to consult with these partners before you talk to me?"

"Actually, no. I can explain what's going on if you want to hang out with me this morning before we take the partners to lunch."

"Okay, but one question."

Frank looked at his watch. "It's a Wednesday. You get three questions."

She only paused to think for a second. She rattled through the questions like an old Gatling gun. "How small is the company you want to incorporate? What is the seed capital? And why did you insist on a lesbian?"

"For right now, it will be three people unless we need a larger board. If so, I have a few people in mind. Second, the seed capital, as of today, is one million."

"And the lesbian?"

Frank leaned in closer. "Do you like working for Murphy?"

"He's not on my Christmas card list. But the company lends some cachet to my resume."

"How big would your first company have to be if you break out on your own?"

"As long as the bills get paid, and more was on the horizon."

Frank leaned back. "I was cursed with my trust when I was ten. Murphy came along while I was in the navy. The only good parts of the trust were this café and my two-by-four shack down on the edge. I live next to the cove I like to surf or just float in. My nearest neighbor is more than a football field away. My pension from the sheriff is full and permanent. But people always treated me differently because of the trust. Or so I thought. I recently realized I could do something useful with the trust that I couldn't do otherwise. And if the how makes Murphy squirm, all the better."

"Are you finished with the paper?"

"Yeah?"

"Good. Go get your shower. I'll read the paper while the rocket boy gets me more coffee."

Frank stood and leaned in. His growl was sincere and low. "His name is Danny. Think of him as my son." He looked down the café. "Disrespect him, and your motorcycle won't save you."

She smiled. "Noted. But can I be your daughter so I can poke him in the backseat?"

Frank looked back over his shoulder as he drew in and let out a long sigh. "You're on probation."

As he headed for the back door, he passed Danny. "You kids play nice. I have my eyes on you two."

The screen door squealed.

Danny turned. "Hey, Frank?"

The man paused with his T-shirt half off. "Yeah?"

"Real long guns or reproductions we can just bolt up there?"

Frank let go of the door. It snapped twice to close. "Either one. You're the decorator. As long as it looks right." He walked a few steps and turned. Danny was still in the door—thinking. "But no pussy whips or ball gags."

"What about the leather maid's outfits?"

Frank turned as the finger floated above his head. "Talk to your sister about those things."

She looked skeptically at the torch-cut removal of the Bentley's top. "Wouldn't it have been easier just to get a convertible?"

Frank smiled as he slid in and inserted the key. "It was in the impound lot. The engine, trans, and dashboard were removed. The top was where the crushing ball hit. That's when I offered the yard boss a handful of bills."

She slid in and buckled up. Her voice was incredulous. "Five hundred?"

Frank turned the key. "Nah, I think they were only twenties. Maybe there was a fifty in there." The large engine kicked over and rumbled into life.

She pointed at the dashboard. "*That* is not a Rolls Royce engine."

"Nope. He also had a four-twenty-seven built for flat-track racing. His son never finished the car. I think the engine and trans cost me about a grand."

She ran her hand along the rough-cut edges. "Who did the cutting?"

"An FBI friend named Granite."

She mussed. "Typical Fed job. Quick and leave the cleanup to someone else."

As they nosed out on the highway, Frank filled her in on the case.

He turned to her as they parked at the Coast Guard Station. Thinking, he reached in his shorts pocket and took out a bill. He handed her the falling-apart five. "You're now on retainer. Anything happens here, anything we learn, anything we see—"

"Is privileged information. Yeah, I know. I work for the firm you retain, so you're already covered."

He stared at her. "Maybe not for long. And if you take the five, you can come in. What I'm doing here and the next place has nothing to do with the firm."

She took the bill and held it up with a sour curl to her lip. Her voice dribbled sarcasm. "Oh, just the bill that I can't wait to put in a big fucking gold picture frame."

The seaman was a miniature knockoff of Danny. A warning look from Frank closed Jazz's mouth. While the seaman explained how they had set up the photos to display in an array, Jazz asked another seaman if it was possible to get a tour of the cutter.

The arrays were of twenty headshots stacked four high and five wide. Hitting the down button refreshed with a new set of twenty. What Frank didn't know was he was viewing every Coastie in the Pacific. It didn't matter. Frank was used to scanning through worse mug shots with worse-looking subjects. It didn't take long before he needed coffee.

He stood waiting for the coffee to run through the little plastic cup in the machine. If Danny ever asked, he knew he'd have to shoot him.

"How goes the search?"

Frank looked up at the silver-haired man with the brush cut and stood. He noted the polished eagles. "Slow but steady, Captain." He stuck his hand out. "Pounds, Frank Pounds. Orange County Sheriff's department."

The man smiled and shook. "I knew more about you the minute you drove the chopped Bentley through the gate. I have at least six serious surfers here. I understand you favor the longer boards."

Frank smiled as he pulled the standard navy heavy white mug out of the machine. "Long gun. It's called a long gun. Anything over nine feet is a long gun. The eights and nines are longboards. The term supposedly goes back to the Wild West. The difference between a Winchester lever-action and a Sharps fifty or seventy was about two or three feet."

"So why a long gun over a longboard? Does it surf different?"

"A board can get up and use a surf running three to five. A long gun starts maneuvering with six to eight. When the winter storms are tearing up the Alaska fishing, we get long gun surf. The kids stay home."

The man looked at the bottom of his empty mug and motioned at the machine. "I wish the kids around here minded the small craft warnings as well."

Frank nodded at the man's pain. "It's why I like long guns."

The panels of faces were starting to blur. The saving grace was most of the panels were of men. It cut Frank's time.

"Anything?"

Frank shook his head. "I have three more panels. How about you? Anything?"

She dropped into the chair next to the desk. "Nothing I'd own."

He side-eyed up at her. She snorted. "And probably wouldn't rent. But a nice boat… and captain."

The last two panels were only men. He cleared the screen. Nobody. He sat reflecting on the meaning. If not guard, who was close enough?

He pulled out his phone and dialed Ming.

"Deep Six." The voice wasn't Ming or Tree—it was male. Squeaky young, but male.

"Ming Lee, please. Orange County Sheriff's Detective Pounds calling."

The "Oh, shit" was muted. The next voice was whiney.

"I'm hungry."

Frank decided to play along. "Who. Is. The. Boy?"

The giggling was what he was looking for. "Just a boy…"

"Tree has twenty minutes to disinfect the sanctuary and be dressed for a public outing."

"Yes, sir. Twenty minutes. You coming up or just honking from the curb?"

"I think my guest will need the five-minute dog-and-pony show before I ply you with food."

"One overview coming up. Tree, he says you have to wear a shirt." The disconnect was a saving grace. His eyes met the squinting scrutiny of Jazz.

"And just how old are the partners of this million-dollar corporation?"

Frank stood to leave. "Good question. And exactly the one disqualifying Murphy and firm."

Frank was still marveling at the transforming two girls—black leggings, matching T-shirts advertising some Deep Six Corporation in light aqua, hair more done than a fast comb could perform, and a touch of makeup had turned the two teens into serious young women. He wanted to know where they had found the thick, black-rimmed glasses to finish the studious-scientists look.

The presentation was a tag team. One was supplying the screens from a slaved laptop while the other explained what Jazz was seeing.

Frank smirked at Ming. Her fingers were pointing to the right places on the forty-inch screens, but her eyes were dancing all over the profound mystery Amazon wrapped in leather. The questions coming from the mystery woman even had him amazed. Her grasp of the significant software on a global scale was almost instant. With each question about ability, the two nerds swapped, and the new laptop jockey rode home the displays.

Frank checked his watch. The five-minute dog and pony show was already running a half an hour over. His stomach was starting to wear a hole in his growler.

His phone vibrated in his pocket. He fished it out, seeing the text was from Lieutenant Ramirez.

He pushed the call-back button.

He leaned over Tree at the laptop. The other two had hit pause and were watching him.

"We're just about there, Lieutenant."

"I've set up a link, but they'll need a passcode to get past the firewall."

Frank looked at Tree. She fished her hand at the phone. Knowing he was outgunned, he handed her the phone.

"Hi, Lieutenant, this is Tree, like a pine tree. We're at real-time fourteen-twelve. I'm ready for the link." She typed the long string and hit enter. The screen burped, and the cursor was in a box. "Passcode?" Only a row of asterisks appeared as she typed. She hummed and commented to herself. "Third-grade coding…" She suddenly sat up. "No, ma'am, just thinking about something else." She leaned forward and looked at the screen of title stacks. "I'm at the stacks. What am I looking for?"

She typed in a string and hit enter. A small box in the lower left of her laptop and the larger slaved monitor started scrolling green lines of ascending codes.

"Yes, ma'am. I'm going ahead and downloading the entire mapping, so we don't have to disturb anything you need to do." She typed in another line of something not showing on either screen Frank could see. She paused and then typed some more. It didn't seem to have anything to do with what was on the screens until Frank noticed another of many screens in the room. The coast of California was overlaying with other mappings about every three seconds. A column of identifiers on the right was matching map and identifier.

Suddenly, what Frank had thought was a dark chalkboard came to life. The wire map of the coastal shelf and the beach line expanded in detail as a continuously drawing map. It started at the border of Mexico and was already past the San Onofre nuclear plant. A second wave was passing over the mapping and added dots of color and shapes. The legend on the right gave the characteristics.

He looked over at Jazz as she slowly stood, gawping at the large screen. What she was watching was the real dog and pony show. They were watching the girl's program work in real-time.

He felt a poke at his hip. He looked down at his phone and then at Tree smiling. She held out her hands at everything going on. "You like?"

He put the dead phone to his ear and then dropped it in his pocket. "This is your program putting all the raw mapping together?"

Ming stood. "It's called stitching. Deep Six takes the little maps of the whole and stitches them all onto the entire map. Don't worry. It's also saving everything as it was in the raw." She stepped over to the large screen and pointed to a yellow dot. "Gollum is taking the known statistics of the size and estimated weights and coding them on the map. The colors code and mirror in the legend over here. We aren't going to dredge them. But if we were bidding this for cleanup, Deep Six would pull all of these into a compiler to build the estimate for time, labor, haulage, and any other four thousand items needed for an accurate estimate."

Jazz stepped over and examined the growing legend. "And your program already does all those four thousand items?"

Tree typed a few other passages to somewhere else. "Are we dredging only, or will there be some blasting allowed?" Suddenly, a cursor arrow popped up. She started pointing. "This set of boulders is larger than a tract home... and there are a few shelf crushes the size of this building. A shelf crush is where the winter surf battered the shelf hard enough to calve off a piece."

Jazz laughed. "Oh, hell, what's a party without a few fireworks."

"Fireworks it is."

Ming turned toward Tree, thinking. "This build will be in a time frame precluding a single company, so let's throw in Mickey Mouse and Donald Duck."

"Goofy is on the break." Tree typed in some more, hit return, and stood. "Time for lunch."

Frank looked at his watch and fished out his phone. He thumbed a number.

"Hi. How late do you serve lunch?... Thanks. Party of four in about twenty minutes."

Jazz turned with her confused finger still pointed at the mapping. "What about...?"

Tree shrugged. "This is going to take a while. It's still sucking down all the data the coast guard had, and some they didn't tell us about..." She turned a coy look at Frank. He zipped his fingers across his lips. "And then the compiler is matching all the stuff we had. Afterward, Gollum will paint all the debris, and then the numbers nudibranchs can work up the estimate"—she turned back to Frank—"which is going to break the fucking bank. Army Corps of Engineers doesn't have that kind of budget for the entire United States."

Frank's face pulled back on the side only Tree could see. "And all of this happens while we're at lunch?"

"You didn't expect me to sweat over a keyboard for a week or more, did you? There are oysters to suck down and nails to paint pink."

Jazz blinked. "Pink?"

Frank wiggled his eyebrows as the two girls bracketed him. They looked down. It was the first time Jazz realized Frank's footwear exposed his toes.

Frank looked up with a soft laugh. "With sparkles." His team squeezed in with challenging smirks.

~

JAZZ's verbal dog and pony show over oysters Rockefeller had started in simple, understandable language. Rapidly, Jazz found out what it was like to deal with true geniuses. By the second round of oysters, the napkin drawings had been replaced by printer paper and three pens of different colors provided by the manager.

A unanimous vote of the founding board expanded the provisional membership by one.

After a report by the taller nerd of already lined-up contracts, the board's size would be expanded to twelve on advice by counsel. The report launched a unanimous vote for round three on oysters and round two on root beer.

As they later relaxed on the beach high above the Central Park, Frank watched between the two towers across the university. Ming and Tree had agreed to each take a foot. Jazz found herself outnumbered and soon slumped down in the chair to enjoy.

Frank rumbled softly, "I'm not sure the school will let us hold all the board meetings here."

Jazz smiled. "The view is seductive, but I'm not sure how much work would get done. It may sound like a simple business, but there are many reasons for the larger board. I think we might need someone with international business law experience. There's also a division of law dealing with land use, ecology, riparian rights, uses, and easements."

Both girls looked up from their painting. "Are you two talking shop again?" The twin scowls carried the warning.

Jazz laughed. "Counsel tables discussions."

Frank harrumphed. "Can I still ask about the large map?"

Tree looked back up. "Sure. Deep Six did all the work. We're just along for the glory."

"You said you were going to have to bribe the boys down the hall to write some code to tweak the system. What still needs to be tweaked? I mean, the map looked amazingly complete to me."

Ming snorted without looking up. "It better be. It cost us eight pizzas, five cases of Pop-Tarts, and two cases of CaffDeath drinks. They had a war coming up, so they crunched all the code in fifty-one-hours over the weekend."

"You didn't have to supply diapers?"

"Eew, no. They order those online."

Jazz rolled her head over toward Frank. "I'm lost."

He snorted. "Roll with it. This is going to be a company with an interesting expense account."

Tree and Ming pulled the cotton toe separators off. "Done. Time for the photoshoot."

Jazz's eyes blinked large at Frank. "Photoshoot?" She started picking at her hair.

Frank chuckled. "Wrong end. Up against the wall, counselor."

27 DEEP SIX

The day had started with all the possibilities of a cesspool, but as breakfast arrived, things took a turn for the offbeat and cruised their way into what Frank liked to think of as an Orange Mix. One part offbeat, one part *What the fuck was that?* And another part *It's a sunny day, so why not?* The kind of day never to make it into the *Orange County Register* or the L.A. *Times*. The *Laguna Beach Sentinel*—only maybe on the back of page nine.

After the long lunch and compulsory toenail polish bonding, Frank dropped off Jazz to pick up her bike. She was going to pull everything together for the incorporation and make a few exploratory phone calls.

Frank dropped in to read to the Tinks, but they were curled in the bed sound asleep. The duty nurse said they had conked out early after Blue had a panic attack, and they gave her a shot of Demerol. She asked if they were real identical twins. Their nervous systems seemed to be in mirror attachment. When one was given Demerol in their IV, the other drifted off to sleep as if they had given the drug to both.

Mickey was awake but was playing chess on his pad. Frank

guessed it was Randy on the other end. He could see they were playing with the two-minute rules.

~

As HE NOSED the large car off the highway and onto the road leading down to the Shack, he chuckled with an image of a mother hen checking her chicks and then fluffing to lie down and sleep. Only the white bag of meat-laden bones from Poco Loco was left to deliver. He knew the dog wouldn't be around for a few hours, but he'd leave it on the porch.

As he passed the dark café, he noted Danny's car was still parked behind the building. It was not an unusual event, but the man rarely entertained a friend without at least some notice.

Frank softly snorted as he parked at his shack. *More mother hen.* Who would have thought he would become so caring about a gawky kid with a flaming afro Frank didn't think would make it through the week? *Five thousand six hundred and forty-seven days.*

Frank stopped at the corner of his shack. The dog was standing at the other corner. Her tail was low and unmoving. She didn't growl, but her head moved to one side. She was trying to see around him. He stepped in the way—blocking her sight. Her head moved again.

Frank looked back up the hill to the café. Something was wrong.

Frank walked back to the car. Laying the bag of meat on the seat, he reached into the back of his pants. The Beretta slid out. He eased back the slide to check for the bullet in the chamber. Easing the slide home, he holstered the weapon. So many years, the gun had lain in the drawer. But then the old habit had resumed. *Fifteen days.*

He walked up the original track. It led straight up the grade to the side of the café. When people started thinking it was a back way down to the cove, Frank dug a trench across it, leaving a berm. Only one drunk had driven over the berm into the trench. The car sat for weeks, totaled by the insurance agent, with its door open, and the weather turning nasty. It had been a warning to others. Nobody tried the road again.

Watching the back of the café, Frank stepped down into the trench. The cut wrapped around where the backhoe had carved it to stop any runoff. It left Frank exposed only from his rib cage up. He looked for the moon—dark night.

The shape was blacker in the black trench. Frank more sensed the object than saw it. He slowly hunkered down. Focusing along the trench, he let his peripheral vision fill in the shape. Nothing moved, so he eased forward.

The motorcycle was all black. No chrome to reflect the few stars showing through the ambient city lights. The engine was still warm, but not hot. It had been there for a couple of hours. Thinking about the black leather and matte-finished helmet, Frank drew his weapon. He hoped his senses were as good as the coyote.

His fingers scaled along the weathered whitewashed board-and-batten siding. At least with white, he thought, he would be able to see the biker.

At the window, he stopped. The secret to presenting the least of a silhouette was to keep your nose facing away. The starlight made his table glow in a dead bone gray. There are no colors in the dark, only shades of gray. He could hear his training officer at Silver Strand Ventura talking them through their first night-drop into the water from a low altitude. *'Your oversized chute will pull your shoulders from your cock and balls. Don't worry. It's just before the ocean slams them back in place.'*

Seven thousand eight hundred and eighty-seven days.

Frank drew back. He thought about the ocean. And the rise of the hill on the other side of the café. At least from the other side, his head would blend more with the background.

As he moved around the back, he gently twisted the door-knob on the back door.

It turned freely.

If the front door was locked, the back door was the entrance to the kill box. Frank kept moving around to the uphill side. The runoff years before had caused Frank to pour a narrow sidewalk around the side and front. Four feet of gravel covered the French drain. The stone would be noisy. He hoped Danny's OCD cleaning extended to the small rock occasionally kicked up onto the walkway.

Frank slid his loose huaraches off. His feet were tough, but they also gave him a better grip if he needed it.

He crept to the edge of the landward window. Nothing was moving in the café. But he had seen enough people tied to a chair to recognize the shape in the middle of the large room. He weighed his choices.

The back door was open, but he had to get through the kitchen and backroom first. Next came the space behind the counter. Either space was a natural kill box. His guess was the alleyway behind the counter.

He sunk to his hands and knees, a position every drill instructor would rake his coals for. It is the least maneuverable, slow, and presented the weakest defense against an attack from above. Frank was betting on his attacker being on the other side of the weather-scoured plate glass.

The front door was locked.

He knew the killer knew he was here, just not where. He looked at the one piece of glass thicker than the rest. The front door was as old as the Shack. The only window ever to be broken was the one a burglar always breaks—the most accessible to the lock knob inside. It was the one frame a previous owner had installed laminated glass in. It would take a club or bat to break—but it wouldn't be quiet.

Frank stood. He didn't care about quiet. His right foot shattered the muntin between the armored glass and the next pane. The noise wasn't as loud as he had feared, but the glass was not shards on the floor. But, close to the door. The next trick was going to expose his arm. He slipped his pistol into his left hand as he reached through the hole to unlock the door.

A black shadow moved from behind the counter as his arm snaked in. It bounced off the side station and approached the door.

Frank fired left-handed through the hole. The shadow spun and leapt at Danny. But Danny stood. His legs, still tied to the chair legs, bent him over as he stood. The shadow hit the chair's legs, sending Danny crashing forward into other chairs and a table. It was the first time Frank was glad they had wooden chairs. He heard cracking wood and at least one chunk of smaller wood skittering across the floor.

The shadow turned to the opening door. Frank sensed more than saw the machete or sword. The shadow was professional; there was no intimidating swishing blade through the air. It only moved guardedly, circling toward where Danny moaned on the floor.

Frank aimed for body mass with his right hand. Shattering the large window at the end of the room told him he had missed. A triple tap panning back into the mass only resulted in more damaged wood and shattered glass.

The shadow spun in a cartwheel as Frank tried another triple tap.

Bullets rattled the hanging pans in the kitchen as Frank moved low toward Danny. He felt the leg with his foot, the chair having shattered from the man's weight and the forced straightening. He felt for the chest or back, and the back moved. Danny was alive.

His SEAL sense caused him to flick his head back as the sword crashed down and through the tabletop and apron. Frank was sure it was a weighted machete. He fell back and poked a triple-tap through the air. The ghost was gone.

Frank grabbed Danny's belt and dragged him back toward the hill end of the café, a place he hoped he could defend.

A blur crossed from the counter to the front window. The ghost was silent.

A darkening shadow bulged over the booth. Frank dropped two more shots into furniture as he longed for the security of night goggles. He stayed low. The large windows only supplied a shade lighter than the interior, but it did provide hard edges between the black and almost black.

The one straight edge moved. Frank double-tapped the bulge. The thud of a body crashing back through chairs and a table was his reward. He aimed for the center of the crash. The gun fired once, and then the slide stayed open.

He crouched. Placing the now useless pistol on the floor, he felt for Danny's pulse. His hand came away slippery. He hadn't gone quietly into captivity.

Frank spoke low, but he hoped reassuring. "Don't worry, buddy. Help is on the way."

Danny moaned a single word. Frank wasn't sure if he heard it right or not. Right now, it wouldn't matter if the alarm was set or not. If the alarm went off, help was barely a half an hour away in sleepy Laguna Beach.

He felt along Danny's body, trying to clear it of the broken chair. As he got to the lower legs, he cleared the chair leg from the ropes.

The sound was only a soft groan at the other end of the room. Frank changed the chair leg from his left to his right hand and then duck-walked toward the sound. The body crashed into him as he reached the end of the tables.

Frank flailed at the body or head and only swung through the air. Something had changed.

He stumbled toward the counter. The thicker ash chairs were the latest addition. One had scrape marks from where it fell off the truck on the highway. A little sandpaper and nobody had noticed. He grabbed a chair and swung. He connected with a body in the dark. He dropped and continued the swing up and over his head with a slight left aim. Air.

The foot caught him in the side below his rib cage. It was weak—testing or targeting.

Frank ducked.

The air rippled through his hair, but before he could stand and swing again, the blade had hinged its arc and bit squarely into Frank's back.

The pain shot up and down his spine. The sword, which could have severed a normal spine, now buried a full inch into titanium alloy. It was as if the blade had welded there. As Frank stood, the links shut around the blade—locking it in place. Frank pushed into the surprised attacker, knocking them back, their hands slipping from the handle of the sword. Frank swung the chair, but only connecting with air again.

Suddenly, the world turned into red light. The uncanceled alarm had triggered into the secondary mode and turned on the backup security lights. There were only three red floods outside, but it might as well have been daylight.

The Latina grabbed a chair and swung it at Frank. The older chair shattered on his shoulder and back. Frank stumbled.

The pistol was loud—triple tap.

The Latina had stumbled with the first two, but the third gave her red-eye in her forehead. She tumbled back. He didn't have to look to know the woman had been wearing body armor.

Frank leaned on the chair in his hand. His head ground toward the front door. The black leather stopped at the neck. The mystery of *el Notche* had soft brown hair almost covering her ears. The pistol disappeared behind her.

El Notche stepped over to Frank. "Don't move. You have a machete in your spine. You need an ambulance."

Frank sighed exhausted. He didn't move. The pain was torturing. "Check Danny."

"But you—"

Frank growled through his teeth. "Danny." He watched her

legs move. His mutter was only to himself. "Doc, it's only a scratch."

He reached into his pocket. He knew the Laguna Beach number by heart. But he also had a new number. He looked at the recent numbers and chose the one he needed.

"Corona del Mar Station."

"This is Frank Pounds at The Shack just south of Crystal Cove. I need a medical dust-off. Two males, one with a sword in him. They need to transport to UCI Medical."

"One moment, sir." Frank could hear a radio at the other end of the desk he called. The voice came back. "Sir, the chopper is spooling up. Is there anything they are looking for?"

"The red safety lights are on. They flood the empty parking lot. They can put down there. There are no overhead wires. They were buried years before you were born."

"Can you give me the cond—"

"Son, I'd love to chitchat with you, but I need to call UCI before I pass out."

He severed the connection and hit a speed dial.

"Frank. I was just getting changed—"

"Pan. Stay there. Let them know they have two casualties coming by Coast Guard chopper. Danny is thirty-four, but I'm not sure what all she did to him. He was conscious for a minute, but I'm not sure." He turned his head to look up, but the woman knelt.

"He's unconscious. My guess is his pulse is eighty but thready. I could barely find it. His right pupil is blown. Left is pinned and fixed. Massive blood loss, she cut him up bad."

Frank turned back to his phone. "Pan?"

"I heard, Frank. What about the other guy?"

Frank snorted with a cough. "Call my mechanic. I need some metalwork. It seems a machete got caught in my spine."

A tornado swirled in the parking lot as the landing lights lit up the entire area. The wheels were just in sight.

"Honey, I gotta go. Our ride is here. See you in a few minutes."

Frank looked at the Night Rider. The staring contest was mutual. Finally, she unzipped her jacket and peeled open a secret pocket, hiding just behind the teeth of the zipper. Frank had seen the ultrathin wallets before. She flipped it open, finding two thin metal badges on the top half and a matching identifier below.

"Interpol via DEA. I'm impressed. Therefore, you had freedom of movement back and forth across the border."

She put away the wallet. "Something like that."

"Well, Agent Grant, what now?"

"Is there someone I can call to secure the café?"

"Because you were never here?"

Her look was pure stone. He looked in his phone and dialed.

"Hey, Granite. Frank Pounds. Yeah, the chopper is for Danny and me." He looked at the EMTs with the stretcher. He pointed at Danny. "I'm ambulatory. Get him. I'll be right out."

He groaned as he sidestepped a few inches for better balance. "Granite, I need a favor. I need someone to babysit the Laguna cops while they try to figure out the crime scene. There is a dead woman, but we're headed for UCI. I shot out a window, and the front door is busted…"

"Yeah? I owe you, dude." He looked up. "Oh, and hey, there'll be a motorcyclist in the parking lot when you get here. They were just passing by. So they'll take off when you get here. Thanks." He put it away as the EMT came back.

Frank winked. "He was FBI, so we're good." He looked back at the other woman crumpled on the floor. "And thanks. Someday I'll love hearing about what I don't know."

She smiled. "Maybe."

28 SERVING TIME

The view from the Stryker bed was like coming home. Frank had watched the same view for months before they tested the experimental spine support. The bones had to heal and mesh around the centipede legs buried deep in tiny holes. Only a layer of plastic food wrap sealed the fourteen-inch wound down his spine for the first month. It discouraged any forming of skin. The docs would come to *ooh* and *aah* over the healing daily. He knew enough about research geeks to realize it was the charge and floor nurses who kept them at bay. If they had their druthers, they would have set him up in their laboratory instead.

Frank smirked at the black marker printing on the white shoes. The five nurses had gotten tired of his grilling them to verify who they were, where they went to school, and what book they were reading. They wrote their names on their shoes instead.

It didn't stop the detective's questions, but it did cut to the chase. "Have they burned her at the stake yet?"

Tiffany giggled. "Are you asking about the Hunchback of Notre Dame or Joan of Arc?"

Frank wished he could rub his chin. There were two nurses

now with the name Tiffany. The only name fitting on the white Danskos were the four letters—*Tiff*. He smiled evilly. "I thought you were reading about your great-great-great-great-grand-mother or however many greats she was."

The woman leaned over and gave him a stern look. The blond bangs were all the hair moving in Frank's purview.

He moved his eyes to glare back at her. When you're strapped not to allow movement, it's hard to be intimidating.

"*The Scarlet Letter*?"

She straightened. "Two more days of demerits before you get turned. You are way off base. I'm reading about stealing fine art."

"Which kind?"

"Paintings. Early Impressionist with the current book."

"Any author I would know?"

"Local guy. My sister works at the Buena Park Library. He's from there or something. She got it for me."

"Get me the name and stuff. Maybe there's a way I could read instead of watching this dumb TV. I'm not exactly an Ellen or game show kind of guy."

FRANK SENSED MORE than heard the person arrive. It wasn't because of quiet shoes. The boots were as black as the leather pants.

The boots turned slightly. The wheels of the metal stool squeaked softly. The cushion gave a soft whoosh as the woman sat.

He could see her knees. "Good to see you again, Ms. Grant."

"Now I see why such a killing tool didn't work. I did some research on you. I'm impressed."

"You could have saved some time and asked Ralph down in Rosarito. He dates to long before the centipede."

"We had lunch in Palm Springs."

"So he knows who you are now?"

Her legs crossed at the knee. Not entirely female, not quite male. "I was wearing a dress. But I think he knew anyway. For a bumbling Baja buffoon, he's extremely savvy."

Frank waited. He was out of small talk.

The legs uncrossed. "*El Hache.*"

Frank wanted to nod, but the bracing kept him to only a twitch of the neck muscles. "Born Maximillian and somewhere along the way became her. Probably to blend in. Nobody expects the woman to be a brutal ax murderer. How am I doing?"

"Missing a few fine points, but I would almost say my trip was a waste of time."

Frank felt around for the drawtube and sucked in some water. The meter kept him at only an ounce at a time. "I think the word you could have used was 'redundant' or 'confirming.' I've had a lot of time to think."

"In light of that…" She stood.

"Is that it?"

"Do you have any questions?"

Frank was incredulous. "Just one or a dozen."

"Shoot."

"What did Mary Shores have to do with the cartel enough to send *El Hache* after him?"

"We don't know."

"Why kill him on the water and then drag him to the beach and scatter all of his diving gear?"

"We don't know."

"Where are the heads?"

"We don't know."

"Don't know… or won't share, Agent?"

He watched the boots turn and disappear. His right finger twitched on the call button as he heard the monitor rapidly change.

"What the heck is going on here, Frank?" The white shoe read *Kat*.

"Knock me out."

"Frank… we've had this discussion be—"

His teeth were grinding. "Knock me the fuck out or get off my roster."

The position of the feet changed. The darkness drifted over him.

"I HEAR you will turn over a new life tomorrow?"

Frank struggled to open his eyes. The morning fogginess couldn't be rubbed away. It would take minutes of him blinking to see clearly. The boney feet resting on the sidewalks of the wheelchair were the dead giveaway. Both feet rested flat on the sidewalks. Both legs were almost as white as the sheet Frank couldn't see. The one leg appearing slimmer than the other scrawny limb told him exactly who the chair-bound person was.

"Good to see they finally got you up and seated. Now your ass can get as fat as a walrus to match your head."

"Doing fine, Mr. Flat On My Face, fuck you very much."

Frank almost harrumphed, but the bands across the back of his chest stopped the air needed. "Your father was in a few days ago."

"He stopped in. It was good to see what a southern California tan was supposed to look like."

Forty-seven days.

"Relax, kid. You're not even halfway there. Besides, I solved the case, killed the bitch, and only threw two of us in the hospital. Case closed."

"Uh-huh. I'll believe it when I read your write-up."

"Fuck you. I already filed it with the sheriff himself." Frank had never wanted so much to use his right middle finger to write in his left hand the way his training officer was known to. He knew his son was intimately familiar with the gesture.

"Has he come in to visit?"

"Spit-and-Polish? Fuck no. They won't let his helicopter land anywhere it might get dirty."

Mickey shifted in the chair. Frank recognized the shift. He was at the end of the pain killers, or they had stepped down the narcotics. "I thought you two were best buds?"

"Just like herpes. Are they sending you up to Rancho Los Amigos?"

"I think Rancho is only for you vets. They're looking at a new place over where El Toro base used to be."

"Have you seen Danny?"

"Naw. I was still in traction. He was in and out in a week or so. Lightweight. A few cracked ribs, broken arm, punctured lung, and some cuts here and there and there and there and there…" The gallows humor conveyed more about the deep respect for the man and what he had endured than the disrespect in the humor.

Frank hummed in acknowledgment.

As the chair moved both feet, he let the dark drift him back. He dreamed of the coyote and fog and the cold flat water like a sheet of old lead.

THE LARGE PAD was connected to the buttons rigged to his left hand. As long as he could control the pages shown on the screen without turning to breaking news or just off, he was fine. Once he got the hang of the controls, he was reading at least a book a day.

Tiffany, the older, had gotten the information on Lance Charnes. He had plowed through all his books in a couple of days and wanted more. So, he returned to Hemingway.

"I hear you filed your report with me personally."

Frank ignored the voice with no feet and kept reading.

"I know you're not asleep. I can see your fingers twitch."

A pair of white shoes appeared beside the bed. The shoes didn't have a name on them, just a yellow sticky note. *I need a massage.*

Frank smiled. If she wasn't talking, neither was he. He knew she was just coming on. The scrubs were light blue and clean.

The feet turned and stopped. Pan's voice was soft and soothing. "Don't be an asshole. There's the seat, and your feet need to be in the box where he can see them. No wonder nobody wants to work for you." She walked away.

He didn't sit but did step into the box.

Frank snickered softly. "Good afternoon, asshole."

"Fuck you." The sheriff stepped slightly closer. The shine on his shoes would have made a drill instructor proud. Frank could almost see the man's face on the right toe.

"What did they replace?"

Frank figured he was looking at the centipede, still exposed so they could check the inclusion of the system to his spine. "All of it. This is known as Centipede two-point-hoho-Oh. It's a Christmas gift from the inventor."

"He's still around?"

"It's not like government service. There's no compulsory age toss onto the trash heap. He'll probably still be around playing golf on Wednesdays when I need three-point-seven or nine."

"Hmm." The man took half a foot back.

Frank found the file he'd been looking for. He had dictated it to Pan as she typed it into the pad. He attached it to the text with an image of a flying fickle finger of fate. He hit send.

The sound was off, but he could hear the phone vibrate. The number was closely guarded and never showed up if the man called you.

"What is this?"

"The report you're sniffing around for."

The man stood silent for a few minutes. The sound of the

phone being returned to his coat pocket was soft. "You're late. Don't let it happen again." The feet turned on heel-and-toe and walked away.

"Fuck you very much, Sheriff."

"Likewise, Pounds."

Other than a commendation, it was the best he knew would ever come of their friendship. Other than a beer shared on the deck of his shack. *Six thousand ninety-one days.*

THE BLACK SHOES weren't large. The gray slacks only hinted at a break where they hit the shoes. Frank could hear more than a few people clustered around his bed.

"Good morning, doctors."

"Good morning, Frank. Today you will get a new back. We just take one last look before surgery."

"Are you doing the graft?"

"I'm only attending. My niece will be doing the grafts. It will be long day. You have many muscles to reattach before we give you skin."

"Will I be able to play the piano again?"

"Sadly, no. You awfully bad at music. This time, please, not to sing in operating room. It scare nurses last time."

"I'll try hard to control myself, Doc."

"Any last questions?"

"Yeah. Who won the big one?"

The bed started to move. Frank knew he would never feel the transfer to the operating table.

"Answer is nobody. No movie worth watching since *Man With Golden Gun*. They consider doing away with Oscars altogether. No more good actors."

"Yeah, I'll miss your brother."

"We all do."

29 FLIPSIDE

The ceiling around the mirror was still the same acoustic tile with what Frank always thought of as buckshot holes. Any time he was in a hospital, he hated looking up. The problem now was looking up was a large mirror. The mirror looked out the large door. The nurses' station was right there, which meant they could watch him. To the left of the mirror was his computer monitor. Unfortunately, most people used it as a TV to watch the least objectional programming of the moment. For Frank, it was about two feet too far to read even the largest type.

He pushed the call button. He watched the nurse look up and shake her head. He tried the button again. Finally, she got up and came into the room. "I told you before. They will adjust the monitor tomorrow. And before you ask, the answer is no. The doctor says no more knocking you out."

"Will you feed me orange sherbet with chocolate sauce?"

Tiffany gave him side-eye. She had heard every nasty ending to every question.

"How long do I have to lie flat on this bed?"

"Two more weeks." She ran her hand under the blanket. The airflow kept him at the ideal temperature while the tiny beads kept stimulating his skin. They had found four decubitus ulcers on his front side when they finally flipped him over. With the skin grafts, they couldn't run the risk of more. "Then we will bolster you for short spells during the day, but honey, you are on this bed for the next two months."

Frank rolled his eyes into closed.

The day-to-day of the ward droned on. The phone rang or buzzed almost on a set schedule every four and a half minutes. The nurses spoke whole sentences only once an hour. No visitors until after six at night. And then it was somebody down past the station. The people were rarely the same, and they never spoke to the nurses. Frank didn't remember it being this frustratingly boring before.

The nurse turned the corner and stopped at the doorway. She sagged against the glass partition edge. Frank had never seen her dressed in full operatory regalia before, but there was only one person who would seek him out dressed for a restricted area. The glasses had telescopic attachments to let her see exceedingly small parts of the anatomy at arms distance. The clear face shield covering her entire face, past her ears, and over the dark blue cloth helmet reminded Frank of the burqas he saw in parts of the Middle East. The N95 mask was white. Or had started the day as white. The blood splatter only reached the bottom side of the mask. The surgical gator had more. The patterns on the dark-blue scrubs told him she had shed the yellow Tyvek shield gown and booties. He couldn't see, but she had probably been wearing shield pants as well. Whatever she had been doing for the last several hours had involved a bloodbath.

He held his hand out just above the floating blanket. She shrugged off the glass wall. He heard the metal stool on casters. The cushion woofed as she sat down heavily. Her hand was soft and warm as she took his.

She wasn't there for talk—just the contact. There had been a few nights like this before.

Frank's eyes closed, and he floated. The only thing tying him to reality was the warm hand. It wasn't squeezing in demand or limp in exhaustion. It was just securing existence.

Sometime in the night, one of the nurses asked Pan if she wanted something to drink. Frank didn't hear the answer. When he woke again, he could sense the carbonation. He guessed at something more lemon-lime or gingery. It didn't have the cloying heaviness of the darker soft drinks.

As the light became brighter from behind his head, Frank could feel his hand was empty.

Meals or trips to the bathroom never regulated his day. Under the blanket, the mysteries of the universe worked their magic. The man drifted in and out through the days.

He felt the small hands on each of his. His eyes fluttered. There was a blonde in his vision. Well, the bust of a blonde. She wore a white T-shirt. Frank tried to adjust his eyes, but they were still blurred and seeing double. He wondered if she was only holding one of his hands, and the sensory from the hand was registering double.

He guessed at Occam's razor. "You're cheating."

The two smiled. The one on the right winked. "I'm taking her into work. We need to fill out paperwork. They won't let us work until the shrinks clear us."

The left finished. "We thought we'd come by and check in on you first. They're sending us out to a facility in Palmdale. It's strict and no makeup or hair dye. It's kind of open-ended, but we'll probably still be out there when they let you out of here."

"That may be a while…"

The right squeezed his hand gently. He turned his head a slight degree. "They showed us a picture of the woman. It was her. We think she worked in maintenance or something. But it was her."

Frank gently blinked. "She didn't work for Disney. Or the coast guard or anyone else." He looked at the left. "It wasn't about you. She was an assassin for one of the more ruthless drug cartels in Mexico. Her job was to protect their pipeline for sending drugs up here. They were aiming for me. You just happened to be in the way."

The right's lower lip curled, and he could see the tip of teeth scraping at the skin. There was a lot of work still to happen there.

"I'm glad to see you up and walking around. I'd love to tell you it will all eventually fade away... but it doesn't. You'll just find ways to cope with it. With time, you get to spaces of days or even months where you never think of it. But then, it comes back. Not like now, but different, in a way you learn to look at it and put it back in the box. Then you put the box back on the shelf."

She thought a moment and then nodded once.

At the door, they turned and looked at the mirror. With just the blond hair and matching shirts, they really were identical. "And thank you for the flowers. They helped. They didn't tell us who they were from, but we figured it was you."

"What kind?"

"Blue and pink. They didn't look like any flowers we recognized. But they were always our colors."

Frank raised a thumb. They waved small, turned, and disappeared.

Frank's hands drifted on the blanket. The air held them floating in midair. He thought about lying on the long gun—the sun just the right temperature almost into fall. The ocean warm from the long summer, matching the sun, and the board floated in the middle. It was closest to hanging suspended weightless in the warm water of the Persian Gulf. Close your eyes and don't breathe—it's the closest to the feeling of being dead.

Seven thousand two hundred and eighty-seven days.

30 BANG IT SHUT

O*ne hundred and thirty-seven days.*
The ten-pound weight rolled out of his hand. Thudding to the carpet, it rolled another two feet. Frank silently raged at the lump of iron and chrome. At the seventh curl, his hand had suddenly gone blank and stopped holding the weight. He sat on the bench, thinking. It wasn't his first rodeo, but he promised it would be his last.

He looked around the gym. Three other guys bent into their personal hells. Nobody worked out with anyone else. Your hell is only a subset of my hell, and you have no idea how hard I have it.

Except looking around and knowing the only people at the rehab center told them the same thing. They honestly had no idea the hell the others had gone through just to get in the room. The black guy in the southwest corner, working the rowing machine to death. Frank recognized the latest electronic leg from just above the knee. The hard part was adjusting to a knee that responded better and faster than a human knee from what he heard.

The beat-to-shit prosthetic on his left leg was pimped out many years before with the screaming eagle. Frank guessed the man recycled to prove he still had it. But the new company wasn't the same as the old company. Stories.

The guy with the shaggy blond beard was bald above his earlobes. Whatever had burned him and taken his left arm had also taken his left eye. The pink-and-purple surgical scar circumnavigating his skull told a far different story than burns. Frank had noticed the large card hanging from his lanyard a few weeks back. *Hi. My name is Doug. I live in Rm #147.*

The blond with spiky hair and a face looking like he just stuck his dick in a light socket always sat by the window. Never in front of it—beside it. Like he was taking cover. But Frank could tell his focus was outside with each repetition of the dumbbells or kettle weights. Frank had the feeling the guy would find a tree for cover if he were outside. If he had a fear, it was a phobia. But this looked more like a psychosis set for life.

Frank closed his eyes and focused on his breathing. His right hand clenched and unclenched. He could feel the pads of the fingers and nails dent into his palm. He focused on the skin on the side of each finger as they rubbed along the other finger— the feelings. The hand was working again. He had been here before. He knew it would happen for the rest of his life, but it didn't mean he had to accept it.

He rocked forward onto his one outstretched foot. He stretched his body along the thigh. Reaching, he snatched the weight from the carpet and sat back. His weight rested on the three points. His elbow dug into his lower thigh. Then he restarted the count.

The soft sound of greased bearings on a wheelchair is distinctive. Frank ignored whoever was crowding his bench and continued his curls. His count was a breath with no more sound than his soaked T-shirt pulling over his back. *Three.* The wheelchair was still there. *Four.* He wasn't going to look. *Five.* They would go away. *Six.*

The voice was high and innocently sweet. "Excuse me. Is this here the library?"

Frank froze. He bit his upper lip. Hard.

He could feel every other eye in the room had turned their way. His hand and weight froze near his chin. His right eye cracked as he side-eyed the direction of the voice.

Ming pointed her finger at his eye as she leaned back into Mickey. "See, I told you he had some Chinese in him. He have the inscrutable slit eye. He see everything. He watch me, and he watch you." She roll-turned and bounced her finger in the man's chest with each word.

Frank noticed the red leather arms on the wheelchair. The blue plastic fake leather was on the crap chairs for use by those who didn't have a chair of their own. The red leather belonged to only one man.

"Whichever bathroom you found the chair outside of—take it back."

Mickey started a mealy-mouthed excuse. "We were just… Ming wanted a ride—"

"Now." The vein on Frank's forehead was bulging or about to start. Mickey knew the look. He turned the chair.

The man with the metal legs sat up straight. "Leave the girl."

Doug parroted. "Yeah, leave the girl."

Ming looked over Mickey's shoulder with wide eyes and a look of panic. Frank slow-blinked and softly jerked his head for her to stay.

She slid out of the chair and stood. Frank noticed the laptop bag.

Frank continued Mickey's education as the young man disappeared into the hall. "And when you find the man with no legs, you apologize, don't touch him, don't offer to help him, and for God's sake, don't offer him a beer."

Ming turned, frowning. "Why not a beer?"

The legs breathed in deeply and let it out loud and long. "Because one beer becomes two, and two becomes four, and then pretty soon you have Bud Scikpak on your hands."

She looked to Frank for help.

"The man's name is Scikpak, Bud Scikpak." He looked up at her and rolled his eyes. "He's not touchy about his name. But he becomes a screaming asshole if you offer to help him in any way."

She sat on the bench. Her voice softened quietly. "Why would you offer to help him?"

Franks rolled his eyes and looked over at the man with two prosthetic legs. "You see how much legs he has?"

"Yeah…?"

"Bud doesn't have a tenth of the short leg. The only reason he doesn't drag his balls and cock is that he doesn't have any."

The subject of their scrutiny glanced over. His voice was more of a loud, slow bark. "You're hogging the girl, Frank."

"Yeah, you're hogging the girl, Frank." Anything spoken would be parroted. Doug wasn't even looking at them or paying attention.

Frank raised his voice enough for the man to hear. "Ming, this is Felix. We call him Crapshoot. Whether the docs take his other leg or not is still a crapshoot."

The man waved shyly. "Just call me *Crapshoot*."

Frank smiled as he looked straight at her. "He's also hard-of-hearing. Getting blown up in a Hummer can do it to a guy."

Frank's hand quit, and the weight dropped… again. He smiled at Ming and stood. "I need some coffee and a donut."

She stood as Mickey turned the corner. His eyes looked almost peeled up to the hairline.

Frank chuffed a single laugh as he walked past Mickey. "You stupidly offered to help the clumsy half-monkey." The side-eyes followed him as Frank kept walking. He stuck his left elbow out. Ming targeted it and acquired it. Frank could almost feel her skipping. It had been too long.

One hundred and ninety-seven days.

Mickey frowned and walked faster to catch up. "Where are we going?"

Frank spun his right index finger in the air. "You're taking us to lunch. It's in the contract."

~

HALF OF THE STRAWBERRY WAFFLE, most of the eggs, and three of the bacon strips stayed on the plate as Frank laid the fork at the five and pushed it away. He closed his eyes and sighed softly.

Mickey remembered Frank only eating three small bites of a fish taco or the small chunk of a fillet mignon from the first time around. His mother never made extra. Just enough for the three of them, and two or three small bites off her plate for Frank. Mickey knew the center would strap him back up to an IV for the night.

Frank's mouth hid in the edge of his hand. The only movement was his eyes dancing around the table. But it wasn't the table he was seeing. He took a deep breath and quietly finished. His gaze came to rest on the quiet young woman. She wasn't sure what was going on. She was out of her element.

Frank's eyes drooped. But his head rose to expose his mouth. "Talk to me."

Her face and hands froze in expressing *What?*

Frank blinked. "How's Tree?"

"She went home for the summer. It didn't go well."

Frank frowned. "What happened?"

"She met a boy. Had a little fling. Hung out at the family's lake house. Ate real food. Did the Fourth of July. Broke the guy's heart. Started hanging out with another guy. Learned to water ski. Did the big family barbecue. Ate a bunch. You know the drill."

Frank leaned back and studied her. "While you stayed at school. Worked. Ate snack bars. Worked. Crunched computer code. Reached out to the companies. Did more work. Ate shit out of the machine. Yeah, I think I know what sucked."

He looked at Mickey silently pushing the last bits of his

omelet around his plate. The man was unusually reflective as he focused on his plate. He seemed to be quarantined in his own world.

He looked back at the wet-rimmed eyes of a budding teen facing real life. She grew up light-years ahead of her age group, but now her similar age group was growing up like her age. Time, reality, and obsession for hiding in the computer instead of taking a walk in the world now scissored her. The cuts were deeper than her emotional understanding.

His voice was soft. "You could have had Mickey or Jazz bring you up to spend time with me."

The girl looked at Mickey. It wasn't a look searching for help. Her eyes cleared without a wipe of her hand. It was a transition Frank had seen only in the military. The hurt child sucks the moisture back into the grit of a SEAL. No crying. No whining. No mewling about fair and not fair. *Die before you cry.*

"I did. We came up many times. I now have intimate knowledge of the science fiction alien in your back."

Frank sat numb. His shoulders fell the thickness of his shirt. "Did they explain about standing in the box?"

Mickey stirred. "Most of the time, you were knocked out. Their words. Your words. Not mine."

Ming's eyes narrowed. "There is a fine line between needing sleep and being antisocial."

Frank wanted to cry out about the pain. Protest his crawling into the oblivion where there was nothing. No voices. No images. No memories. No pain. Just black. But it wasn't just about the pain. He thought about lying in a bed, in a room with no door, just a large opening in the wall where anyone, anything, any… could just walk in…

His eyes focused on the edge of her plate. "I would have liked it if you had woken me up…"

She blinked. The corner of her lower lip was askew in her upper teeth. Her voice was more whispered-scary-drill-instructor than hurt-little-girl. "Anytime?"

He nodded. "Anytime."

"Even now?"

He sighed as he parsed his breath. "Especially now."

"I can take a taxi."

He thought about her age—his lost time, the red hearts tacked up everywhere, Thanksgiving and Christmas with their pumpkin pie that he had spent on IV meals. The nutrients and holidays had flowed through him.

"When do you turn sixteen?"

She chuffed once. The smile was only half there. "You missed it. First of August."

He realized he hadn't been the only important person to miss it. "Why not drive?" He realized the second he had said it how Southern California privileged it sounded.

"I don't need to."

He decided to push. "You don't need to or don't want to? Does Tree drive?"

She shook her head and looked out the window at the street. Frank couldn't tell from her face or eyes if she was looking at two-ton monsters or carefree people going wherever they want.

"Do you want to drive?"

The silence extended. He could see her eyes tracking on the cars. He waited.

If he hadn't been waiting for it, he would have missed it.

"I don't know."

Mickey bent forward with his brow furrowed. Frank waved him off.

Frank tried another track. "Before we go find out"—he pointed at her bag—"was there something you wanted to show me?"

She looked down. "I don't have to show you. I can just tell you." Her arms crossed on the table as the waitress picked up the plates.

Frank shook his head at the waitress's next question. He looked back at Ming. "Humor me. I'm old."

As she pulled the laptop out of the bag and booted it, Frank slid his left foot out of the booth and looked down. The toenails were pink with sparkles. He smiled on one side as he side-eyed her. Her smile was small but telling. *Had he slept through the best part?*

She clicked on the small mouse and opened the program. She selected a file, opened a portion of the Californian coast, and highlighted a smaller part.

The cursor waved back and forth under a glowing orange dot. "This is the southernmost bus. This trench is narrow, but it isn't as deep as some of the others. It's currently about half-full of weed and about a hundred pounds of hard drugs."

Frank's forehead furrowed. But, as his mouth opened, she held up her hand. "We'll get back to it in a moment."

The cursor moved along the trench. "The bus sits about one-twenty. So we think they are pulling the stock out using divers only. Probably pushing out the product in waterproof bags and floating them to the surface with lift bags. Nobody is going to pay much attention to another sportfishing boat floating around out there. But you can see they have easy access to San Diego, the inland county, or moving north. Not to speak of the Del Mar racetrack."

The cursor slid to the upper part of the map and turned to a hand. The hand symbol gripped and slid the map down. The next orange dot appeared. Frank recognized the beachhead. His eyebrows mowed much of his forehead. He looked at her. She nodded.

"This isn't as much of a bus as it's a short bus. This was a thirty-two-foot container. It has limited space for hard drugs. Right now, it's full of small bales of weed. Probably only two to five kilos each bag."

Mickey grabbed the air like he was holding a large basketball. "That's small?"

She reached over and moved his spread hands closer

together. "From the photos, they think they're only cleaned buds and vacuum-packed."

Frank was getting uncomfortable with all the knowledge a sixteen-year-old girl had about some serious contraband and its smuggling. "Photos?"

She again held up her hand. "I'm sure you probably know this beach and where it goes in this tunnel." He nodded. "They don't think the drugs leave the base."

She expanded her eyes and held up her left hand as she moved the map. Frank shut up.

"This was the first bus. When the boys went down, it was empty. Now, it looks stocked for spring break. At least on the weed side. Again, this one is heavy on the smaller packaging. Maybe for moving directly to pot shops. It's anybody's guess. But they think this is the directed feed source for south Orange County."

She sat up and leaned back as she moved the map again.

"Which brings us maybe to your friend."

Frank studied the location of the orange dot. He was aware of the trench and what it did to the surf. The northwestern wall was higher than the southeastern wall. The fifty or more feet of disparity caused the forming surf to close suddenly.

If you're on a long gun, shooting a fifteen- or twenty-foot swell, just about the time you would expect the wave to curl, it drops to a low flat surf. If your nose is pointed downhill, you drill the flat, and the back end throws you into the grinder. It's not a stretch for the faint of heart. It's known as 'dead man's ride.' Mary Shores was one of the hard-core riders who knew the stretch well.

He nodded at the laptop in askance.

"The floor of the cut is just shy of one-fifty-seven."

Frank nodded. "That would explain the triple tanks and the mixed gas."

Her head bobbed small.

Mickey softly sewing-machined the table with his index finger. "What's the mix of drugs?"

She looked at Frank and then Mickey. "Full. Low on buds, mostly shelved for the hard drugs."

Frank ran his hand through his hair. "But the depth…"

She rolled her eyes closed, nodding. "The whole setup's rigged for small subs."

Mickey wrenched his head to one side. "Small subs as in one-to-two-man recreational subs you can buy online, or larger?"

"They think it's a mix. But one-to-two-man subs able to hold a third man of payload or to loads with balloons would be the locals. But the supply subs are closer to something Jacque Cousteau would be jealous of. Maybe in the sixty- or hundred-foot range or more. They would have to be oceangoing to make it up from Mexico and back."

Frank held up his hands in the crossed "T" of time-out. "Okay, so who is this 'they,' and how are you getting photos inside?"

She smiled. "That would be Jazz's wheelhouse. She figured they built all of this because someone in the DEA was dirty. She wasn't comfortable with taking it to the FBI, either. But she made a friend last summer…"

Frank smiled and leaned back. "Her tour on the Coast Guard cutter here in Corona Del Mar."

Ming nodded and smiled.

"But the Coasties would have just turned it all over to the DEA. Their mission is interdiction, not action… per se."

Ming held up her index finger. "Ah, there are those words of conundrum—*per se*." She leaned in and smiled. "Finding out how drugs are moving into the country is part of interdiction. Mapping out the routes, finding stashes, and setting up surveillances are all part of interdiction. Anything short of raiding falls under the heading of…"

The three chorused, "Interdiction."

Frank smiled. "So this is what you did with your summer vacation…"

She smiled. "No. I moved. I'm living with Jazz now. Better rent and living conditions. Since she quit her job, she needed a roommate. And because I'm technically not in the master's program, I needed a place to live off-campus."

Frank leveled a stink eye at her.

She crossed her index fingers as a ward sign. "You're a dirty old man. No. Besides, I like my bed to myself—for now. She doesn't bring anyone home either. She works nearly as many hours as I do, but she knows how to cook." She tossed her head to catch the rolled eyes. "More than protein bars and smoothies. But her apartment is across the street from the university. We're looking for a three-room so Tree can join us."

"But you set all this up with Jazz and the Coasties?"

Her face shied coy. "Not entirely… One of the Coasties reached out to your old team. They have been doing the diving and setting up the monitors."

"SEALs?"

"No… Retired SEALs. Well, for the most part. I think there are a couple of current guys too. But yeah, it's a small group with no connections to be compromised. One of them also runs a small dredging company in San Diego. Also, a John Tenpin said to tell you hi."

Frank smiled. "He was a smart guy. More into the tech side of the team. I figured he would go into the computer industry or something."

"He has a small but successful security and survey company in Long Beach."

"Survey?"

She smiled. "Not like for roads and stuff. He surveys large boats and ship's hulls. He helps companies decide when to scrap their hulls in place or dry dock and make other major repairs."

"I'm impressed. So what's he doing for us?"

"He placed some spy cameras inside the buses. There are also monitors on the outside to tell when more than a hundred pounds of metal is approaching the bus. So we know when it's getting serviced, by whom, and what is inside. We have some pictures of people, but divers all look alike." She held her hands in an oval, squishing her face and bulging eyes.

Mickey frowned. "You have all this information. What's the holdup?"

She snorted softly at him. "Why do you think I called you this morning?"

"You wanted me to bring you up here to see Frank..." His eyes suddenly grew open as he turned to look at a smiling Frank.

Frank looked at Ming. "I can't do anything. They said I'd never be able to dive below ten meters again."

She licked her lips like a lion watching a crippled gazelle. "Want to go for a boat ride?"

31 FLAT TIDE

The Bentley nosed into the parking slot. Frank killed the lights, and the engine grumbled to silence. Frank loved this time of day. The darker gray buildings and boats set against the only slightly lighter gray of the predawn sky. The water between the shore and Balboa Island reflected the same sky and houses.

"It's like it's holding its breath."

Frank looked over at Tree. She had drawn the short straw for riding shotgun. He could read the awe in her face. No computer or boy would ever cause a gut-punch response like this. You either paid the price by getting up at oh-dark-thirty, or you never knew how astonishing and still the world could be.

Ming leaned forward from the back seat. Her arms crossed over his shoulders. Her head rested next to his. Her voice was little more than a quiet thought. "You told us. But I could never have imagined."

Jazz hummed. "When I drove in from Riverside every day, this was the time to fly. Most of the traffic moved at seventy or eighty. Going home was an extra two hours of slog." Frank remembered the young Jazz sleeping in the sheriff's parking lot. She wasn't alone.

The gray Jaguar slipped quietly into the parking slot next to them as Mickey's tan unmarked bracketed the other side. Their doors opened and closed. Frank smiled at the other two men's clothes. It looked like they had gone shopping together. He noticed them eyeing each other's clothes. The khaki chinos matched the casual windbreaker. Only the shoes didn't match —one mirror-polished black, where Mickey had opted for a traditional brown deck shoe. The ball caps were matching OCSO issue. They wouldn't be getting their hands dirty, but there was a certain air of official presence needed. Frank pushed his hands deeper into the pockets of the crude, woven poncho hoodie that surfers from Mexico to Tamales Bay favored.

"Sheriff, this is Deep Six. Ming Lee, Tree Bando, and Jazz Perlmutter."

The sheriff nodded politely, only slightly in over his head. "Ladies..."

Frank smiled at his discomfort. "Ming and Tree wrote the program used to uncover what we call the buses—underwater drug stashes. Jazz is the corporation's legal representation. She'll oversee the proprietary sonar's legal use, search, identify applications, and processing algorithms. Just so there are no repercussions down the road when the county, coast guard, navy, or others involved today need to be sued."

Jazz raised her mirrored glasses. "Unlike the raid eleven years ago on the Bolsa Chica Senior Center instead of the drug house on the next street over..."

The whistle was short and melodic. They turned to see the captain of the ship being piped aboard the cutter. Frank smiled. It was a custom partially eschewed for modern times, but the whistle was a notice to the entire ship that it was time to be about the day. Most ships now opted for a general announcement that the captain was on deck.

Frank put out his hand. "That is our call, people."

As he stood at the end of the gangway, his pocket vibrated.

He pulled out the phone and read the text. He looked at the seaman. "We have one more."

"Are they close, sir?"

Frank looked out at the highway. Two vehicles were traveling close together. He smiled.

Turning, he nodded to the seaman. "We might need some help with a few packages."

The seaman waved at three others. They followed Frank to the cars. Moments later, they boarded, each carrying large garbage bags in their hands. After saluting the officer of the deck, Frank and Pan didn't need to say a word, but the smell of baked sugar and donut dough filled the air. "We have fresh donuts." He pointed at a smiling Pan. "And she's with me."

The man saluted with a toothy smile. "Yes, sir. Very good, sir." The crew set to stowing the gangway. Quietly, the moorings were cast off and hauled in. The cutter made headway and began to turn to sea.

THEY HADN'T TRAVELED FAR but eased to a stop or took up station about a quarter mile from a large barge with a tall crane attached. They could tell it was larger than any crane they might see on land even from a distance. Tied to one side was another barge rigged to a tugboat. The deck was clear, except for a few men.

Pan leaned against Frank's shoulder. They held matching white mugs Frank was certain the government bought by the millions. "I'm glad you texted me."

Frank smiled and leaned his head over onto hers. "I'm glad you texted back. The donuts were a big hit."

"I thought there would be a bunch of cops around..."

"Deputies and feds."

"It's all the same when they get to my office. And sorry about unloading on you that night."

"Unloading on me?"

"The night I came up from operations. I should never have left wearing the contamination."

Frank bobbed his head and glanced at her. "I'd forgotten."

He pushed against him. "Bullshit. How many days?"

"One seventy-six."

They watched the inaction of the little dark figures moving around the decks. "Her husband came home drunk. He had been fired. After he beat her half to death, he dragged her out to his truck. He drove them into a freeway upright. She was a thirty-two."

Frank felt a hard-hot shock to his spine. He looked over at the side of her head. She wouldn't look at him. She was struggling to hold it all together.

They had already run thirty-one units of blood into her leaking bag. When they call a death from thirty-two, the team had a vested interest in saving the person they worked on for hours. There is nowhere for the pumping adrenaline to go. It burns in place. For some surgical nurses and surgeons, it is the final straw, and they find another place to use their training. Others are runners. Never races. But single figures running lonely trails.

Jazz and the captain walked up to the rail. Frank slowly ground his head around. The sun was still hiding behind low clouds over the Angeles mountains. The ocean looked like poured lead. The ripples were less than a hand's breadth.

The captain nodded toward the barges and boats. "The USS *Haddock* tracked a small sub leaving Mexican waters at nineteen-hundred hours last night. Station One and Two haven't reported any action last night. So this leaves Number Three and us. Now it's just a waiting game."

"No more word from the *Haddock*?"

"Tracking the sub wasn't on their duty roster. We didn't want to cause any more interest than we already have."

Frank smiled. It was the same old routine of the military. "We hurried out here to wait."

The captain smiled back. Military is military.

The walkie-talkie squelched on her hip. She pulled it up. "Captain. Go."

"Captain, we have activity. Two minnows. Advise?"

She looked at Frank. "Any word from Station Three?"

"Negative."

"Let's give it a while. Monitor. Can we track the minnows?"

"Affirmative. Divers have tracers."

"Let's trace them just in case. We may want to let the little fish swim home anyway."

Frank squinted behind his mirrored glasses. "Divers?"

She nodded. "We have a team of three in a trouble bubble. The two can go in and out for short periods through a moon pool. It can stand station for up to thirty hours."

Frank stretched his eyes. "For a secret operation, this sure has a lot of working parts."

"We don't know anything about the trouble bubble sub or the men in it. They are some survey group from up in Long Beach. I think they were just doing depth-and-time studies on their survey unit. But even if the four cranes blew the legs and pulled the four buses, it is my understanding it will make the biggest drug haul of seventeen tons last summer look like a kiddy party. So secret or not, this is big. If we can haul in the supply sub too... all the better."

Frank rubbed his glasses up onto the top of his head. He yawned. "Sorry. I didn't sleep last night." He looked in his empty mug. "I think I need some more coffee."

The captain smirked. "We set up everything on the fantail. Go on back and relax. I heard there were donuts back there also." She leaned forward and winked at Pan.

As Frank passed Jazz, she smiled shyly. He leaned toward her. "Good taste in dates. She comes with a nice boat."

~

THE WALKIE-TALKIE WAS SQUAWKING INCESSANTLY as the captain came to get them. They could feel the ship moving.

"The supply sub put in at Number Three. We still have one of the small subs here, so the SEALs just blew the legs, and the crane is bringing up everything. The trouble bubble will monitor from below to make sure nobody falls out."

They all lined the rail. From a few football fields away, nothing appeared to change except the figures on the empty barge were now standing on the tugboat. The line from the crane reached a ring as it came out of the water. Several lines were coming from the collective ring.

The bus broke the surface as the captain's walkie-talkie squawked. "We have two in the water trying to swim away."

They watched as a couple of Zodiacs with DEA or sheriff's deputies made their way out and around the cluster of barges. They would take their time. It wasn't like it was a foot pursuit. And worn-out swimmers made easier collars.

The crane gently lowered the bus onto the barge deck. As the steel net relaxed to the deck, the small sub laid exposed. The agents and deputies moved in to secure the evidence.

Frank elbowed Mickey's arm. "That's quite the collar for you." He looked over at the sheriff.

The sheriff's face was a mix of emotions. He was a witness and knew he was just a witness, another passenger on the boat. His face would be behind the forest of microphones, but eventually, he would have to recognize and share the glory with a few others of the alphabet soup. But come election time, the only name to be remembered was his.

Frank turned to his other side and looked around Pan. "Did you bring the right documents?"

Jazz held up the thumb drive. "The good captain gave me access to their printer. We'll give him a few minutes to enjoy the haul before we start cutting it up."

He smirked. "Any cut is going to be enough. Do the girls understand what this all means?"

Jazz rolled her eyes. "They've been cruising the tech sites all night. They're thinking about building some larger computers. So… no."

Frank smiled. Sometimes education was a clarifying experience. Sometimes life could be even more.

Frank drew a piece of paper out of his pocket. Handing it to Jazz, he winced. "Type this up and include it."

She looked at the directive and glanced up. "Are you sure this is what you want to do with this? This is a lot of money."

Frank nodded. "More than a rookie detective's annual salary, but they need an entire library and so much more. I'm tired of bringing my own books to read."

She tapped the note on his chest with a smile. "You've got it, boss."

32 SHE'S WHAT?

Frank's arm lay draped over Pan's shoulders. They stood looking at the new door. There was a solid look to it, but also it looked like it had been there all along. The twelve small windows had been replaced by nine, with the middle windows being tall. The top and bottom rows were small.

Frank opened the weathered-looking oak door. "I think it's more arts and crafts." He froze. "Whoa."

The entire ceiling floated with incredibly old-school twelve-foot and fourteen-foot long guns. The centerline was a massive board only King Kamehameha himself would have ridden. Frank guessed thirty feet. On the walls hung various paintings and posters of surfing contests or movies framed in what looked like pieces of surfboards. The wooden tables had changed and looked like they had suffered a hundred years of beach bums, surfers, lovers, and tourists with knives or sharpened spoons. The chairs were a mix and match of all ages.

Standing in the center was a tall redhead with a new darker Van Dyke over a commemorative T-shirt of the Beach Boys playing the Crystal Cove. The board shorts were khaki and the only thing resembling a uniform.

An older blonde with a ponytail came out of the back, reached for the plates of food, and maneuvered around her smiling boss. Frank watched with an open mouth at the stack of dishes she was carrying to the corner booth filled with seven customers. Her uniform matched Danny's right down to the huaraches and pink toenails. The smile was all SoCal sunshine.

Frank's limp point at the waitress was answered by Danny's nod toward Frank's table—or unofficial office. It was the only table at the water end of the building. The old green Formica table was gone. The new version looked like two longboards glued together, then resin-coated to create a smooth surface. Each leg was four miniature long guns boxing the sides to make the four stout legs. The chairs were tubular aluminum woven with canvas to resemble ordinary beach chairs. The one had a higher back than the rest. It was in Frank's place.

A stunned Frank pulled the chair out as he looked at a laughing Pan. He frowned. "What?"

"Danny said you ran an idea past him, and while they were trying to put the Shack back together, he just ran with it."

"You knew about this?" His finger waved around in the air at everything and nothing.

"Sure. Where do you think I've been sleeping? Someone had to tend to the new momma and her kits when they cry at night."

Frank sank onto the chair. He leaned in quickly before the mastermind returned with coffee. "It's fucking awesome. But don't tell him that."

He leaned back as Danny poured the coffee and dropped the menus. Frank noted the new logo and name: The Surf Shack. He looked around the man's hips at the older blonde waitress, moving like a shark in a feeding frenzy. "I see you hired some help."

"Hired, my ass. I stole her from the Norm's on Beach. She was their top earner for the last seventeen years. It was time she stopped living off her tips and slowed down. She put the word out where she was moving to. We haven't had peace and quiet around here since the dust settled. She's looking to steal a couple of other old surf Betties she's known for years. I might have to take a vacation just to read my paper in the morning." He pointed at Pan's menu. "Do you know what you want, honey? And by the way, great to see his taste in women improving. The last female he had in here tore up the place. Nasty piece of work, too."

She blinked large eyes at the information and tried not to smile. She flipped open the menu and then closed it. "I'll have what he's having."

Danny stowed the pencil behind his ear, slipped the order book in his short apron, and flipped a duck-turn with his butt sashaying. "A pair of straw-awful, eggs on vacation, with road-kill, coming up."

Pan leaned forward with concern on her face. "We ordered what?"

Frank rolled his eyes. "Strawberry waffles with eggs over easy and bacon. God, I hope he doesn't use those terms with—"

The waitress talked and walked back to the cook station as she wrote the order. "One Whack Moko, one hinny in a mudslide, full stack of skimmers, side of cackleberries running from the law, and a heart attack of roadkill."

Frank let his face fall on his crossed arms. "This place is out of control."

DANNY STOPPED by with fresh coffee and to take Pan's cleaned plate. Frank was still picking at it all.

"The dog didn't stop in last night."

He put the pot down. "She's been skittish since the shootout. But then, there were the twins, and she was just worried. The boy ran off, but Pinkie stuck around. She's got a soft tongue and likes me best. But... I think she's knocked up the same as her mommy. But… we'll see." He lifted the plate and coffeepot and walked away.

"She's what?"

Danny looked back at his boss. And nodded. "See what happens when daddy takes a long vacation?"

ALSO BY BAER CHARLTON

BAER CHARLTON

ABOUT THE AUTHOR

Bestselling author Baer Charlton graduated from UC Irvine with a degree in Social Anthropology, monkeyed around for a while, and then proceeded onward with a life of global travel, multi-disciplinary adventure, and meeting the memorable array of characters he would come to describe in his writing. He has ridden things with gears, engines, and sails, and made things with wood, leather, and metal. He has been stitched back together more times than the average hockey team; his long-suffering wife and an assortment of cats and dogs have nursed him back to health after each surgery.

Baer knows a lot about many things in this world. History flows through his veins and pours out of him at the slightest provocation. Do not ask him what you may think is a simple question unless you have the time to hear a fascinating story.

You can find more at
www.mordantmedia.com